Gideon Redoak

Gideon Redoak

 *Anne Fraser* 

By Light Unseen Media
Pepperell, Massachusetts

Gideon Redoak

Cover and interior design by Vyrdolak, By Light Unseen Media.

This is a work of fiction. Names, characters, places and incidents are either the products of the author's imagination or are used fictiously, and any resemblence to actual persons, living or dead, business establishments, events or locales is entirely coincidental.

Perfect Paperback Edition

ISBN-10: 0-9793028-1-1
ISBN-13: 978-0-9793028-1-7
LCCN: 2009924280

Published by
By Light Unseen Media
PO Box 1233
Pepperell, Massachusetts 01463-3233

Our Mission:
By Light Unseen Media presents the best of quality fiction and non-fiction on the theme of vampires and vampirism. We offer fictional works with original imagination and style, as well as non-fiction of academic calibre.

For additional information, visit:
http://bylightunseenmedia.com/

Printed in the United States of America

0 9 8 7 6 5 4 3 2 1

Acknowledgements

First, I would like to thank Inanna Arthen, friend, mentor, editor, publisher and founder of By Light Unseen Media. Don't ever believe your own light is unseen, Inanna. It shines for all to see.

And many thanks go to my friend Sherry Moore, for being my ideas person and listening patiently to the damnedest tripe. Ya da man, babe.

Thanking everyone who ever helped me, read my various drafts, or given me constructive criticism would need a phone book, and I'd invariably leave someone out and they'd get all cranky. So I shall offend you all by groups, some defunct and others still funct. So thank you all to the past and present members of the following (deep breath):

Vampyres, Nightstalkers, Night-l, Night-F, Inklings (still got your t-shirts?), Scherazade, Ghostletters, Quillings, The Toronto Gothic Society, Psychobabblers Anonymous, and because of course I saved the best for last, "The Anne List." I love you guys. You know what you can do with further notice.

Anne Fraser
February, 2008

Prologue

The undead do not dream. When we sleep by daylight, it is the sleep of death. Yet, when I awoke to the darkness, I could have sworn I heard an echo of laughter, as if from a nightmare.

Blackness enclosed me against a watchful silence, both so profound I thought I'd been struck blind and deaf. I had to feel my eyelids with my fingers to assure myself that they were open. I raised my arms, pressing against the lid of my coffin. It refused to budge. I strained with all my unnatural strength against the lid, but failed to move it even an inch. A few grains of dirt trickled in through minute cracks.

Dirt, the absolute silence, and the feeling of enormous pressure I could sense bearing in on all sides—these meant my coffin had been buried. The earth had been tightly packed around it so that I couldn't escape.

I sucked in the stale air that remained in my coffin. I turned my head sharply toward a harsh rasping sound, cracking my temple painfully on the side of the box. The sound was my own, of course, my pitiful attempt at breathing through lungs that no longer functioned normally.

I clawed at my throat. Choking, I tried to sit up and only gave my abused skull another painful blow. I forced my hands to be still. I couldn't suffocate, since I didn't breathe. I listened and heard nothing—not the wind, nor the rustle of leaves, the scrape of tree branches, the busy gnawing of rodents and beetles in old walls, the clink of chains, or any of the myriad sounds I was used to. I would die here of madness and starvation—the true death, not the false one I had already endured before my awakening as a vampire. How long would it take before I went insane? How long before I started savaging my own body, gnawing the flesh from my fingers for a drop of blood?

The wages of sin is death. So my father had often preached, usually enforcing his point with a birch rod. Recalling those painful lectures, I started to laugh. Damned if he hadn't been right.

Chapter One

My father had embraced the Puritan religion with fervour, despite being baron of a large and prosperous estate. He saw nothing incongruous between the two, and there were other noble Puritans, although few as fanatic as my parent. Indeed, he went far beyond the actual tenets of the Puritan sect.

I was born in mid-December of 1622, and managed to survive the threats of plague, smallpox, cholera, and a host of other dangers too numerous to list. My sister Prudence was my only sibling to live to adulthood. As the sole male child, I was the heir and expected to take my father's place.

From earliest childhood, I was familiar with every inch of the estate—every tenant, servant, swineherd, wandering tinker and stray bullock. I was there when seeds were planted, when the fields flooded or lay gasping for water in a drought, when the crops were harvested and the grain threshed. A baron did more than rule and gather rent, I learned—he must know how every labourer worked. My father and I toiled right alongside our tenants. I could shoe a horse, help a calf into the world, slaughter a pig, name the diseases of corn, and walk the Redoak lands blindfold by the time I was twelve.

My father was even sterner when it came to my spiritual education. Forced to memorise the Bible from Genesis to Revelation, and attend every sermon our tame preacher delivered, I could discuss scripture at length when called upon to do so. A vigorous and immediate application of the rod corrected any faltering of my memory. I still bear the scars made by supple birch on tender young skin.

The preacher was my father's hireling and obediently parroted his rigid views of good and evil. Sermons consisted of dire warnings against straying from the narrow path of righteousness as my father saw it. Lust was the worst of the sins, the preacher would inform his congregation, spittle flying from his lips. Fornication would surely land you in the pits of Hell. Sexual intimacy was only permitted between man and wife, and only for the purposes of procreation. Thus were children born in original sin.

One week, he spoke of Sodom and Gomorrah, and the terrible sin of sodomy. Many of the congregation wept with terror at the vivid descriptions of the punishments awaiting the practitioners of this sin. I was badly frightened, all the more so because I didn't know what sodomy was. I somehow summoned the courage, when discussing this sermon with my father, to ask. He struck me across the mouth.

"But how can I avoid this sin if I don't know what it is?" I asked through bloody lips.

My father stared at me, unused to rebellion, even such a feeble one. He sent for the preacher. "The boy wants to know what sodomy is."

We were in his study. I stood near the fireplace, whose flames cast a small reflection of Hell across the wooden floor. My father sat in his black oak chair, and the preacher stood far too close to me for comfort. He smelled of stale sweat.

"Filth! Sin!" More froth appeared on the preacher's lips. "To lust for a woman is a sin. Aye, even if she be your wife. But to lust for another man, that, boy, is sodomy. To take that vile instrument which dangles between your legs and to thrust it into that hole from which filth issues..."

"Yes, I believe that the boy understands now," my father said. "Gideon, retire to your room and pray for guidance."

"Yes, Father. Thank you, Reverend Sir." I fled. In the safety of my room, I prayed not only for guidance, but for understanding.

My sister Prudence, given to our mother's care, fared somewhat better than I did. I seldom saw either Prudence or my mother. I was discouraged from associating with women, even close relatives. My father didn't wish for me to turn to my mother and sister for sympathy and comfort.

I had very few friends. I was seldom permitted to mingle with other noble children. Many of these were Cavaliers and jeered at my short hair and sombre clothing. I longed for bright colours and the gaiety of court life, but dared not disobey my father. My socialising was limited to dull Puritan meetings. Heaven help the boy or girl who fell asleep during one of those interminable sermons!

While I was still a child, my parents arranged my betrothal to a girl of similar background and breeding, a common practice of the day. I never gave the matter much thought, except as yet another future duty to fulfil. My poor sister was promised to one of my father's cronies, cut from the same stern cloth as he. I met my own betrothed, Piety, on several occasions. We got along tolerably well, since there was no point to our being enemies. She was a pretty and agreeable maid, but I felt no attraction to her.

Of course, such attraction would have been a sin, but it was a sin that held little danger for me. By the time I reached fifteen, I understood, more or less, how conception was achieved. I'd seen enough cows, mares and sows put to stud to work out for myself how humans managed it. To me, the process seemed both brutal and messy. How could anyone feel lust under such conditions? Piety awakened no stirring in my loins, nor any desire to disobey all those prohibitions against knowing a woman.

I can't fairly blame this reaction—or lack of one—on my teaching. From time to time, a glance or accidental touch from another evoked a rush of guilty heat in my body. Then I would remember the preacher's definition of sodomy, and my face would flame as my legs tottered.

No woman caused these first awakenings of sexuality. Such longings I might at least have understood. Rather, it was the sight of a man. Men like the brawny blacksmith's son, muscles gleaming with sweat as he pumped the bellows, or the pale, long-locked, seldom-seen son of our Duke. The thresher effortlessly mowing the hay with his scythe held me entranced, as did, most of all, the son of my father's steward and my only true friend, Jamie Carter. Ah, God, the most forbidden form of lust—other men, and the act that was so damnable that it was more than mere sin. How could I, raised by such strict Biblical precepts, possibly be a sodomite? My first confused stirrings were not very explicit in retrospect. The knowledge of how beasts mated and the preacher's definition of sodomy made me uneasy, as well as rather confused, about imagining anything specific along those lines. But I wondered how it would feel to be held in strong arms.

I prayed nightly for guidance, for answers, for relief from the feeling of warm pleasure that swept over me each time Jamie smiled. I prayed until my knees bled, until even my father noticed my haunted eyes and drawn features. Weeping, I begged God not to punish me thus, to show me that He had not abandoned me. God did not answer.

Shortly after my nineteenth birthday, I became the Baron of Redoak.

Travelling in 1641 was a dangerous business. Disease was rampant, the roads were poor and unlit, transportation relied on high-strung horses prone to broken legs, and thieves lay in shadowy ambush. My father avoided his Parliamentary duties as much as possible, but even he could not dismiss a summons from the House of Lords. Leaving me in charge of the estate, my father and two servants took the carriage and our best team to

London. Horses and carriage were never seen again. Searchers discovered the murdered bodies of my father and the servants and returned them to the Hall on a wagon.

We had no doubt that highwaymen had stopped the carriage. These lawless men, not at all the romanticised figures of fiction, abounded on the roads. My father trusted in the Lord rather than in armed guards. Most likely he had started to preach against the sin of highway robbery and had been shot for his trouble. It was an understandable reaction to one of my father's lectures.

I didn't grieve for him.

Though barely nineteen when I inherited the Redoak title, lands and responsibilities, I had been thoroughly trained for the role. I had become a man at fourteen, putting childhood behind me forever.

Although old enough to assume the governing of the estate, I wouldn't be considered mature enough to marry for some years, for which I felt greatly relieved. God had not miraculously cured me of my desire for other men. Indeed, the closer I approached to full manhood, the stronger the urges. Neither prayer nor meditation eased my lust and confusion one iota. I felt terribly alone, since I didn't dare speak of my sin to anyone.

With my father dead, I found that there was no longer a barrier between me and the women of the household. Although they were almost strangers to me, it didn't take me very long to befriend my sister and learn to love my mother. She knew what I had endured under my father's reign, but had been helpless to interfere.

From Prudence, I quickly learned that I wasn't the only one dreading an arranged marriage. The man to whom she was betrothed, a dour fellow named Simon Paxson, resembled our father far too much for Prudence's liking. She tended to speak her mind, a quality that would stand her in poor stead in Paxson's Biblically strict household.

Prudence feared Paxson and feared for her own well-being if she married him. She loved Jamie Carter, who now held the position of steward to Redoak Manor. Prudence thought that her feelings for Jamie were a secret, but both my mother and I knew of them. I prayed that my own attraction to Jamie was known only to me.

Paxson came to call on me in late spring, less than two months after my father had been buried. With his thick build and eyebrows that bristled out an inch from his forehead, he provoked only revulsion. My father's aging wolfhound, Nimrod, gave

 *11*

a token growl and slunk out of the study when Paxson entered. I never did like that damned dog, but I agreed with his opinion of my visitor.

When Paxson entered the study, I rose from the carved black oak chair to greet him, and motioned him towards a stool to sit. His eyes narrowed at this deliberate insult. He took the offered seat as though it were a throne.

His words were more courteous than his demeanour. "My lord, I must speak with you on a most urgent matter."

"I have many urgent matters which require my attention. Can yours not wait?"

"The truth, my lord Baron, is that time's arrows fly swiftly. My business can not wait."

I leaned back, a luxury that Paxson's three-legged stool would not allow him, and amused myself by watching his ugly eyebrows. "Very well. What is this urgent matter that brings you calling when my father is scarce cold in his grave?"

"My lord, your father and I had an agreement about his only daughter, your sister Prudence." His phrasing and tone implied that I might be unaware of my only sister's name.

"An agreement?" I repeated slowly, as if puzzled by the concept. An idea formed in my mind and I wanted to give it some time to achieve its full effect.

"Yes." Paxson ground his teeth, a muscle twitching in his cheek. His eyebrows telegraphed his desire to shake me. "He gave his consent."

"To what?"

"To... our... betrothal." Each word exploded from him and he nearly launched himself off the stool. His knuckles whitened as he fought for self-control. "Your father, sir, promised Prudence to me in marriage."

Wide-eyed, I told an untruth. Although I braced myself against it, the wrath of God smote me not. "I knew nothing of this. My father did not see fit to inform me of it, and he said nothing of the matter in his papers. No doubt, had he foreseen his untimely end, he would have recorded any such compact clearly, but—"

"He gave me his word!"

"Of which I know nothing. Whatever word my father may have given died with him."

"You must honour your father's agreement!"

"Sir, had I known of it, I should have been very pleased to honour it. However, it is impossible for me to grant your request for my sister's hand."

"Impossible!" This time, Paxson did rise.

I remained seated. "Yes. Prudence is already betrothed."

"To whom?"

"James Carter."

"Carter? Is he not your steward? A servant? Your sister is a noblewoman!"

I gave him a measuring look. "I am surprised to hear you raise that objection, since the Puritan faith avers the equality of all men before God." Not to mention that the steward of a large estate had a much higher rank than a mere servant, but I didn't bother to say so. "My word is given, and the banns will be posted this Sunday. Was there anything else?"

A rainbow of colour changes spread across Paxson's face while his eyebrows danced in anger. His fingers brushed the hilt of his belt knife, then clenched into a fist. He forced them open as I waited, heart in my throat, to see if he would threaten me. He bowed, cold and stiff, hating me with his eyes. Had his eyebrows been daggers, I would have been dead. "Then, if you will give me leave, Baron, I must return home."

I stood and returned his bow, my own expression carefully blank. Had he been a trifle more rude, I would have had to call him out. I had never fought a duel. I escorted him out of the Hall, exchanging more bows but no civilities. His anger frightened me, but I didn't let him see that. When Paxson had ridden out of sight, I sent for Jamie Carter. He came into my study. I didn't sit down for this interview.

"I've put myself in a bad position, Jamie. I've told a lie, and I need you to help me make it into truth."

Jamie's broad, honest face showed his puzzlement. He was my elder by less than ten years and had inherited the post of steward when his father died. Jamie had filled many of the roles my father couldn't be bothered with. He'd taught me how to fish and shoot game, put me on my first pony, shown me the pathways of the stars, and been the object of more than a few extremely troubling dreams. Naturally, I had no intention of ever telling him about those. No one save me and God knew of my terrible affliction, my unnatural and sinful lust for men. Jamie certainly must never discover my secret.

"I will aid you in any way I can, my lord." Jamie's voice broke my reverie.

With difficulty, I recalled what I wanted to say. "Jamie, you know that my father gave his word to Simon Paxson that he could wed Prudence. In order to spare her from this man, whom

I believe to be a brute, I told him that Prudence was already betrothed. Will you help me to tell this other man that he must marry my sister or make a liar and oath-breaker of me? He is a good man, and will be a better husband. What say you, Jamie?"

Struggling with his own emotions, which I could plainly read, Jamie said, "If you feel this other man would be a good husband for Prudence, sir, I will help you." Bless him.

"Excellent. This man will care for her, I know. I believe that Prudence admires him." At the look of jealousy that crossed his face, I relented. "The man I speak of is you, Jamie."

His smile lit the room. "Thank you, my lord!" He seized my hand and shook it with vigour.

While I was still numb from my reaction to this, Jamie fled the study without waiting for me to dismiss him. No doubt he ran off in search of Prudence, to share the news. At least I had made them happy.

For my own loneliness, the awful isolation, the burden of my terrible secret, I could see no solution. I didn't even know there was a name for my longings, other than sodomy.

The wedding, held that summer of 1642, was stark and simple. The Puritan preacher was not the same one who had defined sodomy for me, but he kept the ceremony stern. He warned the too-happy couple that this was a solemn occasion in the presence of God. In lonely splendour as the Baron, dressed for the first time in my life in noble finery, I gave my sister away and bestowed my worthless sinner's blessing upon her and her new husband.

Jamie and Prudence were so intent upon each other that they barely acknowledged my blessing. Watching them, I knew that I could never experience such joy.

A month after the wedding, my mother died. I had only just begun to know her, and found her a gentle and loving spirit. When we buried her, I wept.

Now that I was alone in Redoak Hall, Piety's parents pressured me to go through with our wedding. I named a date, with no enthusiasm.

Jamie and Prudence moved to a farm that I gave them as her dowry, an hour's ride from the Hall. Jamie still served as my steward until I could find another. One morning he came to me deeply troubled, with the news that one of the peasant women had been found dead. We rode at once for the cottage of the bereaved family. As soon as they heard the horses, all of the neighbours poured forth. The widowed husband prostrated himself in front of my mare's hooves, so that I was forced to rein in hard. The press of people made my mare dance and twist.

"Stand back!" I said, and the crowd gave me room to dismount. I approached the prostrate husband and commanded him to rise and speak.

"Justice, my lord Baron!" He wept, clinging to my doublet. "My wife has been slain!"

I steeled myself not to pull away from his rank breath. He had nearly twice my years, an advanced age for a peasant. Half his teeth were gone and the rest rotting. I doubted that his deceased wife had been any more attractive, but his grief was piteous to see.

"Where is your lady?" I hoped my voice didn't betray my apprehension. I had no idea what I faced.

Jamie struggled to my side and soon had the crowd dispersed back to their usual tasks, save the new widower. My steward repeated my question.

"She is still in the field where she was found," the Goodman finally said. "None thought it meet to move her until you had seen her, my lord."

More likely, I thought, they had left the corpse to lie where found out of superstitious fear. "Show me," I said. Jamie at my side, I followed the man to the field where the woman's body lay. Her drab-clothed form lay like some weird fungal growth among the glistening wheat. An overturned basket, its contents ransacked by animals, lay nearby. After making my way along the already trampled path to her body, I knelt beside her. I had been expecting something gruesome, and was surprised at how peaceful she looked. Her eyes were closed and her arms were folded across her chest. My nose detected the usual unpleasant aftermath of death, but I saw no signs of violence.

"You said she was slain, Goodman. What caused you to call it thus? She appears to have gone peacefully to God."

"Look at her neck, my lord," the Goodman whispered, crossing himself.

Waving away the hordes of flies, I leaned over the woman's corpse. The sun beat down on the back of my own neck. Birds, unconcerned by death, sang in the distance. A beautiful day, perfect for harvesting, sullied by this odd corpse. I studied her, choking back vomit. There was no blood on the ground or her clothing, but when I examined her neck, I found two small and ugly wounds. I rocked on my boot heels, at a loss to determine what had caused such marks. They were too precise to be any animal bite I had ever seen.

"It was a demon, my lord," the widowed farmer said.

"Nonsense," I said brusquely, standing up. But what had caused those wounds? This was unlike any gypsy trick or witchcraft that I had heard of.

Two more of my tenants died the same way. They were found in plain view, with arms folded across their chests and no wounds save for those two marks on the neck. All of my assurances, and those of the preacher, couldn't keep the people from muttering about demons.

Jamie and I conferred for long hours in my study. I could call on little in the way of outside help in those days. I could have sent a message to the Duke, or summoned the sheriff out of Shrewsbury. But to do either would be a tacit admission that I was incapable of administering my lands. My tenants looked to me to save them from this terror, and I had only Jamie. We decided that our wisest course was to ride armed and ready around the estate at nightfall to see if we could discover the murderer.

What does one take as a weapon for demon hunting? I took my sword and my flintlock pistol. Jamie had his sword and a musket. I possessed some skill with the sword but none with the pistol, and worried that the thing would blow up in my face.

My sweet little black mare went lame just at this time. I had purchased a young white stallion with the thought of breeding him, but had not yet had him mounted on any mare. I ordered him saddled.

How like a fine young fool I looked, in my new slashed doublet, on my white stallion. How innocent, armed with sword and pistol, hunting demons.

If you hunt for something long enough, it finds you.

Jamie and I separated in order to cover the bounds of the estate. I took the path near the field where the first dead woman had been found. The wheat had been harvested save for the patch where she had lain. The stench of rotting grain rose up from beneath the stallion's hooves. I sat hunched in the saddle, one hand gripping the reins, the other hovering nervously between sword-hilt and pistol-butt. The sun had just set, and my eyes were still dazzled by the lingering bands of scarlet on the horizon. I would need the lantern that hung from my saddle, but for the moment the sunset and the grey twilight sufficed. No lights at all shone from the nearby cottages. The tenants were all in their beds, or under them, praying.

The horse whinnied and shied, nearly jerking me out of the saddle. I gripped the reins and peered over his twitching head to see what had caused this behaviour. The dying red light in the west outlined a black figure directly in front of my horse.

There had been no one on the path—had there? Surely I hadn't been so preoccupied that I didn't see this man approach until he was directly in front of the stallion?

"Who are you and what is your business here?" I spoke with all the authority of the Baron of Redoak. My horse continued to act strangely, straining at the bit and pawing the ground.

The intruder, a tall man plainly dressed, spread out his hands to show that he was unarmed. "Be easy, my lord Baron," he said, his voice rich and vibrant on the twilight air. "I seek you on urgent business."

"You have found me." I didn't think it odd that he knew my identity—who else but the lord of the manor would ride the bounds of his estate mounted on a blood stallion? "Give me your name."

"Forgive me, my lord." He bowed. "I am Etienne Corbeau." The name was French, although his accent was barely discernable.

"What is your business with me, sir?"

He had given me no title, but I automatically granted him at least a gentleman's status. His demeanour was not that of a vassal. "This is not a fit place to discuss it, my lord."

I had to agree, and so I invited him to the Hall, although the idea that the house, with its dozens of eavesdropping servants, was more private than a deserted field was amusing. The stranger drew closer, and the stallion went into a fit of frenzy. It reared, frothing around the bit, trying to attack the man with teeth and hooves. Clenching my legs around the horse's midriff, I kept my seat and fought the beast back down under control.

"Perhaps you had best follow me at a safe distance," I said to Corbeau. "I don't know how much longer I can master this animal."

With another fluid bow, the stranger agreed. I cast a glance back at him to try and decipher this new riddle. His clothes were of good quality, and the sword at his side looked unused. His black hair was neither short nor long, and there was a sensuality to his bearing that suggested anything but a pious temperament. I couldn't make out his features clearly in the gathering darkness, and eagerly anticipated the opportunity to see his face. We reached the Hall shortly. I dismounted, and a groom came out to take the stallion.

"He behaved badly tonight. Be sure to look him over thoroughly," I told the groom, who was having difficulty leading the animal off. My father would have ordered such a horse shot. I was determined to prove my difference.

"Yes, my lord," the groom said, almost dragging the stallion away.

For the first time, in the light of the torches on the Hall's front entrance, I found myself face to face with Etienne Corbeau.

He topped me by at least five inches. Years of labouring in the fields and smithy beside the tenants had given me a most unaristocratic breadth of shoulder. But Corbeau's form achieved noble perfection. His black hair absorbed the wavering torchlight. Dark blue eyes, like a deep mountain lake, gazed at me steadily. With his high cheekbones and exquisite features, he was the most truly beautiful person I had ever seen. I reddened under the intensity of his gaze, certain he saw only an awkward farm boy.

I was very young, and didn't know that evil could walk abroad in the guise of a handsome man.

"Will you not invite me in, my lord?" he said softly.

Embarrassed at being reminded of my manners, I stammered an invitation even as a tardy footman flung open the doors. The house I had grown up in seemed as strange to me as a building in a dream. Corbeau showed me to my own study rather than the other way around. Nimrod, the wretched wolfhound, rose growling when I entered, but upon sighting my guest, the dog fled yelping, tail between its legs. I gave this behaviour no thought, but sank into the carved black oak chair. Once seated, some small portion of my senses returned to me. I dismissed the footman and confronted my guest.

"What is it that you have to say to me?"

Corbeau smiled. The immediate effect was to make my head spin, my palms perspire, and my legs quiver. Had I not been seated, I might have completely disgraced myself. I wiped my palms on the sides of my breeches and hoped he had noticed nothing untoward.

"My dear Baron," he said in melodious tones, "I have heard that you are having trouble on your estate."

That the news had spread beyond my borders didn't surprise me. "Yes. There have been three peculiar deaths among my tenants."

Corbeau's voice echoed oddly in my head. "You were out searching alone. Do you not have a steward?"

"Jamie Carter is my steward," I said, although I had the feeling that Corbeau knew everything about Redoak Hall already. "We separated in order to ride the bounds. But he recently wed my sister, and would rather be with her, tending to their farm."

My hands were beginning to chafe from being rubbed across my breeches. I had no idea why I was being so candid with this stranger. My affairs and those of my family were none of his concern. But such was the power of his voice and those eyes that I would have told him anything he asked.

"I will serve as your steward," Corbeau said. He softened the boldness by adding, "If you will have me."

I knew nothing about this man. I opened my mouth to protest, but he forestalled me. "I have experience as a steward. I will serve you well."

"I..." My mouth closed. I could think of nothing to say.

"You are alone in this house?"

"Yes. I am all alone now." The Hall had a small army of servants, but servants didn't count.

"Not any longer, Gideon."

It was presumptuous for him to use my Christian name, but with those blue eyes gazing into mine, I scarcely noticed. "No. Not any longer."

"And I will be your steward?" His eyes never left mine.

"Yes, of course."

He rose. "I must go now, for a brief time. I will return tomorrow evening with my belongings. A small, dark room with heavy window shutters will suit my needs. I am never to be disturbed during the daytime. That is when I must sleep. Is this understood?"

"It is understood." I rose up and walked over to him, stopping just short of touching him, though the desire to do so nearly overwhelmed me.

He put both his hands on my shoulders, an unforgivably intimate gesture for a stranger to make. A flood of warmth and confusion washed through me at his touch. "Should anyone ask why you came to accept me as your steward, you will tell them that you are well-satisfied with my ability to do the work."

"Yes, I shall tell them."

He smiled, and left. With his departure, some of my senses returned. Had I just arranged for a complete stranger to become my steward? Dazed, I walked to the doors and looked out into the night, but Corbeau had vanished. The warmth and trembling desire his touch had awakened in me had not disappeared, however. I spent the remainder of the night on my knees in prayer, begging for forgiveness for my lustful thoughts. For the first time, these thoughts drifted to physical longing.

The next morning, I directed the servants to prepare a room for the new steward according to the specifications he had dictated. While the shutters were being nailed into place, Jamie sought me out.

"I saw nothing last night," he said, propping his foot up on a stool and looking at his boot with interest. He was fighting against a grin, oddly enough. His mouth kept twitching upwards. "Did you?"

I couldn't imagine what to tell him, but he continued speaking, not noticing my failure to answer.

"Gideon." Jamie had earned the right to use my name when he became my brother-in-law. "I have something to tell you." A smile broke out on his features.

I stared at him, his excitement finally penetrating the mists of my own inward turmoil. "Out with it, then."

Jamie flushed, looked again at his boots, at the floor, at the servants, anywhere but at me. He was smiling again. I wondered what ailed him. He coughed into his hand while I began drumming my fingers on a small table in impatience. My father used to do that, and recalling it, I stopped.

"Prudence is with child," he finally said, his beaming smile threatening to split his face.

Nothing in the way I had been raised prepared me for this event to be greeted with such joy. The birth of a child meant pain and suffering. I summoned up a smile.

"Bless you both," I said, now even more excluded from what my sister and her husband shared.

"Thank you." Jamie looked at his feet again. Something down there seemed to fascinate him. He obviously knew that I felt his joy was misplaced.

I resisted the urge to look down. "And I have news for you. I've found a new steward, and can, with a full heart, bid you tend to Prudence and your farm without depriving me of aid."

Jamie wrung my hand. "But this is excellent news, brother! I'm glad that you have found an able assistant. Truth to tell, Prudence has been worried about leaving you alone in the Hall. She will be relieved to hear there is a stalwart fellow looking out for you. What is his name, and how did you find him?"

"His name is Corbeau, and he found me. He heard of the troubles here, and came to the Hall hoping for an opening." Even as I said it, it sounded too incredible to be true. "I am satisfied that he will do well."

"If you are satisfied, then I am. Is he a God-fearing Christian?"

I had no idea how to answer. I doubted if the reply could truly be "yes." Jamie laughed at my silence. I rejoiced that he didn't question me too closely. Besides having been the unwitting object of my unnatural longings, Jamie had been my good friend and guardian since I'd been in leading strings. It hurt not to tell him the truth.

Jamie once more grabbed my hand. "I cannot thank you enough. My heart yearns even now to be with Prudence. I am glad that you have found a steward. Can he aid you to find the demon that slays our people?"

I hadn't thought of that. Once I had met Corbeau, all concern about the murders had fled. "Yes," I said, thinking of that liquid voice, those deep eyes. My shoulders still felt the pressure of his fingers. "I believe he can." I believed he could do anything.

Jamie beamed. "Then I can go to Prudence with a clear conscience."

"Go, then." I smiled.

Later that same day, the head groom sought me out. First he stated that he had thoroughly examined the white stallion and found nothing wrong with the beast. It was his opinion that the horse would be better behaved after it was bred to a mare. Once I had given him permission to attempt this, he didn't depart, but stood twisting his cap in his cracked hands.

"Was there something else?"

"Your father's dog is dead," he blurted out.

It took me a moment to realise what he'd said, and another minute for it to sink in that I hadn't seen Nimrod since the night before. "Nimrod?" I asked, rather stupidly. My father had owned no other dogs.

"Yes, my lord. One of my lads found him, my lord, in that copse on the north border." His cap was in danger of being destroyed by his nervous hands.

I knew the copse in question—it was on the very edge of my land, practically in Wales. If one of the stable lads had been in those woods, he had undoubtedly been poaching. I decided to overlook this crime and concentrate on the death of the wolfhound. "Old age, I suppose?"

The head groom trembled. "No, my lord. Killed, my lord. Had his throat tore out."

That certainly warranted my full attention. "Get all your lads, and any other young men or older boys that can be spared. Search that copse, every tree, every bush, and every hole. If there are wolves or wild dogs on my land, I want them found."

The stable master looked relieved to have clear orders. "Yes, my lord. And the dog's body?"

"Bury it where it lies."

He tugged on his forelock, and departed. The respect in his eyes bothered me, for I couldn't imagine how I'd warranted it. I had not only failed to protect my tenants, I couldn't even protect a dog. Although Nimrod's violent death troubled me, I certainly didn't mourn his passing. The search turned up neither wolf nor stray dog, and no tracks offered a clue as to the identity of Nimrod's Nemesis.

For an eternal afternoon, I paced the Hall until finally the sun began to sink and Corbeau arrived. In my relief to see him I barely noticed the large box he brought with him. He permitted none save himself to handle this container.

I accompanied him to the room that had been prepared and watched him slide the mysterious box over against a wall. He expressed satisfaction with the arrangements. I flushed with pleasure at this praise, and wished there were something else I could do to earn it. His measuring gaze swept over me.

"Such eyes," he murmured. "Beautiful."

"I beg your pardon?" He could not have meant that my eyes were beautiful, surely. I had misunderstood him.

"Perhaps you would not mind giving me a tour of the estate, my lord?"

"Of course." I felt stupid that I hadn't thought of it.

The waning day shed soft grey light across the fields. Corbeau blinked painfully and pulled his hat brim over his eyes, but made no complaint. Grooms and footmen hovered nearby, awaiting orders.

"Best not use your white stallion, my lord," Corbeau said softly, for my ears only. "It is a fine beast, but likes me not."

I accordingly asked for another horse to be brought. I asked Corbeau if he wished any of my stable for his use, but he replied that he had his own mount with him. The groom fetched the horses, a placid old red nag for me and Corbeau's tall chestnut gelding.

"Horses don't like me. I have never known why," my new steward said. My red mare shied when I mounted.

"Your own is quiet enough," I said enviously, giving the mare a sharp flick with my riding crop and finally settling safely in the saddle.

"He is used to me."

Despite the antics of my mount, the ride with Corbeau proved pleasant. He listened attentively to all that I had to say, and asked intelligent questions. Although he was several years my elder, he treated me with deference and respect.

As the last rays of the sun slanted across the sky, I introduced Corbeau to the tenants. They had turned out in a cluster for inspection, and all of them greeted me with a mixture of familiarity and reverence. None of them seemed to like the new steward, however. They spoke politely, but with no warmth. I took Corbeau to the dower farm, and introduced him to Jamie and Prudence. A certain chill permeated the proceedings. Again, I witnessed politeness but not acceptance. I alone, of everyone on the estate, actually liked my new steward.

Time passed and the new steward settled into his duties despite the reluctance of the tenants to accept him. Some seemed afraid of Corbeau. I caught more than one crossing himself or making the sign against the Evil Eye behind the steward's back. When I confronted them about this, however, the tenants refused to explain.

All I dreamt about was Corbeau now. No longer did I notice attractive young labourers. No longer did I fantasise about Jamie declaring his love for me. Only Corbeau, with his handsome face and bottomless eyes, drew me. His voice sang in my ears. Fever surely boiled in my veins, for I would flush hot and red whenever he looked at me.

Sins of the flesh! Sodomy! Lust! Driven to prayer and tears, I begged God for guidance. Why did I so long for a touch or even a look from Corbeau? Why did Satan lead me into damnation? Had the Devil himself sent Corbeau to try me? Why was I so weak, so despicable?

Corbeau and I dined together every evening. This was the time to discuss the affairs of the estate, to see how crops, beasts and tenants were faring. He ate sparingly, almost nothing at all. My appetite was usually keen, honed by hard work, making me ashamed of my gluttony. Often his eyes were fixed on me. If I noticed, the blood rushed to my cheeks.

Corbeau knew everything that happened on the estate, despite his inability to function during the daytime. I depended upon his help, relieved to have someone older and stronger to turn to. He eased the burden of being Baron. When he smiled at me over the lip of his wine cup, I no longer felt alone. He must have known. But if he caught me admiring him, he would say nothing, but only smile.

There was a small room next to my bedroom, what was then termed a closet. Before retiring, I went over the books and accounts there. Late one night, when I couldn't sleep for the tortured thoughts of my confused soul, I went to the closet. I lit the brazier and a few candles and tried to occupy myself with the accounts. The door opened, making the candle flames dance. I looked up, startled, to see Corbeau smiling down at me. He carried a flagon of wine and two goblets. I'd heard no sound of his approach.

"You burn your candles late, young lord. I've brought some refreshment. Perhaps I can aid you with those accounts."

I gestured to the other chair in the small room. My heart began to pound, but my voice sounded steady. "Pray seat yourself. I would be glad of a wiser head at these accounts, and gladder still of the wine. This is thirsty work."

He set his burden on the desk and poured the wine. He passed one goblet to me, his fingers brushing mine. I jerked back at the touch, nearly spilling my wine. He filled his own goblet and raised it.

"To your long life." His eyes met mine.

Warmth flooded me although I hadn't yet tasted the wine. Head reeling, I lifted my cup. "And to yours."

We drank. The wine, dark in the candlelight, was fruity and spicy, with a musky aftertaste that wasn't unpleasant. I had a good head for wine, yet this one sip swirled in my veins like flaming ice. Hastily, I set down the cup. Corbeau's fingers curled over mine, and my whole body tingled at the touch. His fingers felt cool on my burning skin.

"If the wine is not to your liking, young lord," he smiled as his index finger caressed the inside of my wrist, "perhaps I know something that is."

He raised my unresisting hand towards his mouth. His lips touched the pulse point of my wrist. I nearly swooned from the rush of pleasure. Blushing, I tried to break free of his grip but could not. A voice in my head warned me that this was sin, but I no longer listened.

"It's no shame or sin to desire men," Corbeau said, releasing my wrist. "There are many who find pleasure in the company of their own sex."

"How..." He had read my deepest thoughts.

"I've seen you watching me. You are confused and guilty about your feelings, are you not? No need. I return your desire, young lord. You are beautiful."

"No." I was not beautiful. An awkward, blushing farm boy, far too muscular and browned from the fields, couldn't be beautiful.

"Yes. You don't believe me, but you are. I will teach you the ways of such love, Gideon. Have some more wine."

I drank, savouring the strange mustiness of the wine, but certain that the little I had consumed wasn't the source of the heat and giddiness. Corbeau stood up and came around the table. He gently pulled me up from my chair and kissed the taste of the wine from my lips. The soft pressure of his mouth on mine, the lingering flavour of the grape on our tongues, the trembling heat that threatened to melt me, these are what I remember of that first kiss.

"To bed, I think." He swept me into his arms as if I was a mere babe.

The ceilings and floors whirled before my eyes as he carried me into the bedroom. He set me down on the bed and began undressing me. Although this shocked me, for even my most disturbing dreams had not involved being naked, I didn't protest. I couldn't move of my own volition. I lay limp as any rag doll of my sister's childhood. The surface of the bed beneath me could as easily have been a wooden plank or a cloud.

Soon I lay as naked as Adam when he awoke in Eden. Oh, sin! I trembled in fear and confusion. Corbeau touched me on the head, and then his hand slowly traced the outline of my body. Strange stirrings in my groin surprised me, and when he touched me there, I moaned. I began to understand the words that the preacher had spoken when he defined sodomy.

Corbeau took off his own clothing slowly, letting me accustom myself to the sensations my body was undergoing. I had never seen another man totally naked before, and fear began to nudge under my ribs. My reaction must have been noticeable, for when he was completely undressed, my seducer came once more to my side.

"The first time is always difficult." He ran his hands over the muscles in my shoulders. "How you have escaped being taken long before now, I don't know. Look at these beautiful muscles of yours, and that slim waist. Anyone would want you, Gideon."

Embarrassed, I tried to protest against this unseemly praise. But his lips stopped mine and his body stretched beside me on the bed, pale and smooth, not at all like my rough, sun-browned skin. Unlike me, he had the sculpted form of a true aristocrat.

His tongue touched my right nipple and I gasped. My father's voice began a litany of "Fornication! Sodomy! Sin!" in the back of my mind, but the pleasure cascading through me drowned it out. Corbeau's lips moved lower and kissed me. His body covered mine, and his hands gripped my legs before moving up to cup my buttocks.

"You're so much more attractive without your clothes on. Under those dark Puritan wrappings, I find a treasure."

His words distracted me from what his hands and fingers were doing. I blushed, uncomfortable with such praise. Then a crescendo of pleasure, as he tuned my body like a fine instrument. His lips folded around my manhood, and I cried out. His tongue teased and coaxed, until I shuddered. My first orgasm left me amazed at the power of my body. Corbeau gently turned me over and inserted his fingers, making me gasp. He held me, kissed me, made me tremble, and then he entered. At last I comprehended the full meaning of the word that had so troubled me at twelve years old. If this was sin, so be it.

Trembling despite the sheen of sweat that coated me, I lay in his arms after that first awakening and didn't think of sin at all. The pleasure he had shown me, the places I had gone in my head at the critical moment, these far outweighed the pain and discomfort I had initially felt. Corbeau stroked my damp hair and murmured sweet lies about me into my ear.

"There is one more thing I must show you," he whispered.

Exhausted, but willing, I looked up at him. The things he had shown me thus far had been exquisite. Most of all, I knew I was no longer alone.

"I have a power." Corbeau's lips tickled my ear when he spoke. "I can make you immortal."

The words meant nothing. Half-asleep, I tried to reconcile my actions with my upbringing. Most assuredly, I faced damnation for the sins of sodomy and fornication. This dire knowledge made me want to giggle. Then his sharp teeth found the vein in my neck, and in that crashing instant of realization, I knew I truly was damned.

By drinking my blood, Etienne Corbeau revealed himself as the murderer of those three tenants and the killer of old Nimrod. Here was the demon: my lover. This caused me no alarm. I would have forgiven him anything by then, offered him my own life. I lay quietly in his arms while he drank, and soon slept.

The servants couldn't wake me until noon the next day. I shivered violently, vomiting, weak and dizzy. Blood and worse stained the bed linens. At the frantic beseeching of my valet, I allowed the physician to be sent for. He could find nothing wrong with me—unsurprising considering the state of "medicine" at the time. I was fortunate that he didn't bleed me.

Word of my illness reached the dower farm, and Jamie came to see me as soon as he could. He came to my bedside and peered down at me, as I lay unconsciously clutching the bedcovers. "What ails you, brother?"

"Just a chill," I said, glad that the linens had been changed and that my nausea had passed. How could I ever have had "those" feelings for Jamie? He was no Corbeau. His eyes held only honest concern and his hands were as rough as any labourer's.

"Prudence is worried about you, Gideon. As am I."

"I'm touched by your concern."

"Something is wrong here," Jamie said with certainty.

That frightened me. Nothing was wrong, nothing at all. Someone had finally given me the love I yearned for—what could possibly be wrong? The only thing I feared was discovery. "What do you mean?"

Jamie lowered his voice to a whisper. "It is said that your new steward..."

"What of him?"

He shook his head, unable to repeat whatever rumour had reached him. "I fear you have made a mistake in him."

"Nonsense. He is an excellent man, of great help to me." Last night's revelation was a bad memory. Corbeau could not be a killer.

Jamie looked dubious, but forbore to argue with me any further. He stayed a little longer and didn't mention Corbeau again. When I fell asleep, he left.

Corbeau came to my room that night. "I regret that you are ill. You have distressed your dear sister. Sleep, and be stronger tomorrow." He kissed me, then his fingers brushed my forehead and I immediately fell asleep.

The next morning found me able to rise from my bed, though I still felt chilled and tired. By afternoon, I rode my mare over to the dower farm to visit.

 27

"Prudence," I called out to my surprised sister, who had come out of the farmhouse when she heard my horse approach. "Here I am, well again. No cause for worry."

She hugged me, and peered at my face. "But you're so pale!"

"I have a slight chill. But look how round you are after so short a time!"

Prudence laughed, not at all shocked, and cradled her belly. "I shall have an heir long before you marry Piety."

I frowned. "I would postpone that duty forever, if I could."

"But why? She's a lovely girl, suitable to be your Baroness. Do you love another, perhaps?"

What could I say of my secret, of the happiness that surged through me when I thought of Corbeau, of the answers I had finally found in his arms? "No, I don't love any other woman."

Jamie came from the fields to greet me, and heard me say this. He looked at me sharply as he bid me come into the house. Prudence insisted that I dine with her and her husband that night. I felt lonely and out of place at their table, missing Corbeau's company, and I found little enjoyment in the food. My hosts exchanged meaningful glances throughout the meal, full of love and secret communication. The meat stuck in my throat. I was strangling, all alone.

I slept alone that night, but not the next. Corbeau and I had gone riding together. Somehow we found ourselves racing, despite the danger of riding so quickly at night. I clung tightly to the reins, urging my mare forward, reckless with the anticipation of pleasures to follow. My horse clattered into the yard well ahead of his. Flushed with triumph, I laughed, and so did he. How I longed to kiss him then!

When the household had retired for the night, Corbeau joined me in my bedroom. He kissed me, sending that heady array of emotions in whirl again. I fell into his arms, and he carried me to bed. This time, I responded passionately to his caresses, acting more the aggressor than the ravished innocent. The sharp bite on my neck aroused me when I had thought myself truly spent, and he laughed as he bent to drink.

"You will do well as one of us," he whispered. I didn't ask him what he meant.

The ceiling whirled. Waves of pleasure crashed over me. His tongue, darting across my bleeding neck, gave me such bliss I cried aloud.

It took me three days to recover my strength. I couldn't get warm. Servants hovered, murmuring fearfully, and I heard that the tenants were uneasy. Jamie visited me, saying that Prudence had wanted to come but her condition wouldn't allow her to travel. The physician muttered and mixed potions and bled me once. When he saw that it only made me worse, he had the sense to desist.

Weakness was not a condition I was accustomed to suffering. I had seldom been ill as a child, in part because I would have been whipped for malingering. On the fourth day of my illness, I staggered from my bed and ate a little solid food, and the estate rejoiced.

By the next day, I tended my neglected duties. The tenants I dealt with looked at me sadly, pressing my hand when I allowed it, and some even wept. None of them would tell me why.

Corbeau returned to my bed that night. I'd never really recovered my strength, and I always felt cold and lethargic. His lovemaking, though, roused me out of my languor, and I willingly bared my neck to his deadly kiss. He drank only a little, then pulled away.

"It's your turn, young lord. The change will not be complete unless you drink."

I didn't question his words, though I didn't understand them. He took a small bodkin from the bedside table and used it to cut himself on the inside of his thigh. I gasped, for I couldn't bear to see that beautiful skin pierced. He stroked my hair to quiet me, then pressed my head against his body so that my lips touched the blood that flowed. The taste of it, hot, metallic and salty, shocked me, but I drank greedily.

"Enough." Corbeau pushed my head away and bent to lick his own blood off my mouth. My lips were numb. I couldn't feel his tongue. "The change is assured now. You will be immortal, young lord." His grip on my arm tightened briefly. "And you will be mine."

Morning brought agony. The servants tiptoed around the house and ensured that not one ray of sunlight entered my rooms, for I screamed myself hoarse if it did. I could keep nothing, food or liquid, down. The physician came again, but was helpless against this unknown malady. I shivered and moaned in my bed while the doctor whispered with Jamie. They shouldn't have tried to spare me. I knew I was dying.

As soon as Prudence heard of this, she damned propriety and came to the Hall. Pregnant ladies were not supposed to travel, but I was her brother. She arrived a little after dusk, to find Corbeau blocking her way to my room.

"Your dear brother is ill, my lady." I looked up upon hearing his voice so close.

"I know that, sir." Prudence? Why was she here?

"It would be distressing for you both if you saw him in this state." Corbeau's words might have indicated concern, but his tone was pure malice, and confused me. "In your condition, my lady, I don't think such a thing would be advisable."

Prudence's voice stiffened. "My husband, sir, gave me leave to come, and he is lord over me and the babe I bear. My brother is the Baron. In case you have forgotten your place, you are but the steward, and an ill one you have been. Your services are no longer required. Leave this house."

I heard his footsteps go down the hallway. Prudence's lighter step came into the room and she soon sat beside my bed. Her face, now slightly swollen with emotion and her pregnancy, showed me all. It was hopeless for me. She reached down and hugged me, but I couldn't return her embrace. Tears ran freely down her cheeks as she squeezed my hands. "I should have come sooner. You must get well again, dear brother. I shall see to that."

"Let us not mince words, sister. We both know that I shall die soon. The pain is very bad now, and death will be a release."

"Do not speak so, Gideon!"

But my mind had already drifted to other things. I didn't want to die. It saddened me, to think of leaving my sister and brother-in-law, never seeing their babe. "Poor little Piety. Her parents must be enraged that I haven't married her, to leave her a wealthy widow."

Prudence still wept. "Hush now. Don't concern yourself with Piety. Try to sleep."

I think I did, for when I next opened my eyes, there was a little light showing through the window coverings. I quickly turned my head, since even that trickle hurt terribly. A servant closed the gap, and I managed to look at Prudence.

"Where is Corbeau?" I had forgotten the conversation I had overheard. "He hasn't been to see me." I wanted his touch, his kiss.

Prudence held my hand. Hers felt like a fire on my cold palm. "He has left the house. I sent him away."

"But I want him." In pain and dying, I didn't care if I revealed my secret.

"Look, here's Jamie to see you."

Jamie spoke with me for a few moments, then took Prudence aside. My hearing was acute, though, and I heard what they said.

"How is he?" Jamie asked. "He seems quiet."

"He's in great pain, and the least light makes him scream. Jamie, he's asking for Corbeau."

"We're well rid of him." Jamie spat, which would have shocked me had I been capable of feeling anything but pain.

"But what has he done to my poor brother, that makes Gideon ask after him in such a tone?"

"What tone?"

Prudence lowered her voice. "As if there was more than a master's affection for his steward."

If anything else was said between them, I didn't hear it, for I fell asleep again.

I awoke screaming. Jamie and two servants had to hold me down while Prudence poured syrup of poppy into my mouth and convinced me to swallow. She didn't leave my side save for dire necessity all that day, and I felt at peace knowing she was there. At least I wouldn't die alone.

I was so exhausted by the struggle that at last I surrendered. I refused any more opium, even though the pain was intense. I sensed that the drug was keeping me tied to life. Prudence wept when I pushed away her administering hand.

"No," Jamie said, sensing my distress. "Do not weep, or force him to take the syrup. Enough, dear Prudence. There's a time to let go."

I couldn't speak, only nod. Prudence kissed me. Much to my surprise, so did Jamie. Then I closed my eyes against the pain.

Chapter Two

When I opened my eyes, there was no pain, only darkness. I hadn't expected to awaken again, and I didn't know what to think. I had known I was dying when I pushed Prudence's hand away. No taste of poppy remained in my mouth, no smell of sickness clung to me. The absence of pain was a miracle. Had I died? If so, then where was I? Certainly not in heaven, but hell must be more fearsome than this dark nothing. The questions crowded one upon the other, with no hope of answers.

I had to determine where I was, at least. No sensations of heat or cold, no rush of air, no light, no sound, nothing told me where I was or what had happened to me. I couldn't even feel the clothes on my body, although there seemed to be some sort of covering over it. My hands reached out and I felt rough linen under my questing fingers. Under the linen, I felt only skin. I had been cast naked, wrapped in loose cloth, into a dark and silent place.

A few inches away from either side of my body, my hands met a cold, hard surface that gave back a dull thud when I hit it. It wasn't wood, but what was it? My fingers groped, trying to read this puzzle. Some metal, I thought, something coarser and colder than steel. It was lead.

Coffins were lined with lead, to keep down the smell of rotting corpses. Bodies laid to rest in these coffins were wrapped in shrouds, but otherwise left naked—the law so dictated. It was my coffin that I lay in, and my shroud that parted under my fingers.

Had my sister and brother-in-law, in their grief, entombed me alive? Oddly, I didn't panic. Instincts I didn't yet know I possessed were awakening, and a cold voice in the back of my mind counselled patience.

I noticed that I had no need to draw breath, nor could I detect the familiar rhythm of my heartbeat. A man whose heart doesn't beat and whose lungs draw no air is a dead man. Dead, but waking? What did it mean? What torment of hell was this? My eyes widened in the darkness. I heard footsteps approach. The lid was pried from my coffin, and I blinked painfully against the sudden intrusion of light. Blinded, I didn't see the hand that reached in to pull me out, nor the face of the man who lifted me. But I knew his voice.

"Excellent," said Etienne Corbeau. "You have awakened. Your damned sister might stop me from entering a house of the living, but she can't bar me from the house of the dead. Especially as I come to claim my own."

"Am I dead, then?" My eyes had finally adjusted and I saw him smile.

"You are undead, young lord. A vampire."

The word was unfamiliar to me. "What is that?"

"You'll learn. Oh yes, you'll learn. And it's time for your first lesson. You must feed. But dress, first." He threw a bundle at my feet.

Looking around, I discovered myself within my own family's burial crypt. The dark grey stone walls dripped with the moisture of time. All around me lay the dead. My coffin, I now saw, lay on a slab of white stone next to the one that contained my father's murdered body. My mother's box lay next to his. Further in the cobwebbed recesses, ancestors quietly rotted. Generations of dead Redoaks, and I was the only one waking. My knees threatened to give way.

"Put the clothes on, Gideon, and we can leave this place sooner. The dead cannot hurt you. You are the living dead."

The iron gates yawned open into the night beyond. Dear God in heaven, what did all of this mean? What was I, that I had wakened to this...this death in life? Numbed, unable to think, unable to cope, I could only obey Corbeau and be grateful for his guidance. I dressed clumsily. The clothing was not my own—it was peasant garb and there was blood on the tunic. I didn't ask where the clothing had come from, fearing the answer.

"Ready?" Corbeau asked, and I nodded.

He led me out of the Redoak crypt to a dark patch of road where a carriage waited. Two long boxes, like coffins, had been placed on the top of this conveyance. The driver, muffled in an old cloak, leaned over his box to gaze down at us as we approached. He drew the cloth away from his face and bared his teeth at me. I cringed back, startled at the sight of gleaming fangs.

"Is this the one, master?" he said.

"Yes. Remember that he is mine. You cannot have him. Not yet."

That 'not yet' sent an ice spear plunging into my heart. I didn't like the looks of that driver, with those horrible fangs and his great staring colourless eyes. Since he had pulled me from my coffin, Corbeau had been cold and impatient with me. His smile held no warmth, and his voice had lost its mesmerising quality. What had happened to me, that I saw my love so differently? I must have done something terribly wrong, offended in him in some way.

Corbeau spoke to me angrily. "Get in the carriage! Graydon will not touch you without my permission." His blue eyes locked with those of the driver, and that fearsome being bowed his head.

This change in Corbeau's manner hurt. He had never spoken to me so harshly, never presumed to give me a direct order.

His cold hand clasped around my neck. Fingers like iron shook me. "Second lesson, before you have even learned the first," he snarled in my face. "I am now your master. Listen to your blood, and it will tell you that. You are nothing but my slave, and I expect instant obedience. Get in the carriage." He booted the door open with his foot and flung me into the interior, one-handed.

I landed on something that was hard and soft at once, and that gave a gasping moan beneath me. Pushing myself up with my hands, I looked at my landing cushion. It was one of my tenants, just a lad on the verge of manhood. He had been bound, gagged, and left like baggage on the floor of the carriage. His face shone with sweat—his hair, clothes and the gag were dark and rank with it. His fear had caused him to soil himself, as well. The stink in the carriage would have made me ill, had I still breathed.

But beneath the sweat and the human waste, I sensed another smell. Copper-bright, it sang a siren song in his veins that made my mouth ache. I ran my tongue across my upper gums and felt two sharp, pointed teeth emerging from hidden recesses.

"Ah," said Corbeau's voice from the other side of the open carriage door. "Feel them, do you, my little catamite? Your fangs have come in, answering your need. You can smell the blood, can't you? That is your food and drink, your breath and life, forevermore."

Without even realising it, I had once more covered the young peasant's body with my own, this time with the intention of pinning him in place. His eyes...oh, his eyes! Sometimes, I can still see them, the fear, the pleading, the shocked recognition. For was I not his lord, the Baron of Redoak? He and his family had served me, paid their rent and taxes, tilled my land, tended my beasts, and watched with bowed head as I had been laid in my early grave. Yet here I leant over him, in league with the very devil, demon's fangs sprouting from my mouth and his death written in my eyes.

"There's a vein in the throat," said Corbeau's dry schoolmaster's voice. "You can feel it beat beneath your fingers. Yes, just there. Listen to the blood, Gideon."

A red butterfly fluttered under my questing fingers. The blood spoke straight to my new instincts, and I needed no urging from Corbeau to tear open the flesh that hid the great vein from view and drink. No honeyed wine had ever tasted so sweet, no clear well water had so quenched my thirst. As the warm elixir slid down my throat, the butterfly pulse trembled, faded and was still.

I tasted his death in his blood, felt the life sigh out of him. The realisation that I, his lord, his protector, Gideon of Redoak, caused his death brought me out of the crimson dream where I'd been carried by his blood. I dropped the body, and the boneless way it flopped to the carriage floor sickened me.

"Take the carrion and dispose of it in a ditch," Corbeau said. "Graydon will help you. Bring your coffin back with you when you return."

I would have preferred not to have the driver's help, for he frightened me. He leered at me, fangs bared, as I dragged the poor boy's corpse from the carriage. I could scarcely bring myself to understand that I had committed murder on one of my tenants, but the awkwardly flopping body was too real to deny. Graydon had a spade, and thrust it into my hands once we had reached a suitable burial spot. Numb with shock, I recognised the same copse where Nimrod's savaged body had been found. I had no doubt now who had slain the dog. My heart and mind were screaming with pain and confusion, but I dug a shallow grave and tossed the peasant's corpse into it. What in God's name had I become?

What type of night that was, I couldn't tell you. Still or windy, warm or cool, starlit or cloud-covered, I have no memory of the weather. A chill had wrapped itself around my heart. Why had Corbeau, whom I had loved, turned so cold and cruel? Where were his tender looks, his gentle voice, his kindness to a bewildered boy? It must have been something I had done that had so displeased him. There had to be a way to make amends.

Graydon dragged my coffin back to the carriage once I'd filled in the grave. I followed, too bewildered to do otherwise. I recalled laying my mother and father to rest in the crypt—it had taken eight strong men to bear even my mother's coffin. Yet Graydon carried my coffin with no visible effort. Corbeau studied me as his servant pitched me inside. I lay flat and submissive, aware of his eyes on me. Oh, let him touch me, soothe me, I thought helplessly.

"I expect obedience, young lord," he said. "You haven't learned the first lesson sufficiently."

I heard something whistle through the air and felt a sharp sting across my back. I risked a glance at Corbeau, and my heart quailed when I saw the riding crop he held. "This is but a taste, Gideon," he said, flicking the whip almost casually across my legs. "You belong entirely to me now."

"Please, I don't understand. What have I done?"

The crop caught me on the buttocks, twice. "You are mine! That's all you need know. Obey me, or you'll suffer far worse than this."

Bewildered, I promised my obedience and loyalty. I remained huddled on the floor of the carriage, trying to make sense of my new state as a creature that drank blood to survive. I could feel the blood I had taken from that boy flowing through my own veins, giving me strength and nourishment. The word "vampire" was a new one to me, but I had no doubt at all that I had become one of the legions of Hell.

We left Shrewsbury far behind that night. When we stopped, it was nowhere I recognised. From what little I was allowed to see, it was an abandoned manor house. I was curtly ordered to drag my coffin into the house and get inside of it. Fearing reprisals for further displeasing Corbeau, I obeyed. I found that I could move the heavy, lead-lined box with little effort, but I didn't understand what this meant. Whimpering quietly to myself from sheer terror, I wondered what horrors the future held.

Corbeau took me to France. Every night on the journey, he would supply me with a new victim to drink from. If I refused, he beat me mercilessly and killed the victim himself, then shoved my face into the flowing blood. I never saw the boat or ship we used to cross the channel, for I had been told to stay in my coffin. I could feel it being lifted by outside forces, and I could feel the movement of the boat across the water. The motion made me feel ill.

When we docked, I was allowed out. My box was once more lifted and placed on the roof of a carriage, along with those of Corbeau and Graydon.

I saw little of the countryside through which we passed, for I was kept away from the windows of the carriage. Twice we had to stop travelling while the sun made her daylight journey. The coffins were carried from the coach into abandoned buildings. There never seemed to be a shortage of such structures. Corbeau must have made a survey of them, out of necessity. At dusk Graydon and I would load the boxes back onto the roof of the carriage, and we would be off again.

I spent most of the journey in numb silence. Neither Corbeau nor Graydon spoke to me save to give orders, which I obeyed. My father had taught me too well. I tried to make sense of my lover's new behaviour. I deemed it better to please him.

We also stopped in order to feed. Some poor fool human, out at night when most souls were tucked safely in bed, would be set upon by Graydon and dragged into the carriage for our mutual refreshment. Although this gory feasting disgusted me, blood was the only substance that satisfied my cravings.

The third night, we reached our destination. We had travelled across a large valley and were coming now into some hills. I had no idea of our geographical location, save that we were still in France. The sound of the horses' hooves and the wheels of the carriage changed suddenly, as if there were cobblestones underfoot where there had previously been packed earth. From what little I could see out the windows, stone walls had risen around us. We had entered the courtyard of a large building.

The carriage halted and Corbeau curtly ordered me out. Climbing down, I found myself inside the gates of what appeared to be an ancient keep.

Many storeys tall, it stood upon a barren hill, its crumbling stones once part of a larger fortification. I could hear and smell a nearby river, although the grim walls hid this from my view. Torches in tall stands illuminated the courtyard, the occasional whiff of breeze from the river making the flames gutter.

Two great ironbound wooden doors, black and cracked with age but unbreakable as steel, barred the entrance to the keep. These suddenly swung open from the inside, and several people emerged.

There were perhaps a dozen of them, mostly men although I could see at least two women. Most were dressed as nobles or wealthy merchants. One or two had lowlier garb. But all of them, even the women, had a greedy, feral look to them that frightened me.

Two of the men led the horses away, hooves clattering on the cobblestones, empty carriage rumbling behind. The others all stared at me.

I felt my master's hand descend on my shoulder and grip it. It was not a reassuring gesture. He said to the gathering in the courtyard, "This is Gideon. He is mine until I say otherwise."

My heart sank at those words. Someone snickered, someone else murmured something. Very little scent came to me from that wild clutch of strangers. Only three of them, at most, had the scent of mortal blood in their veins. The others were all vampires.

His hand still on my shoulder, Corbeau steered me into his home. Graydon and the others followed. The doors were pulled shut and barred. I was trapped.

We were in a great, draughty hall. The far wall to my right had a large fireplace, which cast a dull red glow across the bare, cold stone floor. The only furniture, other than the ubiquitous torches, was a large trestle table with some benches. A few square, featureless stone pillars supported the soot-stained ceiling. The altogether cheerless room did nothing to raise my spirits.

The small group who had greeted us in the courtyard gathered around. I came to think of them as the minions. They leered at me, and made disgusting noises and worse suggestions, but none dared lay a finger on me. None, that is, save Graydon, but he did so only at Corbeau's command. He stepped forward and forcibly stripped the clothing from my body.

Shocked and humiliated, I instinctively and foolishly covered my genitals with my hands. This caused a ripple of laughter, which Corbeau silenced with a gesture.

"Graydon," he said, "the chains."

My master's trusted henchman nodded, and left the hall. I stood there, wishing that I could blush, trying to maintain my dignity. I was the eighteenth Baron of Redoak. My family dated back generations and had served kings on battlefields. I knew that in truth I was a simple country boy with pretensions of nobility, but that seemed little cause to humiliate me before this feral pack of jackals.

Graydon returned. I could hear the chains clanking, and flinched when they were brought to me. My wrists, ankles, neck and waist were shackled and the chains run through the shackles. Only now did I notice that the pillar nearby had a rusty iron ring sunk deep into it and that the stone was stained. My chains were affixed to this ring, and Graydon tightened them until I was forced to stand on tiptoe with my arms stretched far above my head, my naked body thus displayed for the titillation of the room.

"You have no life, save the one I gave you," Corbeau said, beginning to pace around my pillar. He didn't look at me. "You do not move unless I give you leave. You do not beg, you do not protest, you do not attempt to escape, you do nothing without my leave. Do you understand?"

I did not. I could only grit my teeth against the pain in my arm muscles, feeling the tendons stretch and threaten to snap, and wonder what I had done wrong to make the man I loved turn on me so.

No pity showed in any of the glittering eyes of the minions. Even the women leaned forward, waiting for the next amusement. Corbeau took a length of chain that had not been used to bind me and thrust it into the fire. When it had been heated so that it glowed red, he beat me with it, head to foot.

Frightful burns and welts sprang up. I screamed, unable to help myself, for the pain was intense. I knew already that a vampire could feel physical pain, but not that it could be this terrible. I could feel bones in my arms and legs snap under the blows of the heavy chain. All the while, the minions applauded, whistled and laughed. Some called out suggestions.

Pieces of my flesh hung in tatters. The pain was unbearable. I could smell cooked meat and knew it was my own. My right eye had been destroyed and my left was flecked with blood, so at least I could no longer see the next torment. The chains clanked to the floor at last as Corbeau tired of this diversion. Over the sound of my own whimpers, I heard him walk to the fireplace, but I couldn't see what he did there. I could hear excited cries from the jackals that watched, however, and even through a broken, blood-clogged nose I could smell hot metal. Surely not more chains? There was nothing left of me to beat with them.

No, not chains, but a hot poker, and a part of me still remained to be burned and tortured. I screamed until my throat bled, but Corbeau was unmoved.

When the chains were released, I was too broken to even sink to the floor. I think Graydon held me and pried my torn mouth open. I could feel blood being forced into me, and out of instinct I swallowed. At once my strength began to return. My eyes were the first to heal. I blinked painfully in the torchlight and whimpered as the blood spread to all the injuries, forcing them to mend, forcing me to be whole again. More and more blood slid down my throat and throughout my abused limbs. Even the burns disappeared, and the strips of hanging meat sealed themselves back to my body. I found I could stand and walk again.

"Now do you understand?" Corbeau asked me.

"Let me go. I've never wronged you, that you abuse me thus. Let me go."

"You dare." He reached out and grabbed me by the hair. "You dare!"

He marched me out of the hall, away from the gaping minions, and towards a long spiralling staircase of steep ascent and narrow width. Prodding me, he forced me up and up this, until my head ached from the dizziness. At last we reached the roof of the keep. Corbeau shoved me out onto it.

Gazing over the broken battlements, I could see some crumbled remnants of walls that must have been part of the original castle. The keep itself was poorly maintained. There were gaps in the mortar, and a greasy patina of dirt, neglect and age lay on the cracked stones. The river that protected one wall of the keep and would once have been a barrier against siege of the castle lay to the left, its deep and wild rapids an equally insuperable barrier to a vampire. The keep stood, as I had known from the way the carriage had travelled, on a high hill, barren of any trees. Not even grass seemed to grow well in its environs. Drear and brown deadness met my eyes in every direction.

Corbeau's hair and clothing whipped in the wind that blew at this height as he pushed me towards the edge that looked over the ruins of the larger building. Great cracked flagstones and sharp chunks of granite littered the ground. I thought I could make out some objects that might be cannonballs. They were a very long way down.

"This is the only way I'll ever let you go." My master put his hand on the small of my back, and pushed.

Downward I plunged, face towards my doom, my limbs spread and flailing at thin air for a purchase. The dark stained walls of the keep witnessed my fall. The ground with its broken bits of castle rushed up to greet me. My mind screamed, but the wind of my passage snatched sound from my throat before it could be issued. I had already endured torment beyond imagining, now a horrible death would be my fate. I could still feel the pressure of Corbeau's hand on my back, hear the grimness in his voice. He had pushed me off the roof of a castle onto a yard littered with stone. Why?

There was no time to ponder. I fell swiftly although it seemed to go on forever. I hit a section of old, jagged wall remnants. I could feel nearly every bone in my body break. Blood spurted from a hundred wounds, and teeth trickled out of my mouth in bloody foam. I couldn't even scream. Surely now I would die?

But death did not come, although I mentally begged for it. Instead, Graydon and some of the others came out and scooped me up. I groaned piteously when moved. This only made them laugh. They poured me—being mostly liquid by then—into my coffin, which had been put in a dark oubliette of a room. I heard my master's footfall, but lacked the ability to move a muscle. Again my mouth was pried open, and fresh blood was force-fed to me. Graydon slammed the lid down on my coffin, laughing.

The daysleep came as a blessing, and I begged whatever strange god ruled the undead that I wouldn't wake at the next dusk. Surely I was too badly injured for blood to have any restoring properties? Surely I could not be made to endure any more torment?

But dusk came, and with it, sentience returned. My eyes opened, my mind awoke and my body stirred. All was mended and whole—the bones knit, the abrasions gone, the teeth all present and accounted for, no blood seeping, no pain.

That was when I truly understood. Nothing could kill me. I could not die, no matter how I wished it. That had been one of the reasons why Corbeau had pushed me off the keep—to show to me that no matter what he did, I would heal. I couldn't escape from my existence. I was subordinate to his will. He was my bloodmaster and I couldn't disobey his command. Any attempt to escape or show independence, and I would again be pushed from the roof.

So it proved. Night after night, I endured torture and torment, often sexual abuse—exposed for the amusement of the minions. What reason Corbeau had for this sport, I did not know. Torture for sexual pleasure was a concept unknown to me. But no matter how brutal my treatment, I would be force-fed blood before I was locked away for the day. Thus I would awaken healed in body. Burns, cuts, bruises, missing digits, even missing limbs—all would be healed with the blood. I knew of the raiding forays into villages and towns that kept this supply fresh, and it disgusted me that my food was the lives of innocents, yet I had no choice. I was a vampire.

As I lay in the coffin at dusk, staring at my restored body, this truth stung me. The horror of what I had become and what had been done to me crippled my mind. I had to protect myself the only way I could. My mind went blank. My personality hid itself in a cloak of darkness and numbness. Uncaring, unfeeling, I became an obedient hulk. I went where I was told, did what I was told, submitted to everything done to me. It couldn't touch me because I had nothing left. Corbeau broke me, again and again and again. I must have been very naïve ever to have loved him.

One evening, many endless nights of pain after my lesson in the futility of escaping, it was not Corbeau who came to fetch me from my coffin, but Graydon. This change in the usual routine brought my mind back to awareness.

"Where is Corbeau?" I asked.

"He gave you to me for the night. He has other amusements."

Graydon carried the familiar, hated chains with him but as yet, he had made no move to put them on me. The door to my tiny cell hung open. I needed no more than that. I ran past him and out the door into the corridor, springing for the stairs that would lead me to the hall and thence to the main doors and freedom. How far I thought I would get, naked, weakened by torture and captivity, a foreigner and a vampire, I don't know. I only knew that I had to take the chance. I could hear Graydon laughing.

The pack of minions that always inhabited the keep heard the alarm and gave chase. Laughing and catcalling they hunted me through the dark passageways, around pillars and along the great hall's trestle table. There, at last, I came to bay, all escape cut off by better-fed vampires that had not been beaten every night.

Graydon came into the hall. "Teach him a good lesson."

They fell on me in a swarm, and I remember no more. The spark of rebellion, the faint breath of hope, withered and died and my mind descended once more into protective darkness.

There came a night—I have no memory how many years had passed—when Corbeau came to my cell. He carried no chains or whips or worse implements, no red-hot metal or iron hooks. Instead, he had clothing with him, good stuff and well made. I was a compliant rag doll as he dressed me in it. Then he led me through the keep by a way I hadn't seen before, to a room I had never viewed. I stared in dull astonishment at the high, recessed bed with its black curtains, the chairs cushioned with crimson velvet, the woven rug upon the floor. I hadn't known there was such a room in the keep.

A low table near the bed held a pitcher and two goblets. From this pitcher, still without a word, Corbeau poured wine. He pressed one goblet into my numb hand while I fought hard against acknowledging that this was happening. Surprise was a feeling, and I didn't want to feel. Whatever happened tonight, it couldn't affect me.

His lips met mine and the wine spilled from his goblet unheeded. I hadn't touched my cup at all, and I didn't return his kiss. To think that I had once trembled for it! Now I felt nothing. How had I ever been a naïve enough fool to believe him, to fall for his blandishments, to hire a complete stranger as my steward? How had I loved him?

He never spoke, not once. He took my clothing off as gently as he had put it on me, and made love to me as if it was the first time and we were still back in Redoak Hall. I closed my eyes and waited for it to be over. He led me back to my coffin and put me in it with a kiss. I made no sound. Neither of us had spoken a word the entire night.

The next night, the torture began again. I had been right not to trust that departure from it.

Time passed. I can't say how much time, for I had no way to mark it. But there came a night when I left the keep by the door rather than the roof, for the first time since entering it.

Graydon roused me and gave me clothing, both events unusual enough to make me somewhat wary. But Graydon brought me to the great hall, where Corbeau presided on a chair that had been brought in. Graydon made me kneel before my master's feet.

"You are to go hunting tonight, young lord," Corbeau told me. "Graydon will take you. Obey him as you would me."

The too-familiar iron shackle was fastened around my neck and a length of chain attached to this. Graydon took the other end of the chain and pulled on it. Reduced to following like a dog, I left the keep. We took a cart rather than the larger carriage and travelled to a village a few miles away.

Quiet and dark, the village was an ordinary enough place, consisting of some houses, a tavern, and a church. It was a place of the living, now all asleep, innocents unaware of the monsters in their midst.

Graydon chose an isolated cottage and with me in tow, went up to the front entrance. With foot and fist, he raised such a ruckus that the sleepy householder came to the door and flung it open to see who could possibly be disturbing him so rudely at such an ungodly hour. He hesitated upon seeing the evil-looking Graydon accompanied by a filthy boy on a chain, yet somehow he was persuaded to leave his house. I could feel some force exerted upon the man by Graydon's mind. This was a revelation for me, as I hadn't known vampires other than my master possessed such powers. I had no time to think about this.

As soon as the man had passed the threshold, Graydon had him. I secured the victim with the rope we brought with us, carried him back to the cart and flung him into it. I could see his questioning brown eyes on my chains, but I couldn't afford to let myself care about his fate. All the blood I had consumed since my arrival at the keep had to have come from such poor fools. This was the first whose eyes I had seen since the night I awakened in the Redoak crypt. It meant nothing to me.

We returned to our home with the meat and delivered it to our master. Corbeau fell on the villager, plunging his fangs instantly into the man's neck. That night, none of the minions were about save for Graydon, who watched and licked his lips. When Corbeau ordered me to come and taste the man's blood, I obeyed.

I knelt, now free from the chains, and lapped up my master's leavings. I could feel the man's life draining away, for Corbeau had drunk deep. There would be nothing left for Graydon to drink. While I tried to coax more from the villager's veins, Corbeau seized my wrist in his unbreakable grip. He had a knife in his other hand.

Horror pierced the dark veil I had wrapped myself in for protection. But I couldn't break that grip nor prevent that knife from slicing my wrist so that the dark blood welled in its wake. I once more felt pressure in my own mind, and realised that it was my master exerting his will upon the prisoner. The man, helpless in Corbeau's mental grip, lowered his mouth to my bleeding wrist.

"No," I whispered, but none heeded it. I don't think anyone even heard.

The villager had to swallow, or suffocate. He chose to breathe, and consumed my vampire blood with the air he took in. Once he had drunk enough blood to ensure that he would change, Graydon took him away.

The court hunted him down and killed him the next night, while I watched. At the end, his eyes turned on me. The stake plunged into his heart the next moment.

After that, I frequently went out on raids to fetch home victims. I learned to use my own mental powers of command on them, hesitantly at first and then more surely. Most of the prey were killed after they were drained. A few were fed vampire blood in order that they would change. Some of these were then killed anyway. Others were released to make their way as best as possible. I learned that vampires could, in fact die—by sunlight, by fire, by wooden stake—though I was watched constantly to ensure that I tried none of these on myself. There were those, too, like the minions who had come of their own free will to the castle. Corbeau drew them with his beauty and his depravity alike. They would come and stay for a few years or forever if they chose, taking the master's leavings and playing his games, while he smiled in amusement. I remained a prisoner and a plaything, the only one who survived. I wondered about this, in moments of clarity.

Time passed, and nothing changed. Then, long after the first time he had done this, Corbeau came to me in his gentle guise and took me to his bedroom where he served me wine I didn't drink and made love to me as if we were truly in love. This time, however, he spoke to me. "Do you love me still, young lord?" he asked, smoothing my hair across the pillow.

I looked up at him. Though I fought hard against it, self-awareness returned. Feelings surged through long-unused channels. But the feelings were hatred, disgust, and repulsion. He was a monster, and he had made me one. He had turned me into an abomination. I became a sodomite, a murderer and a vampire because of this man whom I had once loved.

But I dared not answer, remembering the roof, the wind in his hair and the dark walls rushing past me as I fell.

He murmured in my ear. "I never loved you, Gideon. You were pure and innocent, but I didn't love you. Did you think I had? Your soul drew me to you. Some of that purity clings to your soul even now, did you know?"

I had to fight against the impulse to push him away and run until I died. But I knew the only place there was to run was the roof.

"I was so pure once," my master said, but I didn't think he was speaking to me. "Now such innocence offends me. I will have it, my little catamite—I will have those pathetic tatters of your soul. How have you kept them all this time? Answer me!"

I could not.

"Across all the miles, Gideon, you drew me. Someone who shines so must be destroyed, did you know? I've slain better men than you, brought this nation of France to its knees, and yet you remain innocent. How?"

Angered by my lack of answer, he lifted me bodily and carried me back to my coffin.

After an eternity, there came a night when Graydon brought me clothing and bade me put it on. So sure of me now that he

had brought no chains, he took me to where Corbeau held court in the great hall.

"Ah, my dear little catamite," my master smiled at me while I looked at him and felt hate. "I require a new diversion, and I need you to procure it for me. The village down river has been blessed recently by a birth. A brand new child, Gideon, an innocent baby girl who cries and vomits and soils her cloths. Think of the taste of her, young lord! How sweet, how wonderful, to taste such a life!"

Horror filled my mind and heart. An innocent newborn child? I hadn't thought even Corbeau so depraved as to murder an infant. She should be allowed to live and grow, assuming she escaped the more ordinary dangers of childhood, not be fodder for the beautiful demon before me. "No," I said.

"Ah, you have never tasted a newly born babe, or you wouldn't say that," Corbeau said, not taking my "no" as a refusal. "You and Graydon will go to the village and fetch me this child, then you'll see what sport it is."

I raised my head and looked him in the eyes, unwavering. Although frightened to the depths of my soul, I repeated, firmly, "No."

Silence fell over the hall. I heard Graydon start to gasp, but he stifled it quickly. The ever-present hangers-on stared at me. Corbeau's eyes were pools of ice. It was quite possibly the first time anyone had ever said "no" to him.

"What did you say?" Corbeau's voice was silk on steel.

A third time, the charm. "No."

A torch guttered behind me. Nothing else moved or made a sound.

"I expect obedience. I thought you had learned that lesson." Corbeau's fist, lightning fast, felled me to the floor. "Get gone."

I picked myself up and fled the room. The doors offered no escape—a dozen cruel vampires stood between me and freedom. With nowhere else to run, I returned to my grim little cell and my hated coffin. Hunger gnawed at me, for I hadn't fed now for two nights and I knew there would be no blood tonight. I had discovered that it wasn't necessary to drink every night, but the lack of it weakened me.

Let him kill me now. Let me be free of this nightmare. But as soon as that thought fled, I knew it for a fruitless wish. He would not kill me. I would be punished, and all the torments I had suffered through the years in this wretched place would be nothing to what he would do now. Shuddering in my coffin, envisioning endless nights of being thrown from the roof of the keep, I shut the lid and waited for the daysleep.

But torture did not await me when I woke—only the darkness of the buried coffin. No hope of escape, no reprieve, just an eternal hell of madness and starvation. I started to laugh. Was this not, after all, the very doom my father had often foretold? The irony was too perfect to resist, and laughter kept panic at bay.

Chapter Three

Eventually, I stopped laughing and tested the confines of my prison. It would have been a Corbeau trick to block escape only from the most obvious route, and leave me scrabbling despairingly at the coffin lid while the sides or bottom of the box opened to freedom. Cautiously, I tested each panel that I could press my weight against. Head and foot, hand and knee, buttocks and elbows, all relayed the same message. I was trapped.

So...I had no means of escape and no hope of rescue. I had survived without either for an eternity already, and at least there were no whips in the coffin. In the long, endless nights to come, doubtless I would slowly descend into panic, but for the moment I was content to lie in the quiet dark. Each passing hour was the same as the one before and the one after. The earth turned, but I didn't feel it. I slipped unnoticing into a kind of trance, uncaring and unfeeling.

I didn't even hear the first excavations of the shovel. I drifted back to awareness only gradually. The dark confused me—disoriented, I reached out, and barked my knuckles on wood. I remembered where I was: buried, in my coffin. What had roused me? The burden of earth pressing in on me was lessening! Now that I listened, I could just make out the scrape of a shovel against packed dirt and stones, and the thud of each scoop being displaced. Rescue and freedom were at hand!

I didn't bang on the lid and shout. I drew myself up as tightly as possible and made no sound. Who wielded that shovel? Corbeau or one of his minions come to torment me? Some innocent mortal, digging his own grave? I was famished, my fangs protruding, the blood craving hot in my belly. If there was a human with red fluid in his veins at the other end of that shovel, he was meat. Killing sickened me, but my need pressed hard.

Like a spider in a web, I waited to see if my savior was a juicy fly or a hungry bird. Scraping sounds soon told me that the digger had entirely cleared the earth from above the lid of my coffin.

The lid swung back, letting the lesser darkness of ordinary night into my prison. Eyes stared down at me, where I huddled in dread of my seeming rescue, and I stared back up at them. One of the warm hazel eyes closed in an unmistakable wink. Dark reddish hair, that shade known as auburn, framed a strong face. This was not one of Corbeau's minions, nor was it a vampire. The bloodsmell coming from him carried a strange undertone, something odd. I felt cold prickles all over. Neither human nor vampire, my rescuer represented an unknown.

A sturdy, calloused hand reached down to me. "Well?" he asked, in English. He sounded amused and slightly impatient. "Are you getting out?"

This was too much for me to properly process. Of all the horrid imaginings that had crossed my mind when I first heard the shovel, I had not expected this. In my stupefaction, my mind focused on the most irrelevant of its observations.

"But you're Welsh." I hadn't heard that accent since I'd left Shrewsbury, and never dreamed I would encounter it here.

He rolled his eyes. "Yes, and you're English. We could have a debate about which is the superior nationality, which you would lose. But I'd prefer that you just trust me for the moment and let me help you out of there." He reached into the coffin and grabbed my arm. That grip hurt, as the fingers contracted around my flesh. "Up you get!" he said cheerfully.

I had to cooperate, or lose my arm. The pain, in fact, aroused me fully out of the strange state I had fallen into during my imprisonment. I accepted the stranger's assistance, and he heaved me up onto the mound of earth that had been displaced from my grave. Stunned, I stared up at the stars I'd thought I would never see again. They wheeled above me on their eternal journey, uncaring points of icy flame, yet I could have kissed each one. The moon, a thin sliver of cold reflected light, shone as gloriously as the sun I remembered. A soft breeze tickled my hair, a caress far more welcome than Corbeau's. I took another look at the man who had effected this rescue.

"Who are you? Why have you released me?"

"Evan Jones, at your service. As for why, that can wait. We haven't much time. Give me a hand with this coffin, we've got to get out of here."

He didn't have a spare shovel for me to use, but I had my native strength. I went over and helped him by tugging the coffin loose. By now I'd concluded that this was some dreamlike adventure. If I wanted answers to the questions crowding my brain, it seemed I had to go along with whatever Evan Jones had in mind.

Between the two of us, we soon had my coffin freed from the earth. Evan and I dragged it towards a waiting horse and cart.

I approached warily, given the usual reaction of horses to my kind, but the carthorse only swished its tail in a dispirited way when it saw me. It was altogether a sorry-looking nag, and I supposed it had no heart left in it to be alarmed by the undead.

As we put the coffin into the bed of the cart, I said to Evan, "You knew I was buried there. You knew I would have a coffin. Why have you rescued me?"

"Would you like me to put you back? It's never wise to question good fortune, now, is it? Climb up on the seat, and let's get going." He leapt nimbly up onto the seat himself, and took the reins.

I climbed up. What choice did I have? It was assuredly not safe to stay here, and I desperately wanted some answers. I realised I wouldn't get those answers from Evan until we were well away from this spot.

In an agony of doubt and confusion, I sat beside that stranger and wondered where he was taking me. As far as I could tell, we didn't seem to be going in the direction of Corbeau's Keep, and that reassured me a little. Did Evan act on his own? He wore rough, peasant clothing, yet his demeanour was not that of a servant, at least not a thrall or serf.

As the cart began to move, I looked around the scenery. Was I even still in France? Apparently, for this was wine country. I could smell the fruit on the vine in the night wind.

Ah, that scent, of ripening grapes! It pierced through my fear, through the dark residue of my abandonment, and lifted my spirits even more than the smell of blood would have done. The rustle of the grape leaves was the clink of chains sliding, unlocked, to the floor. Freedom, a wine far headier than any pressed from those round globes on their vines, ran through my veins. The dim outlines of

old chateaux could occasionally be glimpsed, far from the path of our cart, and each one caused my heart to cheer. For I knew now where we were—in the Loire valley, the winepress of France, and that meant we were leaving the dark Keep far behind.

Each jolt of the cart, each clop of a hoof, each rut in the road was one more step away from Hell. I ceased to care where Evan took me, so long as it was not back. After a time, we reached a small stone dwelling, an abandoned shepherd's hut or peasant croft. The thatch was in disrepair, and the taint of its rot made me wrinkle my nose. The foundation had a distinct list to starboard. The next heavy snowfall would be the death of this place, yet it afforded shelter of a sort. Evan stopped the cart and climbed down.

"We'll stay here for the day. It's safe enough."

I clambered down from the cart. He unhitched the horse and produced a feed bag from the back of our vehicle. I took the chance to stretch my legs and look around with interest. No scent of vines reached me here. We were down in a little hollow well away from the arbours and prying eyes. I detected no trace of the smell of human blood, either. My stomach cramped from hunger, and my fangs pricked at my lower lip.

Evan finished caring for the horse, and started pulling my coffin out of the cart bed. I moved to help him, and together we carried it into the hut. Since this was an abandoned dwelling, with no mortals in residence, I needed no invitation to cross the threshold.

There were precisely three rooms, making it a luxury dwelling of its kind. But the surplus of rooms was the only luxury this place enjoyed. The walls oozed. Spiders and beetles scurried for cover under rotting debris when Evan and I entered, carrying the coffin. Something had built a nest in one corner. Unidentifiable things crunched underfoot, and small, brittle bones with gnaw marks at the edges splintered when we set the coffin down on them.

It seemed like paradise.

One of the two extra rooms had a hanging of thick, rough, undyed wool in front of the doorway, and Evan indicated that this was where my coffin should go. We lifted it up and took it into its new resting place, a dank closet of a room with no windows. The door covering, when drawn closed, completely blocked light from outside. I went out of this tiny compartment again to more closely examine my temporary shelter. The dismal condition of the interior was a deliberate blind, I realised. The hut was still completely sound, despite the way it seemed to slant. No cracks or fissures marred the walls, and the door to the outside fit snugly and securely. It could even be barred with an iron rod that lay on the floor as if it was just another piece of unconsidered garbage.

Vampires had sheltered here before. How many confused young ones of my kind had Evan brought to this place, and what was his purpose? I didn't attempt to question him. He brushed past me without a word, out into the waning night, and returned carrying a wine bottle. Tired of being continually disconcerted by this odd creature, I spoke sharply to him.

"Wine? You're drinking wine?" The craving for nourishment pinched me, yet I could sense no humans nearby. How could he calmly drink wine, when my eyes glowed red?

He laughed, and the sound made me relax a little. It was genuine mirth, not the brutal laughter that had been aimed at me for many years. I almost liked Evan Jones, especially in comparison to anyone associated with Corbeau.

"It's not wine," he said, pulling the cork out of the bottle, and thrusting the latter at me. "It's for you."

The smell of blood came up to me from its musty depths. Cold, stale blood that reeked of animal—pig, I thought. The blood was heavily mixed with salt to keep it liquid. Imagine anticipating a wonderful meal, such as rare roast beef, and getting cold gristle instead. But when you're starving, any nourishment is better than none. I wrinkled my nose, but lifted the bottle to my lips and drank. It was foul stuff, but it calmed the hunger. I drained the bottle and gradually felt my strength return. I had been dangerously weak and undernourished, I realised. How long had I been buried?

Evan watched me drink. "Did you like it?" he asked when I finished.

"No," I said honestly, and he laughed again.

"Time for bed," he said, indicating the east. No sign of the dawn yet showed, but I could feel the tug of it.

I gave him the empty wine bottle, which he carefully took and carried outside, presumably to the cart. I dreaded the thought of getting back into the coffin in which I'd been trapped, but there was no other choice. What sleeping arrangements Evan made for himself, I didn't know. I decided I was happier in my ignorance.

The interior of my hated coffin was filthy with dirt that had seeped in during my rescue. It would certainly make no difference to the state of the clothing I wore. I climbed in and pulled the lid shut over myself. Closed into the darkness, I started to shiver. Trapped! I was trapped again, with the packed dirt surrounding me. It took a tremendous effort of will to remind myself that I had been rescued. By whom, and for what purpose, remained a mystery.

The lid was drawn off my coffin from the outside almost as soon as I awoke. Fear washed over me until I saw familiar hazel eyes twinkling down at me.

"I didn't think you'd be lazy," he said, grinning. "We've got to get moving, so get up."

I looked up stupidly. "We're leaving?"

"Want to stay here?"

"No."

"Then let's get this thing back on the cart," he said, kicking my coffin.

"Yes, just give me a moment." I clambered out of the hated box.

"So, what's your name?"

"Gideon, Gideon Redoak."

He studied me. "Gideon. It suits." He heaved up one end of the coffin.

"Where are we going?" I didn't really expect an informative response.

"Home."

"And where is that?"

"The estate of the person who sent me."

My heart froze. Who had sent him? Whoever it was, they knew a great deal about me, and about vampires. I backed away from him, though he'd given me no cause to fear him so far. "Do you work for Corbeau?"

He grunted. "If I did, would I tell you? You'd already be back in his keep, in chains. Use your brains, boy. Now help me with this damned coffin."

Again, he heaved up the coffin at one end. I took the other, and we rushed out of the hut as if expecting Corbeau's black coach to descend on us at any moment. The horse was already hitched up to the cart, I saw. Evan had apparently stirred before nightfall. We slung the coffin into the cart and covered it with sacks of grain. Evan produced a long, tattered grey cloak and gave it to me. "Wear this, and keep quiet if we meet anyone."

"How far are we going?" He seemed to be answering questions tonight, at least partially.

He shrugged. "We'll get there before dawn."

I climbed onto the wagon seat and muffled myself in the cloak. It smelled like cow, and several coarse hairs poked me through tears in my clothing, but I was glad of its concealment. Evan jumped up beside me and gathered the reins. He looked to see if I was ready, then urged the horse into action. It started clopping away at a farm cart pace.

"What are you, Evan?" I asked, not wishing to spend the entire trip to an unknown destination in silence.

"You've guessed I'm not human, then."

"No, I *know* you're not human."

He chuckled. He seemed to find me a constant source of amusement. "What are you?"

"An undead thing. A beast that stalks its prey and is never satisfied, but must kill and kill again." That was what I had been taught, and I believed it to be true.

"Oh, we are feeling sorry for ourselves."

"It's true," I said, nettled.

He shook his head. "What you are is up to you. As for me, it's difficult to explain. After we reach our destination, I'll tell you. My word on it."

We journeyed in silence for a while. I hungered, for the pig's blood the night before had only taken the edge off my need. There was little hope of quenching my thirst, however. Nobody traveled at night—nobody human, at least.

The sound of our horse and cart must have attracted the attention of a thief or footpad sleeping rough in the woods we were passing through. The foolish fellow leapt into our path, brandishing a flintlock pistol. Desperation must have made him brave, for I knew that such a weapon was more likely to kill its wielder than its target. Evan pulled the reins and the horse obediently stopped, swishing its tail at our intrepid highwayman. I jumped off the cart seat and landed at the fellow's side before the horse's tail had completed one full swish.

He paid a high price for his daring night robbery. His depleted corpse thudded to the ground at my feet, one more murder added to my nightmare list of death. I felt little remorse over the shriveled thief, however. No matter what had driven him to take up robbery—the failure of his farm, perhaps, or too much of his income spent on drink and gambling—if the *gendarmes* had caught him, his fate would have been a hemp rope.

We couldn't leave the body in plain view. Evan jumped down off the cart and grabbed the corpse by the arms, dragging it into the trees. He waved away my offer of help, and took the shovel from the cart. He came back eventually.

"What if someone finds the body?"

"There's nothing to connect it with us."

"Who sent you, Evan?"

His mouth twitched. "You'll find out."

We were still in the Loire valley, and traveling southwest. The scent of grapes continued to hang heavily in the air, though the chateaux were becoming scarcer and further apart. I fell into a black mood, wishing that I could go home to England and see Prudence and Jamie. How old would their child be now? I had no idea of the year, I realised with a start. I could have spent ten years or fifty in France. It had all blurred into endless nightmare in the Keep.

Not long after the incident with the thief, we were stopped and questioned. Soldiers manned a barricade made of an old haywain across the road, with lanterns and a large fire to keep away the dark.

"Where are you taking this cart?" the captain of the barricade asked Evan. I could follow French, enough to get on with, but I couldn't speak it.

"There is a fair in Angers," Evan said, in French. His accent was perfect. I could only hope that there actually was a planned fair at Angers, the nearest market town.

"Why are you traveling at night? You're breaking the curfew."

My heart sank. If we were arrested, things would go very badly with me.

"If we get there early, we'll get the best price. There's no curfew when there's a fair."

"True enough," one of the soldiers reminded the captain.

The captain grunted, and I thought that the soldier would be in for a rough time of it later for his cheek. The captain took down one of the lanterns and shone it in Evan's face.

"There are killers in the night, farmer. They creep into huts and cottages, chateaux and manors alike. We're hunting for them."

"I am only a poor farmer. I didn't know!" Evan gave a good impression of quaking.

The lantern was thrust into my face. I prayed the soldiers had poor descriptions of the killers in the night. "Who's this?" the soldier asked.

"My brother."

The soldier poked me in the ribs, and I forced myself not to react. "What's your name?" I remained quiet and blank-faced.

"That's Gaston," Evan said.

"Why doesn't he speak for himself?" The soldiers were looking suspicious now. The captain loosened his pistol in his belt.

Evan slapped me on the back of the head. "He can't, not since the cow kicked him. Maman likes him better this way. So do I."

The soldiers laughed and relaxed. The captain ordered the wain to be trundled out of the way, and waved us on with the lantern. "Get along with you. Don't give rides to anyone you don't know. Get to shelter quickly."

We'd left the checkpoint far behind before I stopped shaking. I rubbed my head—that slap had hurt. But Evan had instantly eased all suspicion, fended off a search of the cart, and diverted the questions from me by his statement that I had been kicked by a cow. It was precisely the sort of rural accident that happened all the time.

The cart continued on its slow journey for a few more hours without further interruption. We arrived in the courtyard of an ancient chateau. Its insignia, bunches of grapes growing on a rose arbour, decorated the archway we passed under.

Evan jumped down from the cart, but shook his head at me when I would have followed. "Wait," he said, and disappeared before I could ask any questions.

I sat obediently in the wagon and wondered what would happen next. A survey of the courtyard told me little, save that the chateau was very old and the stones of the yard had been recently swept. Could I trust whoever owned this house?

"Evan told me you were waiting. Welcome." A soft voice from beside the cart interrupted my thoughts.

Startled, for I had heard no one approach, I turned my head and beheld a beautiful lady. I gathered my wits and scrabbled off the wagon seat to stand before her. Shining blonde hair spilled from the hood drawn up over her head. Her height was nearly equal to my own, making her tall for a woman. She was slender but not thin, and dressed elegantly without extravagance. My nose tickled at her scent, some sun-warmed flower long forgotten. My father had disparaged women who wore perfume as "painted Jezebels," I automatically remembered. But I recognized something about this lady. The scent overlaid no bloodsmell. She moved silently, with a self-awareness few humans possessed. Appearing unexpected and unannounced, she might have been an angel—the angel of death, perhaps. She was a vampire.

"Lady." I knelt at her feet.

"Do not kneel to me." She spoke in lightly accented English, but there was a smile in her voice. "What is your name?"

"Gideon Redoak, my lady." I stared at the ground, suddenly shy. My mind churned. I hadn't been expecting Evan to deliver me into the hands of another vampire, even a beautiful female. I had met females of my kind in the Keep, and learned that their gender didn't make them any less cruel. But I was still too numb to be truly frightened.

"You need not call me 'lady'. I am Genevieve de Monet. This is my chateau, Chateau de Monet. There is hot water and clean clothing in the chateau. Will you enter?"

Too well schooled in instant obedience to refuse her, I followed her inside.

The light from dozens of torches and candles hurt my eyes. I blinked painfully, trying to make sense of my new surroundings. Cool, moist air brushed my forehead, scented with torchsmoke, burning tallow and the lady's subtle flower perfume. The floor beneath my bare feet was unexpectedly soft, and I risked a glance down to see carpets in glowing oriental hues. Woven tapestries on the walls brightened the interior and controlled the drafts that plague stone buildings.

The carpet tickled as I followed the lady across it. Evan appeared in a doorway and grinned at me. To Genevieve, he bowed, but it was not a subservient bow. "We have a bath ready," he said.

"Go with Evan," Genevieve said to me, but so gently that it didn't sound like an order. "A hot bath and clean clothes will lift your spirits...and make you more pleasant company."

I wasn't used to being teased in such a gentle manner, and followed Evan in something of a daze. He led me to a small chamber where half a forest blazed in the grate and a large round wooden tub sat on bare stone.

Evan moved quickly. He stripped me bare. His finger stabbed me towards the tub. Another man came in, better dressed, carrying rough washing cloths and harsh soap. Between the two of them, they scrubbed me thoroughly clean. I tensed when the second servant reached towards my groin, but his touch with the soap and rag was as impersonal and thorough there as everywhere else on my body. Evan, his clothing now dark with water, grew impatient at his attempts to untangle my ratted hair and even more impatient at my yelps of protest.

He stormed out of the room and returned a moment later with a pair of sharp scissors. The second man, a vampire who I learned was called Benoit, held my head motionless while Evan snipped. Masses of dark, filthy hair fell into the tub and on the floor. Benoit then dunked my shorn pate under the water and applied the soap to what was left of my locks. I felt a distinct breeze across my scalp when I was allowed up.

Finally, I left the now cold and scummy water. Benoit handed me a coarse but pristine drying sheet. Evan brought me clean clothing. It was, to my surprise, good-quality things such as a merchant might wear, not the peasant garb I expected. I was unfamiliar with the current French fashions. Gone were the slashed doublets, puffy breeches, falling collars and tall wide-brimmed hats of my youth. The tight breeches, waistcoat and coat Evan gave me fitted my body more closely than I was used to. It didn't take me very long, however, to get dressed even in this exotic garb.

Evan looked me over and nodded his approval, his eyes dancing as he glanced at my head. "You'll do." His face softened a little when he perceived my fear. "You're safe here, Gideon."

I didn't believe him, but said nothing. Benoit beckoned me out of the water-soaked room. He led me through the various passages of the chateau. I was completely lost, having no idea which way was out. I had no wish to leave, however. I felt a growing curiosity as to who Genevieve was and why she had wanted me brought to her. She had treated me kindly on our first meeting, but so had Corbeau. I no longer trusted kindness.

Benoit ushered me into a room walled with books. I had never seen so many in one place—there must have been hundreds of volumes. I stopped in the doorway and stared at the leather bindings. There had been no library in Redoak Hall. My father had deemed reading, other than the Bible or sermons, a waste of time and candlelight.

From behind me, Benoit gave me a slight shove, impelling me to totter into the room and stand in the glow from the fireplace. I heard a gasp, and saw Genevieve rise to her feet. Her hand flew to her mouth.

"Oh, Mon Dieu! Vos cheveux!"

My hand reached up towards my ravaged hair. Behind me, Benoit said something in French too rapid for me to catch. Genevieve came to my side and gently touched my hand.

"No matter," she said softly in English. "Evan is many things, but a barber he is not. But what of that, hmm? You are certainly very clean now."

I again had the sense of being teased, but kindly. I stared numbly at the lady, entirely at a loss as to her motives. She seemed to sense this, and when she next spoke, it was far more seriously.

"Come with me by the fire, Gideon. I do not doubt that you have many questions. You have had an ordeal, but it is over now. Here, in Chateau de Monet, you are safe." She gave Benoit a look and a nod. He bowed, and left us alone in the room.

That word again, "safe." I wished I could believe her. I sat in the chair she indicated but dared not look at her. Her beauty and apparent concern were a trap. Whatever the lady's reasons for having me brought here, they could not be altruistic. Vampires were selfish. One vampire would not rescue another out of kindness. The undead had no kindness in them.

"You do not believe me."

I risked a look at her then. The expression on her face conveyed only great sadness.

"I do not blame you. I know something of what you have suffered. But not all of us are monsters."

I didn't believe that, either, but I ventured to speak. "Madame, may I ask you one question? I would know the year."

"It is 1693."

Fifty-one years! I could barely grasp the truth of it. I had suffered fifty-one years of brutality and torture.

She changed the subject. "Where in England are you from?"

"A place near the Welsh border." This seemed safe enough to tell her. "The nearest town is Shrewsbury. Do you know it?"

She shook her head. "I have been to England only once, although I have friends there. Did you have a large family?"

"One sister, Prudence." I felt a twinge of grief. So much time had passed! Prudence would be dead.

"Gideon and Prudence?" Genevieve's forehead puckered. "Your parents were of that reform movement, what was it called? Puritan?"

"My father was Puritan," I said, surprised. "Were there Puritans here in France?"

"We had our reformers here. We have had our wars of religion, Catholic against Protestant. And I receive news of other places, especially England. I know of your Puritans. You cannot have had a happy life."

I laughed, but there was no humour in it. Even I could hear the bitterness and the edge of hysteria, and quickly stopped. "Did you?"

"Yes, for the most part. But we are not speaking of me. We are speaking of you. How did you meet your master?"

I looked away from her again, realising that I had fallen into her trap. "I don't wish to discuss it."

"Very well." That had not been the response I'd expected. "We have all of time before us, Gideon. You do not trust me, nor have you any reason to give me that trust. I hope to earn it. Believe me when I say that I am not trying to trick you or trap you, only to put you at your ease. I will tell you this again: not all of us are monsters."

It was my turn to shake my head.

"I do not see a monster sitting before my fire." Genevieve's voice was velvet. "Do you want to know what I see?"

"A fool?" I said bitterly.

"No. I see a young man who was cruelly betrayed. I see a fledgling vampire who has learned the darkest possible ways of our kind, who knows only the blood and the killing, but who has not surrendered to them. I see someone who is stronger than he believes, who has survived the unthinkable. I see a wound that needs healing, but a wounded one who is not beyond hope." A hint of mischief played on her lips. "I see a boy in borrowed clothing and an abominable haircut, but a very handsome boy all the same."

This last absurdity made me laugh, genuinely this time, and Genevieve looked pleased. She rose up and crossed the room to a sideboard where amber liquid glinted in a decanter. She poured some of this into two round glasses and approached extending one of them to me.

Remembering Corbeau's wine, I made no effort to accept her offering. Understanding and sympathy flooded her eyes. She made that odd almost-movement again, as if she would have liked to touch me. "It is brandy."

"Brandy? But I thought..."

She pressed a glass into my hand. "Just try it. It is not drugged or tampered with, and the alcohol has no power to affect you. But the taste and aroma are pleasant."

I had never tasted brandy. Curious, I sniffed my glass and inhaled the glowing scent. It smelled like late summer. I waited until she had taken a drink before attempting my first cautious sip.

Liquid warmth, captured sunshine, slid down my throat. I felt my eyes widen. Nothing save blood, sometimes mixed with wine, had passed my lips since my transformation, and I expected this first taste of brandy to be rejected. Instead, it warmed me as nothing had in a long time.

"Such small pleasures are left to us," Genevieve said, turning her glass so that the firelight danced in amber. "Wine, brandy, water, tea. Sometimes even fresh fruit, although you are not yet ready for that. But only blood sustains us. That, I am afraid, is true."

"I know." I turned my head away.

"It is not necessary to kill," Genevieve said, so fiercely that I blinked. "We are predators. I will not deny this. It is our nature. But nature can be tamed by intelligence and reason. We are not animals. We need not kill. We need not feed every night. Mortals are not cattle. You have already seen the results of wanton slaughter of humans. We become the hunted. To indulge in such killing endangers us all. There are alternatives."

I recalled the rancid contents of the wine bottle that I had consumed the night before. "Pig's blood?"

Again that slightly mischievous smile that made me want to like her. "Ah, you did not care for the special vintage from the cellars of Chateau de Monet? It is an acquired taste. Many never acquire it. It does sustain us, however. If you would not be the monster you fear you are, I would suggest you learn to drink it. We must also have human blood, but you need not kill. I will teach you."

"Madame, why was I brought here?"

"Can you not guess?"

"I am confused. What are your intentions?"

"Ah, Gideon. You were brought here to save you."

Genevieve set her glass down and smiled at me. I wanted to believe that the warmth I saw in that smile was genuine, but caution held me back.

"It is nearly dawn," she said, glancing at the stained-glass windows set in the library wall. "We must seek our rest. Your head is filled with the lies your master told you about our kind, Gideon. There is much that I must teach you, but not tonight. You have already had, I believe, too many surprises and new things. There is one thing, however, you must learn this morning."

I glanced at the windows, wondering how they looked with the glow of sunlight warming the colours. Even at night, the windows danced with reds, greens, blues and golds—scenes of harvest and planting, scenes that made me feel nearly at home. There was no stained glass in Corbeau's keep. There had been none in Redoak Hall or the parish church, for that matter, but at least agricultural scenes were familiar. I couldn't allow pretty decorations to lull me into believing that Genevieve meant me no harm. What was this lesson she spoke of? I was not fond of lessons.

Again she seemed able to read my thoughts. "I use no whips or chains in my home, Gideon. My lessons are pleasant and I am a patient teacher."

"And should I fail to learn?"

"Then I have failed as a teacher, not you as a student. Here is the first lesson: you do not need a coffin to sleep in."

I dropped my brandy glass. It shattered on the flagstone floor of the library, little teardrops of crystal scattering everywhere. "I-I'm sorry." Expecting a reprimand, I started to kneel to pick up the shards.

"No, leave it, please," Genevieve's hand was on my right arm, coaxing me to stand. "The servants will sweep it up. It is only a brandy glass."

It was beyond my experience for mistakes to be forgiven rather than punished, and I could only stare at her in bewilderment. She made a noise that sounded sad rather than angry, and with her hand still on my arm, began walking towards the library door. I had to follow or shake off her hand.

"The sun is not our friend, Gideon," she said as we left the library and began walking through the chateau. "When you have lived for a century or two more, then you may be able to go out in daytime—but only at dawn or dusk, and well-wrapped against the sun. Too long a time in her rays will bring you the true death, in agony. You would burn slowly, in terrible pain. So it is true that we must sleep during the worst of the sun's reign, but it is not true that this sleep must be in a coffin."

I struggled with both confusion and relief. I hated my coffin, the dark prison of my years of suffering. But fear of the sun made me long for its safety. I could sense the approaching dawn. Surely the only recourse was to hide in that light-proof box?

I had been blindly walking beside Genevieve, not noticing where she was going. The narrow halls of the chateau afforded me tantalising glimpses of various chambers, but we didn't enter any of these. She led me, instead, to a twisting stairway, its passage so constricted that I had to shorten my stride to follow her. We went up two storeys, then down another hallway towards one of the rooms. Genevieve opened the door and indicated that I should enter.

It was a bedroom, with the usual appointments. A huge canopied bed, far more baroque than anything I had ever seen before, occupied a large portion of the room. I knew that several trees sacrificed themselves to provide all that carven wood. The draperies of heavy black velvet created a pool of darkness inside the monstrous bed.

"Do you like it?" Genevieve gestured towards the bed.

"How did anyone get it up the stairs?"

She laughed. "Oh, I was right, *mon cher,* there is hope for you. You see that there are no windows, Gideon? The sun cannot reach this room. You will be safe. And look what I have found for you." She reached inside the shadow of the curtains and brought out a small bundle. When she shook this out, it proved to be a long, silken garment like a shirt. "It is a nightshirt," she said, handing it to me.

I wore such a thing once, but never one so luxurious. As I studied it, secretly enjoying the feel of silk in my hands, Genevieve turned down the covers on the bed.

"I will leave you now, for I must seek my own bed. *Bon nuit,* Gideon." She hesitated a moment, then left, closing the door gently behind her.

Dawn's arrival was imminent. I felt the heaviness of daysleep looming. There was no time to seek out my coffin. I took off the borrowed clothing I wore and donned the nightshirt, savouring the smoothness of the silk against my skin. My father would have said that such pleasure was a sin, but it must have been a very minor one compared to the sins I had committed over the years of my imprisonment. I crawled in under the covers and drew them up to my chin. Dawn came, and I was not incinerated.

At dusk, I awoke, half-expecting to find that the chateau, the lady, and Evan had all been some hallucination. The brooding physical reality of the bed assured me that I had not imagined anything. I rolled out from under the covers and stretched, the silk shirt rubbing soothingly against my skin. I found the clothing I'd worn the previous evening, and put it on. Then I sat on the edge of the bed, wondering what to do. I had not been given leave of the house and didn't know my status.

A knock sounded on the door, and Genevieve entered, smiling. "Ah, you are dressed. Good evening, Gideon."

I rose to my feet. "Good evening, Madame."

"Come and see the house. You must learn your way around. There is no need to stay in this room."

She showed me each room, sometimes citing the history of some piece of furniture or decoration. How beautiful a home this chateau made, full of tapestries and paintings. Colour blazed everywhere I looked.

"Just because we must live in the night does not mean we need to live in darkness," Genevieve said when I commented on the number of beautiful things. "Light and colour are ways to liven up our existence."

"There were no tapestries in my master's keep."

"No. There would not be. Nothing of beauty, I imagine."

My head turned slowly away from the tapestry I was studying, and I looked at the lady. "You know him." It wasn't a question.

"There is something I must show you. Trust me but a little longer, Gideon, and follow me."

We left the chateau, I brimful of questions I dared not ask. We walked through a dead grape arbour, dried leaves crunching beneath our feet. Beyond the tangled vines there was a little hollow cleared of foliage. I saw a gravestone under the shadow of a large tree. The name engraved there drew my attention.

"Claude de Monet. Your father?"

Genevieve's blonde head, gleaming in the moonlight, was bowed over the grave. "My husband. And my bloodmaster. Your master killed him. I received his hand back as a gift from Corbeau."

I didn't know how to reply to this. "Then why did you have me rescued, Genevieve?"

"Had you not rebelled, you would not be here. I have been watching you, Gideon, and although you have been cruelly used, you are not evil. There is much to teach you, however."

"Corbeau really killed your husband?" I stared at the grave. "Even though he was a vampire?"

"Yes."

"Then you truly are his enemy."

"Yes."

"So am I."

Genevieve looked sad. "So you would like to believe. The fact remains that he is your master, and it was his blood that changed you. He can claim that bond any time he chooses, and you would not be able to defy him."

"Then I put you at risk by being here."

"It is a risk I am prepared to take. Are you?"

I looked again at the grave. The slain Claude de Monet had helped me come to know that this lady was truly as she appeared. The grave was too real for this all to have been a lie.

"Yes," I said.

Chapter Four

Thus I became a denizen of the Chateau de Monet. Genevieve, true to her word, was a patient teacher. I never once saw her angry, or heard a sharp word from her. Gradually my fear of betrayal eased, and I grew more confident. I learned that it was possible to live among mortals and not treat them as cattle, nor to be hunted in turn by them. She taught me how to walk cloaked in secrecy through a room full of humans while none of them heeded my passing. I learned how to use the mental powers at my command to lure humans to me, to keep them quiescent while I fed, and to bid them forget once I had drunk my fill. I learned how to take human blood and leave the victim not only alive, but very little harmed. The nights flew by, each one a bright new bead on a string of pleasure. I had not known how damaged I was until Genevieve began the healing of me.

One evening as I awaited Genevieve's summons, Evan came to my room instead. I saw him here and there about the chateau, along with Benoit and a handful of others. Most of these residents of the castle, while not quite Genevieve's equal, seemed to be something more than her servants, but I didn't understand their relationship to her. I spent nearly all my time with Genevieve, listening to her instructions and learning from her, so I had barely spoken to Evan since he'd delivered me here.

"Hello," I said, rising from the chair where I'd been reading and setting down my book. "I wasn't expecting you."

"Hoping for someone prettier?" he asked with his usual grin. "I apologize for disappointing you, but Madame has other affairs that require her attention tonight. So I thought perhaps we should talk. No doubt you're still full of questions you don't dare ask the chatelaine of this castle. Let's go for a walk in the gardens, and I'll give you some answers, if you like."

I agreed that I would like that, and shortly we were outside in the beautiful rose arbours that surrounded Chateau de Monet. He stopped at one bush that produced the purest white roses I had ever seen, now starting to close for the night.

"He developed these for her, you know. They're known now as the Ice Queen, but when he grew them, he called them Genevieve."

"Do you speak of her husband?"

"Indeed. I didn't actually know Claude, but Benoit told me about the roses, and he was Claude's get."

I pondered that for a moment, trying to think which question to ask first. Evan stood patiently toying with the petals of a white rose.

Finally, I asked, "How came you here? A Welshman in France?"

He sat down on a stone bench that stood nearby. "Ah. Very nearly, but not quite the right question to start with. After all, you are an Englishman in France, although we know how you came here. Fortunately, my own reasons for being here are somewhat less grim." He leaned back and looked me up and down, as if judging my readiness to hear his story.

"What would those reasons be?" This seemed somewhat inadequate, so I blurted out the real question I had been longing to ask him since we'd met. "What are you, Evan?"

His face broke into an approving smile. "Finally."

I sat down on the bench opposite his, and prepared to listen.

"I am a Nameless One," he said. As I opened my mouth, he raised a hand to silence me. "Please, no tedious protests that I do have a name, or suchlike. You already know that I am not human. Nor am I a vampire. There are a limited number of other things I could be. I am a Nameless One."

"I don't know what that means."

"The Nameless Ones are a separate race of people. We may have been human once, and changed by some unknown force, or we may always have been as we are. I don't know. We're not human as you think of it, however. You noticed, the first night, that my blood smells different and didn't appeal to you. I'm also stronger and faster than a human, capable of far more physically. But the thing that makes us truly different is bit more complicated to explain. You need to know about it, however, since we're going to be spending a lot of time in close company."

He paused, and I simply looked at him expectantly and waited for him to continue.

"We go through stages, or cycles, that change continuously. We can't predict when we'll shift into another cycle, although on average we go through all three of them in a year's time."

"All three?"

"We're most active in high cycle." He grinned. "We'll eat anything that's not moving and make love to anything that is. High cycle is the only time we can reproduce. We're not fertile with human beings or any other species but our own—but that doesn't mean we don't enjoy the pleasure other species offer."

If I had been mortal, my face would have been burning. "I'm not certain that I need to know quite this much," I mumbled, looking away from Evan. He chuckled.

"I'd rather explain everything in one go and have it over with. In mid-cycle, we feel and behave just like ordinary humans. But in low cycle, we're somnolent most of the time, and all of our appetites virtually disappear."

"It almost sounds like a vampire's daysleep."

"But we're not unconscious and insensible like you vampires. Don't be fooled—the person who thinks that one of us in low cycle would be easy to kill or get past would be making a fatal mistake. We can still move like lightning."

"All right. I understood most of that—or I think I did. But it doesn't explain why you're here."

"Our chief employment is as warriors. We make good soldiers, bodyguards, outriders...wherever there is a position of that sort, with the correct employer, you'll generally find us. We're drifters and mercenaries, going where we're needed. Madame de Monet required extra protection and help after the death of her husband, so I came to France to assist her. And here I am."

"What makes Genevieve the correct employer?"

He crossed his legs and stretched, an image of total comfort. "She's wealthy. The chateau is comfortable, the meals excellent, the wine impeccable, and the recompense for my employment is more than adequate. And she's a vampire—one of great renown. This is not to say that I wouldn't be willing to take employment elsewhere, should there be a better offer."

"That seems somewhat heartless, if the lady has need of your services."

"Of late, my young friend, my main business here at the chateau has been you. Now that you're rescued and Genevieve is training you, I doubt she needs me as badly as all that."

"What do you mean, I have been your main business? I know you pulled me from that grave..."

"Did you not wonder how I knew where to find you, and when?"

"Actually, I did."

"You've been watched, Gideon, since the moment you crossed the border. For many years now, Genevieve has been seeking a way to strike back at Etienne Corbeau. He's extremely powerful, and she was greatly weakened by Claude's death. But she's been slowly regaining her strength, searching for ways to hurt him without attacking directly. She may never be prepared to do that, unless she should raise an army, and she doesn't wish to try. Even a private war would cause too much destruction and death. But then he brought you here. You were young and innocent, and you remained so despite all that was done to you. I was sent to spy, at first only to observe and report back, but then to attempt to free you if possible. For a long time, you were too closely guarded for that, but my race is a patient one. Finally, one night I saw those wretches who serve Corbeau bring out a coffin and cart it for many miles, so that they came perilously close to the Loire and Chateau de Monet. I knew it had to be you in that box. I watched them bury you, and pack down the earth around you. It was then too late in the night to rescue you and get you to safety, so I waited until the next nightfall. The rest you know."

"Thank you. I apologize for not saying it earlier."

He laughed. "Ah, one look at Madame's face, and I was forgotten."

I made no reply, but felt uncomfortable. I liked Evan, or wanted to, and I liked Genevieve very much. It was apparent, however, that Evan didn't know my full history, even though he had been spying on me. If Genevieve knew my perversion, she didn't mention it. It would scarcely have been fit conversation for such a lady.

Then I noticed that Evan was looking at me almost pityingly. "You don't know when you're being teased, do you?" I must have looked at him rather blankly, for he sighed and shook his head. "Madame de Monet and I both know much about you, Gideon. I'm only joking when I say you were struck by her beauty."

"She is very beautiful," I said, unable to think of any other response. Was he saying that both he and Genevieve knew of my proclivities? And yet neither one of them was repelled, nor condemned me?

"Ah, mais oui."

Something in his tone, as he spoke these simple words in French, made me wonder if perhaps he had a more intimate relationship with the lady of the house than a mere bodyguard. It would be indelicate to ask, however. Perhaps something in my expression betrayed my thoughts, for he laughed. "Any further questions?"

I avoided asking the questions that were foremost in my mind. "Are you immortal? You seem to have been with Genevieve for a long time."

"We're not immortal the way vampires are. We age slowly and have very long lifespans, though. That's why vampires value us so much as employees."

"Why are you the Nameless Ones?"

"Oh, we have a name," Evan said lazily. "But we don't reveal it to outsiders, just as we never reveal the locations of our enclaves."

"Enclaves?"

"Only those seeking or serving employment live among men. Our children are raised in hidden villages until they're ready to go out in the world."

"Do you have children?"

"One or two, yes. They're being raised by Guardians—Nameless who have outlived the cycles and can pay attention to such an important task as raising the young. Some day, that shall be my task."

"Guardians—I thought I heard Benoit use that term, but he's a vampire."

Evan nodded. "That he is. What he referred to are those mysterious persons you see wandering about the estates and the chateau, reporting to Genevieve. They are known as Le Societé des Gardiens. I myself am a member."

"And what does Le Societé do?"

"Rescues young vampires from being buried, for one thing. Gideon, Genevieve is more than just a wealthy, attractive woman. She and we Gardiens are engaged in a war. Not a land war, but a more subtle one. Claude began it, and she carries on in his stead. We're trying to rid the world of those like Corbeau, the true monsters. She believes that vampires don't need to kill to survive, that there are alternatives. She's rallied other believers to the cause. Those whom you have seen, talking with Benoit, or walking the grounds, or reporting to the lady, are Gardiens."

"Could I join you?"

"You will have to talk to Genevieve." He raised his nose, like a hound catching a scent. "It smells to me as if dinner is being served. We'd better go in."

I nodded, and fell into step with him. He had decapitated the rose he was playing with, and continued to twirl it between his hands. It looked very abused by this treatment. That reminded me of one more question I wished to ask.

"You said the rose's name had been changed, from Genevieve to the Ice Queen. Why?"

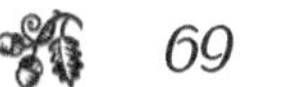

He looked down at the rose in his hand, then gave it to me. As I stood there gazing at it in confusion, he said, "Because that is what she has become." With that, he gave me a curt nod and disappeared into the great hall for dinner.

A few nights later, I wandered into the library in pursuit of a book. Descartes being my latest discovery, I pursued his works eagerly. Genevieve encouraged me to read French, and my grasp of the language improved greatly. A volume caught my attention, and I hooked it off its shelf. The inglenook by the fire enticed me, and I settled there comfortably, Descartes in hand.

I heard voices on the stairs, coming towards my cosy retreat—Evan and Genevieve, deep in a discussion that was almost an argument. If I rose to go, they would know they had been overheard. But if I stayed, I would eavesdrop. Indecision kept me in my chair.

"...that you are lonely." Evan's voice was tender and vexed at the same time.

"That is no concern of yours." Genevieve spoke more sharply than her wont.

"Genevieve, you cannot go on like this. As your friend, I am concerned about you."

"What would you have me do, Evan?"

Embarrassed, I burrowed further into my chair, but nothing blocked out the sound of their voices.

"Let me stay with you tonight."

"Evan." She barely breathed his name. "I cannot."

"Why not? One night. To ease your pain."

"And let you add me to the list of your conquered?"

"I could never conquer you. One night, Genevieve. For both our sakes."

Oh, go with him, I thought. I didn't want to be found here, listening to this conversation.

Evan's voice asked, "Where is the harm?"

Silence fell. I hid behind my book. Then I heard a soft noise, a kiss.

"One night." Genevieve sounded adamant.

"Agreed."

Their footsteps moved off in the direction of that corkscrew staircase. I set down Descartes with trembling hands. But I felt a sense of gladness warm my heart, that Genevieve agreed to even one night of pleasure. She was more alone than I.

I stayed with Genevieve for many years, as humans reckon time. When you're immortal, what is one year, or fifty, or a hundred? I acquired many skills under her tutelage, not just those needed to live as a vampire without attracting attention. I learned to dance, to speak French, to dress well and to socialise without fear. Genevieve taught me all the arcane secrets of wine-making and much about gardening, as well.

I found that, for some inexplicable reason, I was considered a "catch." Young ladies whispered offers to me in the corners of ballrooms, or boldly asked Genevieve if she was my wife. I politely refused all offers, whether of marriage or an assignation for a single night. A few of the offers came from men, but I turned them down, as well. The abuse I suffered under Corbeau had killed desire.

Genevieve once told me frankly that same-sex love was readily accepted among the night-dwellers such as vampires and werewolves. She assured me that it was no sin, and that no shame existed in finding love anywhere, including with others of your own sex. But my harsh Biblical training and the brutal treatment I received over all those years in the Keep inhibited me from testing to see if she spoke the truth.

My mentor instructed me in how to acquire wealth. With a loan from her, and the guarantee of her good name, I set myself up in business. I entered the import/export trade, and rapidly acquired both experience and capital. Within a short time, I made good on Genevieve's loan, with interest. The other debt I owed her could never be repaid.

As I gained business acumen, I grew steadily more self-confident and independent. The scars left by Corbeau faded, although the wounds he had inflicted on my soul never truly healed. The fact that they weren't physically evident didn't make them hurt any less. Genevieve let me try my wings, knowing that sooner or later I must fly alone. She had her own life, after all, and often several nights would pass when I didn't see her. Evan would sometimes keep me company, or Benoit or one of the other Gardiens.

One night as I was returning from a solitary walk in the woods, Evan came to meet me. He summoned me into Genevieve's library. Although years had passed, little had changed in the library. It was still full of books, and the stained glass still adorned the windows. As I came in, shaking the night's dampness from my hair, Genevieve smiled at me. She had put out brandy, as she did the first night we met.

"Please sit, Gideon," she said. "We must have a serious conversation."

I poured the brandy and sat down. Genevieve picked up her drink, but didn't sit.

"Leave us, please, Evan." He bowed and obeyed. Genevieve sipped her brandy, then turned to me. "I will put this bluntly. It is time for us to go."

"Go?" I echoed stupidly.

"Yes. We must leave the chateau. We have been living here far too long. This is the coin in which we pay for our immortality... having to move on. The mortals tend to notice when their neighbours do not age. Yes, we can alter our appearances, but still they are beginning to murmur."

I nodded. I'd already been expecting this to happen. "What should I do?"

"Sell your holdings and leave France. Go back to England, and start over. It is best to take a new name, and do not settle near your old home. Invest wisely. I think you know enough of business now to make the right choices."

"And what will you do?" I accepted our parting as a fact. Although saddened by the thought of leaving her, I was looking forward to my new life.

She smiled. "Would you betray me, then? Come, Gideon, I thought we were better friends than that."

"Betray you? What do you mean?"

"Once you leave my protection, Corbeau will come looking for you. It may not be immediately, but he will come. He will never let you go completely. If I tell you where to find me, you will tell him."

I could offer no argument against the truth. As dear as Genevieve was to me, that love was no proof against the power of my master. "Then I will ask you nothing more. Credit me with understanding the danger I impose on you even now. Only promise..."

"Promise?"

"That this will not be our last parting."

Genevieve smiled, crossed the room, and kissed me. "I promise."

I left the library deep in thought, so preoccupied that I nearly walked into Evan. He tapped me on the shoulder to get my attention.

"She said it was time to move on, am I correct?"

"Yes. She thinks I should move back to England. She says she is leaving the chateau, as well, but she cannot tell me where." I sighed, feeling very bitter against my master. "What will you do, go with her?"

"Actually, I was hoping I could go to England with you. I would like to live in the British Isles again. You'll need a protector and servant once you establish your new home. You might as well take the devil you know. Will you accept my services?"

Of course I wanted Evan, not that I ever anticipated this offer. A Nameless One offered protection against my master. "But Genevieve..."

"Has no need of me. She has the entire Societé des Gardiens, after all. She herself is far from helpless. No, I would rather go with you, if you'll permit."

"I should very much like that. I was worried about returning to England alone."

He thumped my back, in a friendly way that hardly made me stagger at all. "I accept your offer of employment," he said, extending his hand.

We shook on it. "Thank you, Evan." Feeling a bit suspicious, I said, "You and Genevieve haven't quarrelled, have you?"

He stared at me for a moment. "No, no quarrel. Things end, that's all. Now, let's discuss exactly what we're going to need once we get to England." And with that, he deftly changed the subject and we began planning to establish my new household.

Once Evan and I were settled in England, I set about making London my own. In my mortal life, I had visited the city a total of three times, and a great deal had changed since then. The Great Fire in 1666 had destroyed much that I knew, and the reconstructed areas were unfamiliar.

I purchased a small house built in the Queen Anne style in a quiet neighbourhood, well out of the hustle and bustle of London life. While it possessed none of the austere grandeur of Redoak Hall or the comfortable luxury of the Chateau de Monet, it suited me, and I felt proud of it. It boasted two storeys, four good bedrooms, servants' quarters, and a stable in the mews—what more could one want? I furnished it with the plain, simple decor popular at the time, patronising fine cabinetmakers such as Chippendale and Sheridan.

Along with Evan, I kept a few discreet servants in my small home, well paid for their lack of curiosity about their master's eccentric habits. Otherwise I received no company. I preferred the quiet life of seclusion, for in many ways I was still healing. Evan had complete freedom to come and go as he pleased when the high cycle called him, although he was adamant about never leaving me completely unguarded. We got along well together as house mates, although I missed Genevieve and France.

Still, I kept busy. Business interests needed seeing to, and, more often than I would have wished, the hunt to meet my own needs. I had learned well under Genevieve's tutelage, and hunted over a large range of territory as infrequently as possible.

On a foggy night four years after my return to England, Evan and I prowled the streets of one of the poorer sections of town. The fog drove all but the most destitute into whatever shelter they could afford. Pickings were slim. Sometimes I felt we were being followed, but I could detect no bloodsmell and heard no footsteps. Evan, wary and on the alert, kept a small crossbow hidden under his frock coat.

About to give up and go home hungry, I drew my cloak around me and started back towards the more heavily trafficked streets. A shadow loomed in the narrow alleyway to my right—human-shaped, but lacking human scent. Alert, fangs sliding into place in my gums, I stopped. Evan stopped beside me and cocked the bow. Then he faded back into the mist so that not even my eyes could spot him.

"Who's there?" I called. I had not worn a sword to venture into this poor part of town, having no need of one with Evan at my side. Now I cursed that oversight, even though instinct told me that a blade would be useless.

The shape didn't move, but a deep, disturbingly familiar laugh came from it. The fog clung to it in a grey shroud hiding the face, but the blackest depths of my memory knew that laugh. "Graydon," I whispered.

"I see you remember me," said my master's most trusted servant.

How could I forget the cruelties he had inflicted on me? No Corbeau loomed over us to cow me. Snarling, I leapt at the shadowy form.

An arm of iron knocked me to the ground before I even reached him. With a noise like a wildcat being skinned alive, Graydon fell on me, inch-long talons raking towards my eyes. I flung up a hand to protect my face, and felt the skin lacerated. I curled my bleeding fingers into a fist and drove it with all my power into Graydon's gut. He grunted, but didn't shift his weight off my chest. I shoved at him, but he was bigger and I couldn't get my full weight behind my efforts. I sank my fangs into his arm, the nearest part of him I could reach. He screamed then, but still didn't get off. He seized my head and began slamming it against the cobblestones. Struggling uselessly, I began to fear that he would kill me.

I heard, above the thuds of my head hitting stone and Graydon's snarls, a peculiar series of sounds. A sort of stealthy "snick" was followed by a swift whirring noise and a meaty "thunk" accompanied by a gasp from Graydon. An inch or so of reddened pointed wood popped out of his chest. His eyes widened, then glazed. He fell sideways. There was very little blood, just that one horrid sound, and he was dead—truly dead, by the time he hit the cobblestones. I could tell by the way his limbs flopped.

"That took you long enough," I said out in a shaking voice.

The fog coalesced into a human shape, which shrugged. "I had to wait for a clear shot. I would never get invited back to France if I accidentally shot you."

"And if you intentionally shot me?"

"That would depend on the circumstances." Evan surveyed the street, but we were still alone. The fight and Graydon's fall had not attracted any attention. "I think you had best abandon the hunt for tonight, and drink pig's blood, Gideon."

I agreed, but we couldn't leave Graydon lying in the open. The two of us dragged his corpse into the darkest corner we could find and hid it behind some barrels. Evan said that he would come back to dispose of it properly. We left the fog-bound alley and walked in silence until we came to the livery stable and reclaimed our coach. As we did so, a certain jauntiness entered my steps. Graydon was dead. One monster, at least, had been slain.

As much as I missed Genevieve and the chateau, all the Gardiens and the beautiful estate, I rather enjoyed being master of my own household. One habit, however, I didn't change: I remained celibate. There were men whom I found attractive, and I cultivated their company, but never to the point of sharing their beds, which I think disappointed one or two of them. The memory of Corbeau's cruelty held me back.

This state of affairs remained the same for thirty years. Once or twice Evan and I uprooted ourselves and began new lives under different names, although I retained possession of the London house and returned there whenever the neighbourhood's memory of us faded. I heard occasionally from Genevieve, always a welcome event. I owned a fleet of good ships, which provided my main source of income, and spent time in various ports of call, often uncomfortably because of the large amounts of running water nearby. I socialised seldom, but whenever I did so, I found myself invited to share a bed with someone. I refused all such offers.

God help me, I never planned to fall in love.

Chapter Five

The carriage wheels trundled awkwardly over the muddy ruts in the road. I rode alone in the vehicle. Evan sat on top beside the coachman. When he was in low cycle, he claimed the fresh air kept him awake.

I heard Evan call out, "Ho!" A moment later, the carriage jerked to a halt, the jangle of harness bells stopping abruptly.

"What is it, Evan?" The sounds of a struggle gave me my answer. I'd never even heard Evan move.

I leapt out of the carriage. We'd drawn up beside a ditch, and several figures were involved in a melee. Sliding in the mud, I made my way down to investigate. Evan, already in the middle of the action, pulled a man away from a cluster of five or so that kicked and pummelled a lone victim. The man Evan grabbed went sailing through the air and landed face down in the mud. He looked surprised.

"That bastard threw him!" yelled one of the others. "Did you see that?"

"Get on out of it, you!" Another man turned on Evan. "'Tis no affair of yours!"

"I've made it mine." Evan felled the rogue with a blow to the kidneys.

A third man snuck up behind Evan, cudgel in hand. To my amazement, the battered victim of this cowardly assault staggered half to his feet, his lips mouthing a warning at Evan's back. I was within reach, as none of the men had seen me. I reached out and tapped the rogue on the shoulder. He spun about with remarkable alacrity. Before him stood a demon from the depths with glowing red eyes and foaming fangs. His shriek died in his throat as I sank my fangs to open a wound, then drank. His blood tasted foul.

Two of our opponents remained standing. One of them squelched up the side of the ditch, hunting for an escape. Evan firmly planted his footprint on the other's backside.

"Enough, Evan," I said, and he subsided. The three downed men were senseless or dead, and their compatriots were soon out of sight. "Now, where is the fellow these dregs were attacking? He put up a brave fight."

A moan from the ditch answered me. I made my way over to find a mangled heap of flesh and rags that had collapsed in the mud.

"Looks like he's in a bad way," Evan said.

I made a decision. "Help me get him to the coach."

We lifted him out of the ditch and put him inside the carriage. The stranger appeared less than human. He bled from several wounds, yet his heart was still beating. I didn't stop to consider the consequences of my actions, but ordered the driver to continue our journey.

When we reached the house, the footman came as usual to open the carriage door, and looked astonished to see that we had returned with an extra passenger.

"See to his wounds." I watched as the footman gathered the injured man and disappeared into the house.

"Gideon," Evan said hesitantly as we handed our coats and hats to another hovering servant, "What are you going to do with him?"

"I have no time to think of that now, dawn is threatening. I'll make my decision tomorrow. See that he is well cared for, will you?"

Evan nodded, not pressing the issue further.

When I rose the next evening, I bathed and dressed more slowly than usual, pondering the question of what to do with the foundling. Why had I taken a total stranger into my home? Evan was waiting for me in the library. After greeting him, I inquired about our guest.

"He's comfortable," Evan said. "His injuries are not as grave as I at first suspected. Only a few bones are broken, none beyond mending, and nothing seems to be wrong internally. He's bruised and cut badly. Have you come to a decision about him?"

"He stays," I said flatly.

"Why?"

"He tried to fight against his attackers, even though they were stronger and outnumbered him, and he tried to help you when we were helping him. I like that kind of spirit in a man. I know what it is to feel helpless and yet still have the will to fight."

He shook his head. "It's a risk. He's human."

"I'm aware of that. I don't wish to discuss this, Evan."

"It's your decision, Gideon. I'm merely reminding you of the dangers."

"Thank you. By the way, where is he?" I hoped he had not been placed in the servants' quarters.

"The blue bedroom. The servants didn't know where else to put him."

"Thank you." The blue bedroom was the best guest chamber. I realized that I had been unusually sharp with Evan. "Evan..."

He held up one hand and smiled. "Don't. Perhaps you should just go and see if the arrangements are to your satisfaction."

"I will."

I went upstairs to the blue bedroom, to find the stranger washed, and his wounds tended. A nightshirt covered the worst of the damage, but plaster adorned his face, in between the bruises. A large white bandage hid most of his hair. What little I saw was blond. His eyes were closed, but he looked as comfortable as he could be under the circumstances.

"Has he awakened?" I asked.

"Not yet," Evan said from the doorway. "But he's sleeping naturally now, not unconscious. That's a good sign."

I turned and nodded at Evan. "You've taken good care of him. I was unaware you listed physick among your many skills."

He shrugged. "When you work with weapons, you need to know how to tend wounds."

"We'd best let him sleep. Alert me if there is any change."

The next evening I learned from Evan that the patient, though weak, had recovered enough to speak. I went upstairs to meet my houseguest, whose face now bore an interesting array of colours as the bruises began to heal. A pair of vivid blue eyes sunken among the bandages and swelling surveyed me with interest.

"Good evening. I am Gideon Redoak, the master of this house."

"Thank you for my rescue," he said faintly, "I am Jonathan Pearce."

"It was an honour to aid you. Now you must rest and get well, for I'm anxious to hear the story of how you came to be in that ditch."

He opened his mouth to speak. I raised a hand. "It can wait until you are quite recovered."

"Thank you," he repeated, and drifted back to sleep.

Later that night, Evan requested admittance to the library, where I was reviewing the accounts. "Pearce is a very old name."

"So is Redoak. Did you really come here to tell me that?"

"No."

"Out with it. I hope we're good enough friends that you feel you can speak your mind."

"Only in low cycle. You wouldn't want to know my mind when I'm in high." Seeing me glare at him, he sighed. "Gideon, what are you hoping for? Why are you keeping Jonathan here?"

"I'm not hoping for anything. I have no reason to expect that our young guest shares my tastes. Even if he should, that's no guarantee that we would be at all compatible. My only rationale is that it seems important to heal him. I wish to repay the kindness Genevieve has shown to me."

Evan nodded. "My only concern is your security. I told you, it doesn't matter to me who shares your bed. I'm just worried whether or not we can trust Pearce, once he regains his health."

"We'll have to judge that when the time comes."

Several more nights passed before Jonathan Pearce recovered enough to leave his bed. I visited him each night, making sure of his comfort. Not wishing to cause him undue stress, our conversations remained casual, never straying into his past. I caught myself pondering his beauty and how it would return once the blooms of purple faded. A few good meals would soften his cheekbones. The cook made all possible efforts to achieve that goal, especially the first night Jonathan joined us for dinner. Our guest made his way slowly down the staircase, his weight supported by the strength of Evan's arm. His own clothes had been unsalvageable, so Evan loaned him a very lightly worn evening frock coat and waistcoat. The bulk of extra fabric swallowed his emaciated frame. I deliberately kept the conversation light through dinner. Jonathan didn't seem to notice that I ate only a few small pieces of fruit. After dinner, we adjourned to the library.

"Now," I said, "I think we are ready to hear your story. How came you to that ditch?"

"'Tis not a long tale," he said. "I was set upon in the dark by robbers on the road, and they took joy in beating me for the few coins I carried. You caught them still at it." He took a sip of wine. "As for how I came to be on the road at that time of day—that is a longer tale. I was a merchant, but I'd fallen on bad times. I thought to go to London to improve my fortunes. My horse went lame on the high road, and I was riding on shank's mare, leading the beast. I had only a little money on me and I was hoping to save that for when I arrived in London. I thought I might sell the horse for what I could and find another means to travel. I had walked some twenty miles without finding anyone willing to buy the horse or give me any aid. When darkness fell, I kept walking, hoping to reach some shelter that would spare me the need to sleep in a field like a common tinker. Those brigands you fought fell on me without warning. The horse bolted and two of them gave chase. The others began to beat me when they found I carried little money. I believe they would have killed me in the end, save for your timely arrival."

"Have you no family you could appeal to for aid?"

"My parents are both dead, sir, and my other family are all distant and scattered. I am alone."

I looked at Evan. He smiled and nodded in response to my unspoken question.

"You're welcome to stay here," I said to Jonathan.

"I will not take charity, sir, though I thank you for the offer."

"I'm not offering charity. I have need of a private secretary. You are an educated man, judging by your speech."

"That I am."

"Secretary is a suitable occupation for a gentleman. You would be welcome in this household."

"What rules govern this house, if I may ask?"

"Only discretion. I have unusual habits, but I don't encourage questions. Nor do I ask them unnecessarily. Discretion works both ways." I wondered at his reasons for asking. "There's no need to give me an answer immediately. Rest and heal, and observe how this household is run, before you decide. Surely, that much charity is acceptable?"

I held his eyes until he looked down to study his wine glass. He had some fire left in him, for he withstood my gaze longer than most could.

"Very well," he finally said. "Thank you."

Jonathan became a familiar presence in the house. The bruises slowly disappeared, his broken arm mended, and the shadows under his eyes dwindled. A bright, smiling young man emerged from the victim we had rescued. As he grew stronger and recovered more completely, I could tell that he was bored by idle convalescence. He needed very little encouragement to become my secretary.

Nearly a year passed. Jonathan settled into the household routine and took over my correspondence and some business matters. I found myself looking forward to our evenings together. The smile in his eyes warmed me.

I discovered that he had a ready sense of humour, most especially about his own foibles. One night while preparing to work on some business letters, he struggled with the ink bottle. The top refused to budge for him. He swore under his breath. I knew better than to offer to help, since that would humiliate him further.

I watched the top fly off suddenly in his hands, leaving him, the papers, the table and the carpet splattered with black ink. He stared at the mess in dismay then suddenly burst out laughing. I sprang to my feet, but his contagious merriment infected me, and I couldn't help but laugh with him as the ink dripped down his face. He accepted my handkerchief to mop up the ink.

Jonathan was kind and considerate of others' feelings, and always behaved with sympathy. When I made some passing comment about his family, offering to let them know he was here, he shook his head and sighed. "All my closest relations are dead, and those that are left alive have never cared for me. It's better they not know where I am. But what of your own family?" He looked up at me. "You've never spoken of them, nor do you seem to correspond with any of them."

"Some things don't bear speaking of. My family, too, is lost to me."

"Do none of them care for you?" The light of understanding shone in his blue eyes.

"I had a sister," I said, and the hurt would allow me to say little else.

"I'm sorry," he said, and we spoke no more of it.

Since I seldom went into society, the evenings tended to be long with little entertainment. Out of boredom, I taught Jonathan how to play chess. I refused to play with Evan, since he regarded a chess board as an actual battlefield and made the reckless and dramatic moves that he would make in combat. His knights sacrificed themselves for the Queen or his pawns rushed a castle, until the chess board ran with figurative blood. Jonathan, fortunately, played a more conservative game. In return, he offered to teach me how to play cards.

"But gambling is a sin," I said, taken aback at this offer. My father's grim judgmental voice still haunted my conscience.

I felt those blue eyes consider me. "And no sin must ever be committed?"

The mantle clock ticked. Evan, invited to join us to make another hand at the cards, watched us both.

"It's only a game," said Jonathan, his eyes not leaving mine. "No more a sin than chess."

"Then teach me." I was rewarded with his warm smile.

I thought myself too badly damaged by that half century in Corbeau's keep to feel desire again. But the light in Jonathan's eyes and his ready smile worked a healing on me as sure as Evan's ministrations had healed Jonathan's broken arm. Doubts

assailed me, not the least of which was doubt that Jonathan shared my secret affliction.

For all that Genevieve had assured me that it was no shame to desire my own sex, for all that I had met others who regarded sodomy as perfectly normal and free of sin, I was unable to reconcile my feelings. It was a sin. In that year of 1781, it was also illegal and carried harsh penalties under English law.

On a crisp autumn night, the kind that carries the scent of leaves and bonfires and makes one long for apples, I went out riding with Evan while Jonathan remained behind to work on some shipping bills. A brief spurt of rain took us by surprise, and by the time we returned and stabled the horses, we were both soaked to the skin. The groom supplied us with blankets and alerted the kitchen so that hot whiskey toddies awaited us when we reached the house.

Jonathan came into the kitchen as I drank the toddy to make the cook happy. He wrinkled his nose at the dank odor that came off our riding clothes. "You smell wet."

"That tends to happen when you're caught out in the rain," Evan said.

"You should go and get warm. I took the liberty of ordering fires lit in your bedrooms."

"Thank you." I smiled at him. "I shall take advantage of it. Evan?"

He nodded. "Very kind of you, Jonathan."

"If I could delay you just a moment, Evan?" the young man asked, almost shyly.

My protector raised an eyebrow, but nodded again. Wondering what was in the air there, I went on up to my bedroom. The fire had made it warm and cozy, and I was grateful to take off my steaming damp clothes and rub myself dry with a towel. I found that my silk nightshirt had been laid out to warm in the glow of the fire. Still uncomfortable with being naked, I hastily put this on.

I wasn't surprised to hear the gentle rap at the door, as I had heard footsteps climb the stairs and negotiate the hallway. Evan's step was soundless and the servants used the back staircase.

"Jonathan?" I asked as I opened the door. "Is anything wrong?"

"I need to speak with you privately, Gideon."

"I am scarcely dressed."

He swallowed. "It doesn't matter. May I come in?"

"Yes, of course." I ushered him in and shut the door behind him.

I had never been alone with Jonathan in my bedroom, far less while clad in nothing but a nightshirt. He sat down in one of the chairs by the fireplace. He seemed fascinated by the dancing yellow and orange flames.

He wore white and green. The long jackets and tight knee breeches of the period suited him, as they did not suit me. He'd gained some weight under the constant vigilance of my cook and Evan, but was still thin. His hair now hung in blond waves around his narrow face. He spoke to the fire. "Gideon, I haven't been honest with you."

"In what way?" I regarded him seriously, but without alarm. I doubted that his dishonesty was of a harmful nature.

"I didn't tell you the truth about myself. I told you that my parents are dead. My father is still very much alive, damn his heart."

"Ah." I sank into the chair opposite. "And the reason that you lied?"

"I was disinherited and driven from my home in disgrace. Had I told you that, you would have asked the reason, and I feared that you would also drive me out."

A log settled, sparks shooting up from its charred sides. The chair under me creaked as I shifted. "Why?"

He watched the fire and swallowed again, then finally turned to look at me. Streaks of dampness marked his cheeks. "My father caught me with the footman. Naked with the footman."

I understood his meaning immediately. He had been discovered in the act of sodomy. Being disinherited and driven from his home and family was only one of the terrible penalties that could be inflicted upon someone caught in such an act. A man could be hanged or imprisoned if convicted by the court. Exile and social ruin awaited those accused but not brought to trial. Blackmail was common enough to be a thriving industry. No one was immune from persecution, not even the wealthy or noble born.

I studied him, and he didn't look away. "I see. Why have you chosen to tell me this, and why now?"

"Because you've been so kind to me that I thought you should know the truth. I know I'm risking my very life by telling you, but I can't imagine that it's a very great risk."

"No," I said, not releasing him from my gaze, "it isn't a very great risk. I wouldn't have you hanged or imprisoned after taking such care to see you recovered from your beating."

He smiled, jumping slightly as another log settled in the grate. "So I hoped. I'm sorry that I didn't tell you sooner. I should have known that I could trust you."

"Jonathan, I understand. It's no easy thing to admit that you are a lover of men. I should know, for I'm one, as well."

Was that a look of triumph in his eyes? He spoke before I could fully assess what I'd seen. "Ah...I thought so."

I froze. I had been extremely careful not to reveal my shame. Seeing the look on my face, Jonathan half-rose from his chair, hand extended towards me. "Oh, no, Gideon! There's nothing to show it. You're very discreet. It's only that sometimes, you have a way of looking at me..." he trailed off, embarrassed. "And besides, I asked Evan."

"And he told you?" My voice sounded too high. I cleared my throat. "He told you?"

Again, the smile that warmed me more intimately than any fire or blanket. "I had to coax him. But yes, he did. Pray don't be angry with him, Gideon."

If Evan had told Jonathan my secret, then my protector must not only trust my secretary but believe that I would not be unhappy about the revelation. I pondered this in silence.

Jonathan swallowed hard. I watched his Adam's apple move. The fire warmed his blood, and the smell distracted me. I had fed when I was out riding with Evan earlier, but actual hunger had little to do with my feelings. I shifted in my chair, hoping that my other physical reaction didn't show.

Jonathan leaned forward. "You are beautiful. This is too sudden, I know. But I must know if you feel as I do, that we two can be together."

Together, entwined as one, beneath the blankets...oh, yes, I felt it. It was not until I envisioned us together that I realised that I loved Jonathan. It was more than physical attraction—I loved that warm smile, the pleasant personality behind the handsome face, the way he turned his head just so, the fall of his footstep.

"I feel as you do," I said. In truth, I was finally healed. Despite the law, despite the taint of sin and unnaturalness, this somehow felt right. It was cleaner than my feelings for Corbeau. For the first time, I realised that Corbeau had made me love him, used his mental powers to corrupt my emotions. What I felt now, for Jonny, was real.

His eyes widened and he smiled again. "When you came home tonight, wet through and smelling of rain and horse, I wanted you right then and there. I love you, Gideon Redoak. It's more than desire, although I want you. You've shown me that there can be love between two such men as we."

I didn't feel uncomfortable, to my surprise. Excitement rose rather than shyness. He stood up, still smiling, and crossed the short distance between our chairs. He reached out and touched my face. "You are beautiful," he repeated, and his lips stopped my protest. It was too far to the bed. There was a soft rug in front of the fire.

How easily the silk nightshirt slipped off, compared to Jonathan's more complicated garb. But soon we were both naked on the rug, blanketed only by the warm yellow light of the flames. His golden body gleamed in the firelight, sunlight entwined with the pale moonlight of my flesh.

"You're still cold," he murmured as I covered his body with mine. "Let me warm you." The member he seemed most interested in warming raised itself in reply.

"This is wrong," I said even as my body eagerly responded to the touch of his hands.

"Yes."

"We should wait, this is unseemly haste."

He drew in his breath as I explored him with my fingers. "Gideon?" he managed to ask in a broken voice.

"Yes?"

"Stop talking."

That was an easy command to obey. His sweetly responsive body rendered further conversation unnecessary. Besides, there were other things for our lips to do.

At last, on that rug before the fire, the hairs tickling my bare ankles, I found what pleasure and love really were. His lips on my skin, our bodies moving together, his gasp as I took him, my cries as I reached climax, the soft fur beneath us and the fire warming us, this was what love and sex should be. I had been cheated, unless that first night with Corbeau counted, of knowing this.

Lying in bed at night felt odd. I couldn't sleep as humans do, but enjoyed lying quietly while Jonathan slept curled up against me like a cat. I listened to the myriad sounds his human body made: the steady beat of his heart, his stomach rumblings, his snores, his toenails scraping against the sheets. His body warmth enveloped me, and the song his blood sang was the sweetest of music. But no matter how copper bright that bloodsong, I didn't succumb. Jonathan was my lover, my friend and my salvation.

Of course we had to be circumspect about our relationship, but only in public. The servants were all hired for their discretion in the first place, and were paid well enough to make the consequences of bribery or blackmail unattractive. Evan heartily approved of my love affair. Jonathan and I raised no eyebrows by holding hands, touching fingers, or exchanging long glances, as long as we didn't do these things outside the confines of our home.

One dawn as I rose out of Jonathan's bed to leave for my own repose, I felt his fingers encircle my wrist.

"Why are you leaving?" he asked sleepily.

I leaned over and kissed him. "I must."

"But why? You're never with me in the daytime. Evan says you must sleep then."

"That's true. I can't be active in the daytime."

"Why can you not stay with me?"

"Too much sunlight comes into your room, Jonathan. I must have darkness. Please let me go to my rest, and I promise to explain."

"Very well." He released my wrist. "But you must remember your promise."

"I will." I kissed him again. "I do love you." With that I left him.

I felt his eyes on me all through dinner the next evening. His scrutiny was so intense that I wondered if there was some physical sign on me that I had slipped out to feed. But Evan would have told me if I had a bloodstain anywhere.

"What are you?" Jonathan whispered to me when we were alone in his room. He sat on the edge of his bed, still dressed, watching me.

"Did you say what?" Had he discovered what I was? I'd been careful, trying to hide my nature from him. Jonathan, not being stupid, was aware of my idiosyncrasies. He shared my house, my table, and my bed—he would have to share my secret as well.

"Yes. Gideon—please. You say you love me. Don't lie to me. You don't eat. You sleep during the daytime. Your skin is pale, and sometimes it's strangely cold. I've seen you do things that no human could do. But whatever you are, I still love you. I just want to know the truth."

"I am a vampire, Jonathan."

He said he wanted the truth. I gave it to him. The world had come to know the meaning of this word since my turning. Vampire scares rippled throughout Europe in the wake of mysterious deaths, and many perfectly innocent corpses were dug up to have stakes pounded through their hearts and other atrocities committed on their remains.

"A vampire?"

"Yes. I'm no longer human. I must drink blo..."

"I know what a vampire is, Gideon. Why have you never taken my blood?"

I hugged him tightly. He stiffened at first, then slowly relaxed in my arms and gave me a tentative smile.

"Because I love you. I wouldn't do that to you unless you asked me to."

"Do you really love me? Can vampires love?"

"This vampire can, and does." I touched his cheek. "Please, Jonny..."

He stood up. "You've never called me Jonny before. I like it." He kissed me deeply, and his hands grasped mine. "No matter what or who you are, I love you."

Yet, when we lay together in bed and I began stroking his back, I felt his muscles go rigid and he drew away.

"Jonathan?"

"I'm sorry. I know you won't hurt me, but I can't help thinking..."

I continued to massage him, reassuring him that I would never harm him, and he finally relaxed. A little extra magic entered our lovemaking that night.

A quiet year passed in our quiet little house, in which I enjoyed a type of happiness I had never known before. I received a handful of letters from Genevieve, congratulating me on finding Jonathan and giving me news of herself and her new lover, Jean de la Mare. She sounded happy, which made me glad. Replies were entrusted to Evan. Although I feared there would be some reprisal for the death of Graydon, enough time had gone by that it was no longer an immediate dread.

One cool autumn night I awoke to an unusually empty and quiet house. Jonathan, out looking after some business affairs for me, would return later that evening. As I put on the plain, dark clothes that were the despair of my tailor, I found myself thinking about my appearance. I wore my hair long and caught at the back in a ribbon as a concession to fashion, but my clothing had the barest minimum of lace and embroidery, and I wore a powdered wig only when its absence would have caused comment. What had happened to the boy who longed for bright colours and pretty fripperies?

Dressed, I went downstairs and sat by the window to wait. Evan was out pursuing his high-cycle interests, and none of the servants were immediately noticeable. I missed Jonathan, but knew he would return shortly. The ticking of the mantle clock and the steady crackle of the fire on the hearth kept me company. Nothing seemed out of the ordinary.

A feeling of deep oppression caught me by surprise. A summons I couldn't disobey forced me to my feet, even as my mind recoiled from the knowledge of who had sent that summons. Corbeau had found me. My master approached.

I rose from my chair and went to open the door. No one stood on the step. I closed the door and returned to the parlour. As a vampire, and my master, Corbeau needed no invitation to enter my house. He stood in front of my fireplace. *He was in my house.*

Unlike me, he chose to adorn himself in the height of fashion, and the light literally sparkled on his diamond-studded waistcoat. Despite his beauty, I felt only fear. The memory of his cruelty was more than enough to forestall any ghost of the desire I might once have had for him.

And Jonathan returned home soon—disaster in the making.

Corbeau's mouth was curled in a mocking sneer. "Well, I see you got out of the coffin."

I said nothing. What did he want from me? Revenge, or had he come only to taunt?

"Come here."

I obeyed. When I was within distance, he reached out and unbound the ribbon that held my hair in place. Freed, it fell to my shoulders.

"Very pretty. You haven't lost your looks, although you've aged yourself. It doesn't become you. Who pulled you from the grave?"

The sudden change of subject caught me off guard. It took a supreme effort not to tell him, even though I had sworn not to betray Genevieve. "No one."

His blow knocked me to the floor. I narrowly avoided going headfirst into the fireplace. I could feel the flames reaching eagerly for my hair, and managed to pull myself away.

"You never could lie to me," Corbeau said. "Perhaps you need a small reminder that I am your master. You do remember this, don't you, young lord?"

I looked up sharply at his sarcastic pet name for me. When I saw the whip in his hand, I remembered.

He pulled me to my feet, stroking the braided leather lash. "Yes, it's time to remind you. Strip to the waist."

Again I obeyed. "It doesn't matter what you do to me. I shan't answer your questions."

"Such bravado. I think it's high time you learned your place again. You're nothing but a slave, and slaves who forget their station should be whipped."

The lash didn't draw much blood, for I hadn't fed recently, but it hurt. I didn't cry out. Dear God, Jonathan would be home soon, how could I save him from Corbeau?

In his most honeyed tones, Corbeau said, "Come, Gideon. This isn't the worst I can do to you, and you know it. What are you hiding? If you don't want more pain, you'll tell me. Tell me everything, and I may even reward you." Seeing no reaction to this promise, he grabbed me by the hair. "Who saved you? It was her...de Monet. I know it. She took you from me. She will pay. But she can't protect you in England, can she? Who killed Graydon? Who are you hiding? Who lives in this house with you, shares your bed...?"

I must have made some sound or shown some reaction, for he released me.

"So that's it. You're protecting a lover." He backed off a few paces, coiling the whip once more. "You wouldn't have tried a woman, would you, my little catamite? As I recall, the very thought made you ill. So, it must be some pretty boy who warms your bed. Have you told him about me, about the things we did together? Have you taught him what I taught you? What is his name?"

I nearly told him. "You will never know," I managed to say instead.

"Still you defy me."

He tore at my clothes, shoving me to my knees. He kept me down with one hand, ignoring my struggles easily. He fumbled with the fastenings of his breeches with the other hand. I felt him shudder into me. The pain of forceful entry made me cry out. All the indignities I had suffered in his Keep came rushing back to me.

Suddenly his weight and his painful thrusts vanished. He was literally torn out of me and thrown aside. I rolled out of the way and took refuge against the wall.

Corbeau lay on top of a broken chair. He picked himself up out of the ruins. Evan seized him by the throat. Corbeau's fists pounded into my protector's kidneys. Evan grunted and dropped him.

Corbeau lunged for him. Evan moved fluidly aside. He reached for the broken chair. Corbeau slammed his own body into Evan's, knocking him off course. I scrambled to my feet and tried to reach the pieces of chair. They weren't much good as wooden stakes, but they would at least inconvenience Corbeau. Without noticeable effort, Corbeau knocked me back against the wall. Evan grabbed my master by the back of his jacket. I could hear the fabric rip. Corbeau snarled and turned on Evan, his right arm catching my protector full across the chin. Staggering back, Evan took hold of a heavy brass candlestick and threw it at Corbeau's head.

It missed, smashing a hole in the wall. But it distracted Corbeau enough that I shoved him away. Snarling, he whirled to bare his fangs at Evan, then spat on me. With his torn coat tails flying in his wake and his face twisted beyond beauty, Etienne Corbeau raced across the parlour. He pushed Evan out of his way and leapt through the window, glass shattering with the impact of his body.

Evan ran after him, but stopped at the ruined window. He balled up his fists, then let them slowly drop to his sides. "Gone." He turned away from the window and came to my side, helping me into a chair. "Let me get you a blanket. Are you badly hurt?"

I was half-naked, blood still seeping from the whip wounds and the pain of recent rape making it difficult to move. The only answer I could find to Evan's question was a laugh. It had the edge of hysteria.

Evan gripped my shoulders, then released me and swiftly left the room. He returned in no time with a blanket and an unstoppered wine bottle from which drifted a familiar scent. He examined my back before wrapping the blanket around me and forcing the bottle of pig's blood into my unfeeling hand.

"The welts aren't bad. You need blood to heal properly, however. It isn't the scourge that worries me, Gideon. Are you bleeding inside?"

I choked down some of the pig's blood from the bottle, and felt its warmth spread through my cold, distant arteries. I hated this strange detachment from my own body, but it seemed the only way my mind could cope with what had been done to the flesh that contained it.

"I have been violated in my own home, Evan. I am bleeding everywhere." I looked up at him. "Thank you."

He shook his head. "I should have been here. It's my duty to protect you, and I failed."

"You can't remain on guard every hour of every day, Evan. How did you know to come when you did?"

"I am your protector. It's a bond nearly as strong as that between a turnsire and his get. I felt your danger, and returned as quickly as possible."

"Returned as quickly..." I felt my cold indifference melt into near panic. "Jonathan! He should have returned! What if Corbeau discovered him, and has hurt him, or worse?" I bolted up from the chair, the blanket falling unheeded to my feet.

In my distress, I didn't notice the door to the parlour open. But the sound of a footfall made me turn that way, and there he was. The scent of roses followed him in, and my eyes widened as Genevieve entered my parlour.

Jonny threw the blanket over me. He then moved slightly away and stood awkwardly, arms akimbo, obviously uncertain how to react.

"Jonny," I croaked, then, "Genevieve." I wanted to collapse in her arms.

My beautiful mentor approached me, and tentatively touched my cheek. *"Mon pauvre fils."*

My poor son. She had never called me her son before. *"Maman,"* I replied, trying the sound of it. It sounded right.

"Evan and I, we did our best for you. It was not enough."

"Jonathan is safe. It's enough for me. But how came you here, tonight?"

"I knew that Corbeau had found you here in London and that he knew you had a lover. I came as swiftly as possible to warn you, but he was the swifter. It was a chilling race, Gideon, and I apologise for being the loser of it. I knew that Evan would come to your aid as quickly as possible. I took the task of protecting your good friend. Although I had not met your Jonathan, I knew him from your descriptions. I waited in your stables for him to return, and told him who I was and that I must keep him safe. He was most reluctant to stay in safety with me, *cheri*. Most reluctant." She smiled at Jonny as she said this.

He blushed. "I knew nothing of this lady. You had not told me about her, no doubt for excellent reasons. When I heard that you were in danger, my only thought was to be by your side to help protect you from it."

His loyalty touched me, although it would have gotten him killed. "That would have been foolish, Jonathan."

"So I was eventually persuaded. You have a very good friend, Gideon."

I reached a hand out from under my blanket towards Genevieve. "I do," I said as she took the offered hand. "Another debt I cannot repay, *Maman.*"

She kissed me on the cheek. "We do not speak of debts, *mon fils.* But are you well? Did he hurt you?"

"He did, but I am well now that my loved ones are here."

Genevieve looked me in the eyes. "Of course you are not well. But I believe you will be, with time and love. Drink some more, Gideon, it will help you."

In fact, it healed the injuries, at least the ones that showed. But the unseen wounds still bled, both the old scars re-opened and newly inflicted ones alike. Despair, guilt, anger—every possible negative emotion washed over me. How could I ever have been so foolish as to believe I was free? To have made a life for myself, taken a lover, deluded myself so greatly? Why did I dare to dream?

"It is not a dream, *mon cher,*" Genevieve said, and I realised I had spoken out loud. I dared not look at Jonathan. "We are all subject to the whims of fate. What you have is very real. He cannot shatter it. Not even he is immune." A light shone in her eyes. "I think, however," she said, leaning forward with an intense expression that made her very beautiful, "that you should leave England for a time. My chateau is empty at the moment. You healed there once. Perhaps you could do so again? I am certain Jonathan would enjoy France, would you not?"

Jonny jumped at being directly addressed. "I believe I would."

She smiled at him. "Then it is settled. I will give you time to prepare things here, *cheri,* and then I will see all three of you in France. If you do not arrive quickly, I shall ask Evan to carry you. Understood?"

"Understood," I said. "Thank you, Genevieve."

She kissed me briefly on the forehead. "I wish you joy, Gideon."

She turned and kissed a startled Jonathan. "You as well. Thank you for loving my son." She then hugged Evan and kissed him, and not on the forehead. "*Merci beaucoups,*" she murmured to him.

I couldn't catch what he said in return, and my hearing is excellent.

"Must you go?" I asked.

"You have all you need here, *mon fils.* I will only be in the way. And Jean will fret. You shall see me again. *A bien tot.*"

Genevieve left then, without lingering farewells or a backward glance. Seeing her again, and having Jonathan restored to me, brought me out of the dark and cold place where my mind had retreated. Keeping the blanket secure with a judicious tuck and fold, I turned to Jonny. I hugged him tightly, inhaling the scent of leather, horse, dust, and the sweet underscore of warm blood. I opened my eyes in time to catch Evan's smile before he left us.

Jonathan and I went upstairs together. Only in the privacy of my bed, with Jonathan lying next to me, did I once more remove the blanket. He exclaimed over the whip wounds, although the ones I could see had already begun healing, aided by the pig's blood.

Jonny examined me closely. "What happened to you? You have never felt so cold, or looked so pale and weak. It is more than a flogging, I fear, that has made you thus. Genevieve told me about your master, what a brute he is. What did he do to you? You can trust me."

Haltingly, the story came out. When I finished, I turned my back on him, certain that he would reject me. Instead, I felt his hand gently caress my shoulder. I looked at him, and saw only love and concern in his eyes.

"He hurt you. I know what you need. You said your friend gave you blood to drink, but it was pig's blood. You need human blood to help you heal, don't you? Take mine."

"Jonny, no!"

"Please, Gideon. I know no other way to show you how much I love you. Let me prove that I trust you—with my life, and beyond. Take what you need."

He pulled on my shoulder until I rolled over to face him. He kissed me until my lips responded despite myself. I shuddered and put my arms around him, cherishing his warmth. My lips moved to his neck, and my body straddled his, hunger and passion waking at the same time. He gently guided me into him even as my fangs sank painlessly into his pulsing vein.

No wine tasted sweeter or headier than the rich fluid of my loved one's lifeblood. His body arched under me in pleasure while I, kitten-gentle, lapped his blood. Luckily, I kept my wits about me long enough to stop drinking before I supped too deeply. He moaned, aroused, seeking my body. I felt him enter and we rode the waves of pleasure together. The tide of our love crashed over the memory of rape and drowned it.

Chapter Six

enevieve had added new furnishings, tapestries and carpets over the years, but Chateau de Monet itself remained changeless. I stood in the courtyard and inhaled the familiar scents of mud, grapes, old stone, dead leaves and faintly lingering perfume.

"I've always liked it here," Evan remarked as we unloaded supplies from the carriage. Genevieve and the Gardiens had discreetly vacated the chateau for us.

"But perhaps it's not so enticing without the lady of the house in residence," I said innocently.

"I have no idea what you mean." Evan was as straight-faced as a magistrate.

"This is beautiful!" Jonathan said, coming out of the main reception room as I carted luggage by on the way to the bedrooms. "How long may we stay?"

"As long as we like," I said. "I can manage my business concerns from here, and nothing else presses." I set the portmanteau down for a moment, and stood remembering my first night in this room, when the most beautiful woman I ever saw had greeted me kindly. How much I owed Genevieve. Yes, I could heal here again. The process had already started.

"You lived here alone with Genevieve for more than seventy years?" Jonny was teasing, his expression mischievous. "I think I'm jealous."

Laughing, I chased him out of the castle and told him to get back to work unloading the carriage.

We settled in comfortably, making arrangements for the delivery of food, which would be especially important when Evan went into high cycle. The three of us agreed to share the various housekeeping chores to avoid the necessity of hiring servants.

This marked the start of a happy time. Despite winter's arrival, we were snug in our temporary home, living mostly in the library and the bedrooms. Evan, not yet in high cycle, stayed close to the castle. Jonathan and I went for moonlight rides in the snow, or explored the less-used parts of the chateau. Sometimes the memory of why I was here would come flooding back, but my lover learned to recognise these moods in me and held me until the fear and pain passed.

Spring came, bringing little change in our idyllic existence, at least for a while. Evan went into high cycle, and as one outlet for his energy, practised with various weapons. One evening, he tried, not for the first time, to teach fencing to Jonathan. The young man disliked such things intensely, but Evan insisted he learn to defend himself.

"Oh, damn." Jonathan swore as his rapier flew out of his hand yet again. He turned and bent to pick it up. Evan used the flat of his own weapon to swat his opponent across the offered target. Jonathan whirled on him, spluttering.

"You did that on purpose!"

"Certainly. Never turn your back on an opponent. Had I been an enemy, you would be dead."

Jonathan picked up his sword and attacked Evan with renewed vigour, seeking revenge for the swat. An excellent sword fight ensued, until Evan held up his hand to call a halt.

A carriage clattered up the stone driveway, passing under the arch and turning so that the horses nearly ran us down. Jonathan dropped his sword again, jumping out of the way of the carriage with an oath. A smile tugged on my lips, for though I had never seen that carriage I knew its occupant. I glanced up at the driver, who nodded cheerfully at me as if he had not just narrowly avoided trampling us. It was one of les Gardiens, Thierry.

He sprang lightly down from his lofty perch as Evan moved to hold the horses. The carriage door swung open before Thierry could reach it, and a stranger leapt out. He drew his sword, eyes glinting fiercely in the torchlight, teeth bared.

"Hah!" He glared at the three of us, sword held *en garde,* daring us to move.

Evan had not dropped his sword. The hilt rested in his hand with deceptive casualness. His eyes didn't leave the stranger's. Jonny didn't dare move to retrieve his own blade, and I had none. Thierry simply stood watching. I heard him snicker.

A voice spoke from within the carriage. "Jean. Put that sword away."

The stranger sighed, and sheathed his weapon. He stood a little taller than I, with the compact build of a fighter. Long dark hair framed a strong face. A well-trimmed beard and moustache added a touch of fierceness he didn't really need. He looked dangerous enough already. But he sheathed the sword, as Genevieve had requested, and went and helped her out of the carriage.

"*Bon soir,* Gideon, Jonathan, Evan," she said, nodding at us. "I see you've met Jean."

Jean de la Mare grinned and bowed. *"Enchanté."*

This was Genevieve's new lover? I confess I blinked. Oh, he looked handsome enough, but seemed to lack somewhat in gentlemanly manners. I expected someone more refined.

I escorted Genevieve into the chateau, Jonathan following with Jean de la Mare. Thierry and Evan saw to the horses, and joined us inside some time later. We gathered in the main reception room, where Genevieve introduced us properly to her burly companion.

"I saw swords drawn and men fighting," he said by way of explaining his behaviour earlier. "I am a man of action. And Genevieve was in the coach. How was I to know there was no threat to her?"

Evan and Jonathan both stared at him. My eyes sought Genevieve's. Hers were dancing. She winked at me.

I soon realized that Jean's bluster and fierceness couldn't be taken seriously. No doubt he was deadly in a fight, for he carried his sword like one used to bearing arms, but he frequently made us laugh. I thought I understood what had drawn Genevieve to him. He did not dissemble or play politics. Impulse rather than deviousness ruled his actions.

That visit initiated a round of socializing with Genevieve and Jean. They were living in Jean's house in Paris, and the Gardiens had been distributed to various posts throughout France. Jean had, in fact, been recruited for le Societé des Gardiens, by Genevieve. I wondered what the taciturn Benoit made of this brash fellow.

We stayed in France for another three seasons, but when the second winter became a second spring, and there was no word or sign of Corbeau, Evan deemed it safe for us to return to England. I thanked Genevieve effusively for the loan of her chateau, and she assured me that it was at my disposal any time I needed it. We packed our things, restored the chateau to the condition in which we found it, and removed back to England.

The prospect of returning to my little house in Chelsea caused me some grief. It had been violated. I had been violated in it. The shattered window had been replaced before we departed for France, and the broken furniture removed, but it was no longer a sanctuary for me. Evan and Jonathan talked me into returning to it.

Once through the door, I found astounding changes. I barely recognized the parlour where Corbeau attacked me. Sporting new paint, new wallpaper, new furniture in fresh arrangements, new carpets, even new paintings on the walls, it was a different room. Nothing at all remained to serve as a reminder of that night.

"Is it well, then?" Jonathan asked, peering anxiously at my expression as I stood gaping at the changes.

"It's very well. You and Evan planned this, didn't you?"

"We did," Evan said.

"Thank you. Thank you both."

One of the first things I did upon my return to England was to sell my house to Jonathan. This ensured that Corbeau, or any other vampire, including myself, couldn't enter it without Jonathan's invitation. It was only a small protection, for there were ways around the prohibition, but it gave me some peace of mind. Jonathan found it very amusing that he had to formally invite me into the home we shared once he had purchased it.

"And if I don't?" His eyes danced with mischief as I stood on the wrong side of the threshold.

"You shall have a very cold and lonely bed."

"And I shall bounce you down the stairs," Evan growled, coming up behind Jonathan in the entrance hall. Jonathan jumped. He'd forgotten that Evan needed no invitation.

"I invite you, Gideon Redoak. Be welcome of this house."

I stepped across the threshold, the barrier gone. "Thank you. But you shall pay for that mischief."

"I'll leave his punishment to you," Evan said with a grin.

"Then you wouldn't have bounced me down the stairs?"

"Several times." But one hazel eye closed in a wink that Jonathan couldn't see.

The following years were the happiest I had ever known. We lived quietly, Jonathan, Evan and I, at least one of us glad of the respite. I find it difficult to express how much Jonathan meant to me. I loved him dearly, and I know he felt the same. In his arms, I found something I had never known with Corbeau. At last, I was able to make peace with myself.

Jonathan and I designed and planted a garden behind the house. Although I was unable to see it in the daylight, Jonny took great delight in describing each plant to me—how every budding flower, every leaf, every stem would look as the day passed and the sun and shade moved across the beds. We spent long hours over plans for the garden, discussing the merits of this shrub or that vine. He loved flowers and had these planted in abundance. "I regret that I don't have a vast estate for you to plan a larger garden," I said to him one day.

His eyes looked troubled. "I have no desire for vast estates, Gideon. They're only a burden. And the current fashion for false monasteries and new ruins, these gothic battlements, is ridiculous."

I had seen some of the estates he mentioned, vast follies that swallowed the fortunes of impetuous nobility. I thought our little garden of light and colour was far prettier. But his reply intrigued me, and gave me another piece of the puzzle of Jonathan's background. He came from the nobility.

Being found out as a sodomite had disgraced many a noble son. Blue blood was no guarantor against persecution—indeed, nearly the opposite was true, for the higher your social profile, the greater chance of your being found out if you engaged in unnatural practices. Men who desired other men as sexual partners were reviled. This was one reason why I lived as quietly and unobtrusively as possible.

Time passed and the century began to wane. Unlike the years spent at the Chateau de Monet, now I marked time as it fled. I had met Jonathan in 1780, when he was twenty-five. Now it was 1795, and he was turning forty.

He still looked beautiful to me, but I could see the signs of aging on him. Though I ensured that he had the best food and medical care available, hiring an Eastern physician to attend any ills he might suffer rather than relying on English medicine, he was still mortal. How frail he seemed to me! His breath and heartbeat counted the knells of his lifetime. His hair thinned, and lines tugged at the edges of his eyes and mouth and creased his forehead. His step was not quite so blithe as it had once been.

I couldn't contemplate the only cure that I knew for this ailment. To turn a human being into a vampire, a bloodthirsty monster that was forced to kill for sustenance—it was unthinkable. I couldn't do to him what had been done to me. I knew that I had unwillingly caused others to become vampires in Corbeau's Keep, but I had had no choice and they had been strangers. To make Jonathan, my Jonny, into something such as I—the idea made me shudder.

Still, Genevieve told me once that such turnings happened in our night world. She herself had been turned into a vampire by a man she loved and who loved her. She turned Jean out of compassion because he had been dying of a bullet wound, bleeding profusely. She gave him the only blood that would save him, and he worshipped her for it. Love did not always survive the turning, but sometimes it was strengthened by it.

The choice should be Jonathan's. So one night after we had celebrated his fortieth birthday, I came to his bed and sat beside him.

"Aren't you joining me?" He patted the pillow next to his invitingly.

"Not just yet. There's something we must speak of."

"So very formal, Gideon!" He laughed, sitting up, but the expression on my face must have been more serious than I suspected, for the laughter died. "What is it?"

"Jonathan, you're forty years old."

"Yes. How old are you?"

I realised that I'd never told him this. "I was born in the year sixteen hundred and twenty-two. I died in 1642."

"You were nineteen? Twenty?" His eyes registered his shock.

"I shall, in a way, always be nineteen. You will not always be forty."

His blue eyes were very bright as he regarded me. "Ah. I wondered if we'd ever speak of this, but I thought it better to let you be the one to introduce it."

"You know what I'm going to ask, then?"

"I've suspected for some time that you might, Gideon."

"And your answer?"

"No."

I knew before he spoke. I turned my head in pain, and felt his hand on mine.

"Don't mistake me. I love you dearly, Gideon. It matters not to me that you're a vampire, that you drink blood, that you can live only by night and must shun the day. But I can't be what you are. How you find the strength to go on with such a life, I don't know."

"I find it in you, Jonathan."

Pain bloomed in his eyes, pain and love. His hand clenched mine. "I love you. Never think that I don't. But I don't wish to be a vampire."

"I—I can't blame you."

"You aren't angry?"

I managed to smile at him then. "Of course not, Jonathan. The decision was yours, always, and I think I knew your answer before I ventured the question. But surely you see that it had to be asked?"

"Yes, and it has been asked and answered. Let's speak no more of it. Come and love me, my vampire."

I did so willingly, though not without sadness. I would lose him, then. I had always known that, from the first moment in that muddy ditch so long ago, but now the reality stung bitterly.

Twenty more years passed, two decades of peace and happiness in the gardens of Chelsea.

Business called me away in the damp spring of 1815. A ship came in late, there was a dispute with the chandler and some of the cargo was damaged. My agent had thrown up his hands in despair and insisted that only I could sort out the mess. He arranged to have my house prepared for me, being aware of my special needs without knowing the true reason, and I made hasty travel plans.

Jonathan was old, but he appeared hale. I reassured myself that many men of his class passed their three score and ten. He showed no sign of illness, or I never would have left him, if it meant losing every ship in my fleet. I ordered Evan to stay behind and guard him, which caused an argument with my protector, but I wouldn't leave unless I knew Jonathan was safe. I said good-bye to him in the garden. His kiss was an old man's, dry and whispery. I rode my mare away, and I didn't turn to look back.

Once I arrived in Portsmouth, I became involved in a legal tangle that would have exasperated Machiavelli. I paid off the chandler, more than he deserved, and fought the temptation to invite him for dinner. His blood would have been as sour as his disposition.

Negotiating the warped boards in the hold with care and slightly nauseated at the proximity to running water, I assessed the damaged goods. The cargo consisted of furs, tobacco, rum and spices. No ship I even partially owned carried slaves, however lucrative the trade might be. I was not Corbeau, regarding humans as cattle. It was bad enough that I fed on them to survive.

Jonathan was never far from my thoughts. In his younger days, he would have come with me. He loved the sea, and ships. He handled this business better than I, unhampered by my aversion to running water. We shared some enjoyable nights in port lodgings, our passion heightened by the music of waves and wind.

The damage was not as bad as estimated. I could well afford the loss. From my agent's frantic message, I'd expected the ship to be crippled and the cargo sunk to the bottom of the Atlantic.

Straightening out the matter myself proved worth the time, but I sighed with relief on leaving the ship.

I lodged in a small house that I had bought because my business took me so often to Portsmouth. It was safe. All those who conducted trade with me knew that I couldn't be disturbed in daylight. The house was quiet without either of my companions and cold and lonely without one of them in particular.

That evening, I awoke from my sleep no longer whole.

Jonathan was dead.

I screamed his name. I shook, unable to rise from the bed. Grief washed over me like the angry tide even as I denied the reason for it. He couldn't be dead. He wouldn't have left me.

I rose from the bed, so numb that I walked into a chair without seeing it. The echo of its crash went on for a long time. I finally realised that the noise was someone rapping on the door. Somehow I found it and yanked it open, almost sending my shipping agent sprawling across the threshold.

"Is something wrong, sir?" he asked.

"I must go home," I said, but I wasn't speaking to him.

"Of course, if you must..." he faltered, and turned to the one servant I kept in this house. "Bring your master's carriage around. Do it now." He looked back at me. "Is there anything I can do?" Perhaps he wasn't useless after all.

I shook my head. He found some brandy and poured it for me, forcing the glass into my nerveless hand and wrapping my fingers around it. He went up to my room and packed a bag for me while I stood staring at the brandy, unable to remember how it had gotten into my hand. When the carriage came around, my agent put me in it and told the servant to take me home.

The horses caught my mood, as did the servant. The team came through the gates of the courtyard breathing fire. No groom came forth to take them. Only Evan awaited me. He opened the door for me and gave me his hand to steady me.

"Gideon..." His voice broke. Then he wept.

"No." A whisper, when I wanted to scream. I wanted it to not be true. I wanted Jonathan to come out of the house and greet me.

Evan laid a hand on my arm. It burned. "I'm sorry."

I started to run to the house, but Evan held me back. My powers had deserted me, for I couldn't break free of that gentle grasp.

"It was very sudden. No one expected it. Jonathan went out to sit in the garden as usual. When I went out to tell him dinner was ready, I thought he had fallen asleep, but he was..."

"Did he suffer?"

"I think not. It must have been very fast. He went peacefully."

I shuddered, recalling the pain, the haze of opium forced on me, and the suffocating darkness of my own death. "Evan, unless you have died, you must not assume such things." I would never have spoken to him so in my right mind.

He knew it, too, for he said nothing. Angrily, I wrenched out of his hold on my arm. I lifted my head and howled to the uncaring moon and the cold stars.

"Gideon." Evan shook me, ever so slightly. "Come inside. You must come inside."

I followed his direction. The servants stayed well out of sight, terrified by the unearthly noise they'd heard. I flung myself into the library. Jonathan had liked to sit here by the fireplace, the flames playing in his gold hair. There was no fire lit tonight. Instead, the room was full of flowers. The scent cloyed. I wanted to see him. Some of the flowers were from his garden. He would have liked that. Jonathan did not lie in the coffin. I saw a dry, dead stranger. How could this lifeless husk have ever been the beautiful young man I had loved? I didn't touch him. I couldn't bear to.

The door opened and Evan came in. "I thought you would be here." He spoke as if verbally crossing cracked ice.

"It's not fair!" I wanted to weep, but I could no longer shed tears.

"I know. It isn't."

"The funeral?" The words were wrenched from my throat.

"Arranged for tomorrow. It could be postponed until evening, if you'd like."

To watch him be buried in the suffocating earth—I couldn't face that. "No! He loved the sunlight."

Evan nodded. "Are you going to be all right?"

"No. But you can go."

He looked dubious, but left me alone. No sense of Jonathan remained in the room with his body. He was gone. Lost, I stumbled up the stairs to my private chambers. The door to Jonathan's room was closed, and would always remain so.

The sun would rise soon. I could have gone out and stood facing it, immolating myself on the altar of my grief, but...no.

I collapsed on my own bed, welcoming for once the oblivion that came with the dawn.

With the sunset, I awoke. Someone had been in the room while I slept. Only Evan would have dared such a thing. He had undressed me, and put me properly to bed. I rose, washed and dressed, the motions mechanical. A decanter of wine stood on a table, and I poured some. It tasted dry and sour. Nauseated, I spat it out.

Downstairs, there were fewer flowers. Evan came in with a message from my agent, saying all was well with the ship. I didn't care if it sank.

The nights dragged on and on, an endless stretch of loneliness.

Disturbed by my behaviour, Evan sought for a way to get me out of England. Without my knowledge, he consulted with Genevieve.

One night Evan came to me with an urgent message from both Genevieve and Jean de la Mare, saying that I must go to Paris. There was a child vampire loose in the city, and they'd had no luck in locating it. Would I help? A child fledgling is a danger to the community, since they have no idea of the range of their powers or how to control their feeding. A rogue child must be caught and trained or else destroyed.

We left for France the next night. I knew that my grief would overwhelm me if I did nothing. Jonny's loss was a pain worse than any I had suffered in Corbeau's Keep. It wasn't like losing a limb, but a piece of my heart. I answered the call for help, that I might start to feel again.

I had often been to Paris with Genevieve, to balls or to the opera, and it had changed little. In 1815, it was once again safe to visit, the revolution being over and Napoleon defeated. The streets bore marks of the recent violence and the bloodsmell was still faintly discernible in the air.

Jean owned a large house in the Faubourg Saint-Germain, an address that he found amusing for some reason. He agreed to accommodate us there, so that was where Evan and I went first. Withdrawn in my grief, I took little notice of my surroundings. Jean's tastes ran to the excessively opulent. The house resembled a high-class bordello, all red and gold velvet and drapes everywhere. At least, that fitted my idea of what a high-class bordello might be like. I never set foot in one. That Jean had, I entertained no doubt.

Genevieve was ahead of Jean by the fraction of an inch in their race to greet me. She folded her arms around me and held me tightly, murmuring sympathies in French. I rested my head on her shoulder and let her hug me, the familiar scent of roses making me feel at home. It helped, a little.

She released me reluctantly and Jean embraced me. Had I still been a fragile human, I am quite certain that his squeeze would have broken several ribs. He also kissed me on both cheeks. He smelled of wine and velvet.

"Come," he said after greeting Evan. I noticed that he made no attempt to hug my protector. "This child must be found. He or she is not merely a diversion we invented."

"Why can you not find him?" I asked.

My two friends looked at each other and shrugged.

"It is a big city," Jean said.

And there are many vampires here," Genevieve added.

"In other words," I said wearily, "You haven't looked very hard, thinking to use this rogue child to distract me."

Genevieve put her hands on my shoulders. "No one is denying you the right to grieve, *mon cher.* But the world goes on, and you must move with it, or go mad. We are your friends, we love you, and we are very worried about you. Let us help you."

Touched by this display of concern, I said, "Very well. Let us plan how to find this child."

The primary emotions that a newly awakened fledgling has are fear and confusion. Add to these the overwhelming need for blood, and the discovery of supernatural powers, put them all in the mind and body of a young child, and the result is danger—for the child, for other vampires, and for humans. For one thing, it is not very appealing to live for centuries in the body of a prepubescent. Luckily, I'd been old enough when turned to avoid such a fate.

The four of us scoured Paris, searching for the youngster's bolthole. Jean and Genevieve, knowing the night dwellers, questioned them as to whether they had seen a new child. Evan and I split up the likely and unlikely hiding places between us. There were known vampire sanctuaries, for lack of a better term, places where the undead could go when in trouble or in need of respite. I doubted whether the youngster would know of these places, but instinct might draw him there.

When I walked into the Café Chat Noir, I knew this was where I would find my quarry. I sensed the raging emotions from where I stood. The café, a known vampire gathering place, had no mirrors. Tonight, only one vampire occupied the café, broadcast-ing his emotions so forcefully that he scared off everyone else for fear of the attention he attracted.

He sat at a corner table, his back to the wall and his chair po-sitioned so that he could see everyone who came in. I judged his age to be about twenty-four. He was a handsome boy, certainly, with slightly angular facial features, and a square jaw. Jet-black hair adorned his head. Grey eyes, as troubled as a winter sea, surveyed me in panic as I drew closer. Perfectly shaped, long-fin-gered hands toyed with a wineglass and a slender cigar, but he lifted neither to his lips. His slim, powerful form tensed for flight, and I hoped he wouldn't bolt before I could speak to him.

He watched me as I approached, his eyes wide and his hands trembling. "Be easy," I told him in French, "I'm here to help you. I'm Baron Gideon Redoak." As pretty as he was, I felt no desire for him. I missed Jonny intensely.

"Count Alexander Philippe Goldanias." He had an accent that I couldn't place more accurately than Eastern Europe.

"May I join you?" He indicated the empty chair across from him, and I sat down, suddenly aware of how Genevieve had felt to have a newly-made vampire thrust into her care. I wondered how much this frightened young man knew about his new situation. "I can help you."

He tensed, and his eyes narrowed. It was actually a good sign that he didn't trust me. It meant that he had learned to be on his guard. Possibly he didn't recognise me as his own kind, or he did, but knew better than to trust me for that reason alone.

"Why would you think I need help?"

"This is a public place, sir. We should have this discussion somewhere private."

"I think that whatever you have to say to me may be said here, Baron."

"There are others you should meet. You have my word that you are safe with me."

He nodded, and rose without further protest.

We left the café, and walked to Jean's home without speak-ing. "Here is your child," I said as we entered.

Jean, already back at the house, greeted my new acquain-tance effusively. I saw Alexander recoil slightly from Jean's en-thusiasm. "Tall one, is he not?" Jean grinned, for Alexander stood 6'4" in his stocking feet.

Genevieve returned just then. She glanced appraisingly at my foundling. "Ah, the lost lamb, is it? You are somewhat older than I expected."

"I am twenty-four, Madame." Alexander was not at all reluctant to gaze upon Genevieve. He obviously liked what he saw, for he bowed deeply.

"As old as all that!" She didn't laugh, for that would have hurt his feelings. "Your presence in the city felt much younger. How long have you been one of us?"

The young man sat down heavily in a chair that creaked alarmingly at such usage. He put his hands over his eyes. "I do not know," he said, and added something in a language I didn't recognise.

Genevieve answered him in the same language, speaking very sharply for her. Alexander lifted his head and stared at her in frank surprise.

"You speak Hungarian?" he asked her in French.

"Yes. So kindly refrain from profanity in that, or any language."

"My apologies." He rose and bowed again.

"You are Hungarian?" Jean asked, his tone unusually harsh.

We all turned to look at him, and Alexander replied in his heavily accented French, "Yes. Why?"

"Who is your turnsire?" Jean leaned so far forward that he nearly fell out of his chair.

The young vampire moved his own chair back, out of Jean's reach. I could see Genevieve's lips parting to ask a question.

"Please," Jean held up a hand. "I have a reason. Who is your turnsire?"

"Turnsire? Do you mean my mistress?"

Jean sucked in breath, an odd sound in a room with four vampires as occupants. "A woman." His voice was strangled. "A woman. Her name, boy? Her name!"

Looking frightened and trapped, Alexander turned to me for reassurance. "I don't understand. I thought you said you would help me."

"Calm yourself, Jean," Genevieve said. "You are frightening the boy."

Alexander's beautiful head snapped in her direction, and a storm was in the sea-grey eyes. He replied with dignity. "I am not a boy, Madame. I was a married man, with two children and an estate."

"You are so green in the blood that the smell of your turning is still on you. Your mortal age means nothing to us, although you are older than I expected. To us, you are a boy. You cannot forget your family, but you must think of them as dead to you. It is kinder. You cannot go back to them."

Jean had subsided back into his chair, but I could sense the excitement that seethed through him. His hands trembled. Beside me, Alexander sulked at Genevieve's response.

I looked at Alexander. "I haven't betrayed you. We can help you, if you choose to be helped. I know that these two were of great solace to me when I needed assistance."

"You expect to win my trust so easily?"

"No," Genevieve answered, and he turned to look at her again. "Trust must be won slowly." She smiled at me, and I felt warmed. "But we must also trust you. It seems important to Jean that he know the name of the woman who made you what you are. Please, tell us this much."

"Her name is Lucinda," Alexander said, after a long, searching look at Jean. I'm certain that he noticed Jean's shaking hands, set lips, and narrowed eyes. "I never knew her last name."

We all looked at Jean. Slowly, his fingers curled into tight balls of tension. "Lucinda! I shall kill her!"

Genevieve stared at him. "Jean? You know this woman?"

"She is mine," he said through tight-held teeth. "I was in the Empire, you remember? The little fox seduced me and persuaded me to turn her, then broke free of me. She always had an eye for handsome noblemen, that one."

Alexander seemed to be thinking this over. "So, you turned her and she turned me? Does that make you my grandfather?"

"If so, it makes me your great-grandmother and I would prefer not to be quite so old," Genevieve said sternly, but I could see amusement in her eyes.

That startled him. "And you?" He turned once again to me. "Are you some distant relative?"

"I am your adopted great-uncle, perhaps." I surprised myself with this attempt at humour.

Genevieve rose from her chair, and as one, so did we men. "Come, gentlemen. Dawn grows close. Alexander, have you somewhere safe to stay?"

"The café..."

Jean sighed. "No. I would not have it put about in the community that I turned my grandson out to fend for himself. Do you have any belongings?"

He shook his head, and I noticed for the first time that his clothing, though rich, looked worn and travel-stained. "Not even my coffin. I learned that it's only a hindrance, and that I need but hide from the sun to be safe."

Genevieve gave him a considering look. "You learn quickly."

"When need arises."

"Why did you come to Paris?" Jean asked.

"To find Lucinda. She came this way after destroying my life."

"I will find her," Jean said grimly.

I felt myself going numb. The grief was still new, and it had been a long and eventful night. Dawn tugged at me, promising oblivion.

"Let us find our beds," Genevieve suggested. She came over and took my hand. "Gideon is tired."

"Of course. You may have the second guestroom, my grandson." Jean showed Alexander the way to that chamber and then returned. He looked at me tenderly. "Poor little mouse," he said, and gave me a hug.

To think that I had once disliked him. First impressions can be wrong. "My dearest friends," I said, taking Genevieve's hand and pulling her into the hug.

"Now go to bed, my son," Genevieve said.

"Yes, Mother," I replied in English.

She smiled, but with sadness behind it. "I once had children."

Before I could answer, Evan showed up, unasked, and told me it was bedtime. I followed him to the guest bedroom that had been assigned to me. Evan slept in the servants' quarters. I had protested this, since he was no servant, but no other accommodation existed in this household and he claimed to be content. It gave him free access to the house and easy egress to the outdoors.

He turned down the bed for me, got out my nightshirt, and bid me goodnight. Jonny's absence hit me like a tidal wave in this strange bed with its strange smells of slightly scorched linen and musty velvet. Finding the "child" vampire had not cured me of my grief—it made me feel it all the more keenly. Alone and miserable, I waited for the daysleep to take my pain away.

The next evening, we gathered again in Jean's sitting room and planned to hunt for Jean's get, the female vampire Lucinda who turned Alexander. Genevieve sat in an over-upholstered chaise with Jean hovering behind her. I perched on a dainty little tapestry chair that seemed inadequate for my girth of shoulder. Alexander looked equally uncomfortable on a similar chair, which he dwarfed. Evan was the only one who looked really at home, but Evan had the happy ability to make himself comfortable on a shard of glass if necessary.

"How do you know that Lucinda came to Paris?" Jean asked.

"She told me, just before she left me. She said that Paris was friendly to our kind, and much more exciting than a mud hole in the Carpathian Mountains." Alexander couldn't quite disguise the shaking in his voice when he repeated this insult.

Jean pursed his lips while Genevieve gave him a slow, measuring look.

"Did you perhaps give Lucinda your address?" she asked Jean, the closest I had ever heard her come to sarcasm.

Evan coughed, but I could tell that he was covering a laugh. My own mouth twitched, but Alexander merely looked puzzled.

Jean shuffled his feet. "I thought she should know where it was safe."

"We must find her," Genevieve sighed. "And convince her that turning young men with wives and children is not acceptable."

"I doubt if she will agree. She has her own views, that one."

"She will be made to agree. Jean, where would she go?"

He replied with a fluid shrug. "We searched many of the usual places looking for the child. I would have seen Lucinda had she been in any of those." He frowned a little, as if in thought. "I couldn't sense her anywhere, and a master is usually aware of his get."

"But you were not looking for one of yours," I said.

"Even when not actively looking, one feels their presence, Gideon," Genevieve said.

"Lucinda loves light and crowds and music," Alexander said. "The café where you found me was too quiet."

"There are other places with light and music." Jean ran his hand over his bearded chin and upper lip. "I was searching some of those."

I had drawn only the quiet places, like the Café Chat Noir. Those were what I would prefer, but I was not Lucinda. She sounded most unpleasant, and I found myself harbouring the uncharitable hope that we would not actually find her.

"How long ago did you leave your country to come to France?" Evan asked Alexander.

The boy's head swivelled to look at my protector. His eyes narrowed, as if he felt that Evan had no right to address him directly. He had borne a title and managed an estate when he had been mortal—perhaps he thought that Evan was only a servant and below his station. He would have to learn that among the night people, your only rank was what you made for yourself. "I don't know." he said gloomily, when the pressure of the silence made him realise that he had to answer. "I wandered for a time. And I had some trouble leaving the Austro-Hungarian Empire. Perhaps a year?"

"A year?" Jean's hands shot up in a gesture of hopelessness. "She could be in America by now!"

"Why would anyone want to go there?" I said without thinking.

Four faces turned to look at me incredulously. Evan laughed first, and before long, even I had to join the merriment. The tension that had been mounting dissipated.

Jean rubbed his chin. "She could be anywhere, including here, for all I would know. I haven't been in Paris more than a month or two. I've been staying at the chateau."

"So she could have come to Paris while you were in the Loire, and then moved on," Alexander said.

I saw Jean and Genevieve exchange looks, and even I knew that a vampire who found a safe and congenial place seldom moved on after less than a year. Alexander was the only one who didn't appear baffled by the situation.

Genevieve sighed. "We have a serious dilemma on our hands. By this time, she may have seduced another...susceptible young man."

"I am a fool. You may say so." Alexander's voice was bitter.

"I shall not say that." Genevieve said firmly.

A wave of grief washed over me unexpectedly as I thought of my own lost young man. Genevieve rose at once and crossed to my side, rubbing my shoulders and whispering soothing words into my ear. I leaned against her.

"Is he weeping?" Alexander asked in surprise.

"Gideon has just lost a very dear friend. Alexander, Jean: how well did you know Lucinda's habits and tastes as a vampire? Where would she be likely to go?"

I looked at the two men, improbable allies united by a common mistress. The thought made me smile, and seeing it, Genevieve squeezed my shoulder.

Alexander finally said, "I don't know. She spoke only of Paris."

"We can ask if anyone has seen her," Evan said. "I have had some experience at tracking vampires."

"We begin tomorrow night, then," said Genevieve. "For now it is already too late."

Jean brought out some familiar bottles and poured four glasses of pig's blood. I saw Alexander's lips curl. He sniffed the contents of the glass he was given. Evan excused himself to get his own meal in the kitchen.

"He is insolent, that fellow," Alexander said, looking at me. "I am surprised that you, a Baron, would tolerate such familiarity from a servant."

"Evan is not a servant. He's my friend."

"Friend? But he is human!"

"He is not human, but it's not my place to tell you what he is. You are no longer the lord of your estate, young Count." I emphasised his title slightly, and saw him wince. "All claims to titles and estates die with our mortal bodies, Alexander. I gave you my old title of Baron simply to ensure that I had your attention. There is no nobility among the night dwellers such as we, save that which you earn."

He glared sullenly into his glass, wrinkling that aristocratic nose. "And this foul stuff?"

"Foul it may be," Genevieve said, "but you must make yourself drink it. We cannot prey on humans every night, even in Paris. We can subsist on this. It quells the hunger."

He took a sip. Remembering my first taste of the Chateau de Monet's special vintage, I sympathised when he gagged.

"And this is my legacy from Lucinda?" He forced himself to swallow the blood. "This is what it means to be a vampire? To drink the blood of pigs, and be on equal terms with servants and peasants?"

Thunder rolled across Jean's face. "Idiot boy! This is what it means to be a vampire: to drink the blood of pigs so that we do not deplete the humans and kill them all! To live as normal a life as possible, not to succumb to the lure of power and the darkness! To be on equal terms with those who could kill us in an eye blink—you sat there and sneered at a man who was armed with at least three weapons. Because if we do not do these things, do you know what that means?"

Alexander pulled back from Jean's fury. He looked imploringly at Genevieve, as a source of feminine sympathy, but her expression was stony. Having no other recourse, Alexander looked at me.

"What does it mean?" he asked, licking his lips.

I thought of Corbeau, eternally handsome and eternally evil. He would have sneered at pig's blood. To him, Jean and Genevieve must have seemed weak and ineffectual vampires, playing at being human. I knew which way I preferred to live.

"It means we are monsters," I said. I rose up, all eyes on me. "Excuse me. I think I shall retire a little early." I bowed.

I knew they all watched me as I walked to my lonely bedroom. The distance never seemed so great.

However, before the daysleep could claim me and ease my sorrow with oblivion, the sounds of an argument disturbed me. Jean yelled in extremely profane French, casting aspersions on some unfortunate person's hygiene, ancestry and sexual habits. The fuss penetrated my gloom and I rose, pulling on some breeches, to go and see.

I found Evan pulling shut the front doors of the house and bolting them. Jean, invective still pouring from his lips, held Alexander pinned against a wall, the velvet wallpaper crushed under the tall young man's weight. Genevieve, wrapped in a robe of some sort, sat on the edge of the chaise. She looked shaken.

"What happened?" I asked.

"Alexander came out after everyone had retired," Evan replied, when neither Jean nor Genevieve seemed about to answer. "He didn't see me, but walked right past and threw the doors open." Evan was invisible unless he wished to be noticed.

"Jean, let him go," Genevieve said wearily. "Sit down, Alexander."

From her tone, it was an order intended to be obeyed. Jean, snarling, stepped away from the young man and he slid down the wall, leaving a streak of crushed velvet, and sat abruptly on the floor.

"Evan, are the doors secured?" Genevieve asked.

"They are." He didn't stir from them.

"We have but moments before the sun rises," I said needlessly. No one is more aware of sunrise than a roomful of vampires.

"This will take but a moment," Genevieve said. She looked at Alexander. "Why?" The single word sounded like a pistol shot.

He raised his head, looking at us all in turn. He addressed me, sensing sympathy. "If we are monsters, isn't it better to die?"

There was silence. Everyone seemed to be waiting for me to answer.

"No," I said finally. "The answer is to fight."

"It is not uncommon for fledgling vampires to commit suicide," Genevieve said.

"But not to take others with them!" Jean said hotly. "We could all have been consumed by the sunlight! Genevieve, let me beat some sense into him?"

I knew Genevieve's views on punishment, and was not surprised when she shook her head. "No, Jean. It would solve nothing, and only teach him resentment. Alexander, the sun is rising, we must retire or become so many senseless bodies for Evan to put to bed. Give us your word that you will not try this again."

He was still looking at me, pleading for understanding.

"Give me your word, Alexander," I said. "And we'll speak no more of what has happened."

"You have my word. I will not open the doors again."

"Are you satisfied?" Genevieve looked at Jean.

"I want an apology." He still looked angry.

Alexander stood up then, and crossed over to him, offering his hand. "I apologise. It was foolish of me, please forgive me." He bowed deeply and prettily, and rose with his hand still extended.

Jean hesitated a moment, then took the hand and shook it gruffly. "Next time, boy, talk to someone first before you do something foolish!"

"I promise."

Chapter Seven

We scoured Paris for traces of Lucinda. I found myself paired with Alexander as well as Evan, and now I knew how Genevieve felt to have the care of a badly taught vampire fledgling. He knew so little, I marvelled that he had survived. Still, a certain warmth of feeling grew between us, but not the sort of relationship I had built with Jonny. It was more like what I felt for Evan, or Jean: friendship.

As Alexander and I toured the dark streets of Paris and the hidden cafés and other places where the night dwellers went, I began to realise that I liked him. I wasn't even sure why, since his temperament proved moody, prone to sulks and fits of despair that made me a little impatient with him. Yet flashes of the quality within could be seen, and I determined to mine for it. He became somewhat less self-conceited as he threw himself wholeheartedly into helping us search for his turnsire. My own grief abated now that I had other things to occupy my mind.

We questioned the denizens of the places we searched, and heard disturbing rumours. Someone had been through Paris, a year ago, recruiting disaffected vampires. The bored, the displaced, the ones who made no attempt to hide their nature from humans—these had been asked if they wanted to join with others of similar disposition. For what purpose, nobody seemed to know. Those doing the recruiting gave details only to the ones who agreed to join.

Lucinda had been seen speaking to these mysterious recruiters. She had gone off with them, and no one had seen her in Paris since. The recruiters, some witnesses stated with sideways glances at me, appeared to be English and not all of them were vampires.

In a café full of cigarette and cigar smoke, the smell of absinthe and blood mingling together, we five searchers sat at a table over a bottle of crude wine and pondered our findings.

Alexander produced a thin black cigar, like the one I saw him with the night we met. "You do not mind?" he asked, and when we all shook our heads, he lit it. "One habit that did not die with my body." The haze in the café indicated others found it equally hard to quit.

After a long silence, in which Alexander's cigar contributed to the level of pollution in the café, Evan said, "Someone is recruiting vampires."

"And others." Jean sighed, putting his head in his hands. "Remember that they say these strangers are not just vampires."

"But what else are they?" Genevieve asked. "Werewolves? Witches?"

"Witches?" I said. "Like the ones my father's preacher used to rant about? Surely in this reasonable age, harmless old women aren't convicted and hanged because their neighbour's cow has gone dry."

"There are those with real power, Gideon," Genevieve said. "Wielders of magic. The word 'witch' is one of convenience. I assure you, they do not ride broomsticks or sign pacts with the devil."

"Some of them do," said Jean darkly.

Genevieve ignored him. "We do not normally cross paths with the magic users. I do not like the sound of this recruiting."

But although we continued our questioning, we learned nothing new. We found some of the vampires that had been approached by the recruiters, but they refused to reveal why they had been sought. One of them did grudgingly admit that she thought the non-vampires among the recruiters might be *sorcières*—witches. She added that when they told her she would have to move to England, she lost interest, but she would say no more. Pleas, threats and downright bribery couldn't coax another word from her.

One evening after several weeks of fruitless investigation, I awoke with my gums itching and tingling. Pig's blood would no longer satisfy my hunger. I requested Jean's permission to hunt on his turf, and received it—a mere courtesy, but an important one. Evan followed me at a discreet distance.

Time had passed since I last stalked a human for dinner, but some things you never forget. I bypassed groups of two or more. Though I could overcome ten humans, there was no sense in raising an alarm. Even vampires died from the caress of *La Guillotine.*

Finally, I spied a lone figure, standing near an entrance to one of the rougher nightspots favoured by both humans and non-humans. In this hovel of a cellar, death was sold by the glassful or pipe full. We had looked here once for Lucinda—or, rather, Jean and Evan went in and come back out nearly at once, declaring it too degenerate for the rest of us. My potential victim appeared to be in rather the wrong place.

I could smell her blood from where I stood. She was human, with her back turned to me. Her garments appeared odd to my eyes, which were long-used to French fashion: a short, high-waisted jacket over a filmy dress that did nothing to disguise her curved figure. Evan gave a low whistle under his breath.

She heard him and turned, sharp features incongruous beneath a demure bonnet. A knife appeared in her hand. "Stop where you are or I'll gut you both."

She spoke English, with a faint overlay of a northern burr. Was she Scottish?

"Easy, darling," Evan said, keeping his hands still.

Her eyes narrowed. "I am not your darling, and I can use this knife. Stay where you are."

"What are you doing here?" I asked her. It felt good to speak my native tongue, after so many nights of French.

"Looking for vampires."

I bowed. "You have found one." I made the mistake of taking two steps towards her as I straightened out of the bow.

Her body thumped into mine at top speed, catching me off guard and sending me sprawling to the filthy sidewalk. Her green eyes, fierce in the darkness, stared into mine. She sat on top of me, pinning me down and holding the knife at my throat. A knife wound couldn't kill me, but severed arteries tended to inconvenience one.

No human could attack a vampire like that. I raised my hand, seizing her knife arm. She swore, struggling in my grip. I pushed her arm away and levered her off me, sending her flying into Evan, who had just joined the fray after a highly unusual hesitation. As I rose to my feet, I saw her stab my protector in the forearm, forcing him to let her go. She struck him on the back of the head with the knife hilt, then rushed at me before I rose fully to my feet. She kicked me in the groin.

I hadn't known that degree of agony since those nights in the Keep. Groaning, I sagged to the ground, cradling my distressed member in my hands.

"Stay there," she said.

As if I could move! In an instant, Evan grabbed her. He seized her from behind and took a firm grip on the arm that held the knife, then picked her up as if she was a toddler and slammed her into the wall of the building. Before I could protest such treatment of a woman, he did it again and she dropped the knife, swearing and cursing in a totally unknown language.

Evan released her, staring at her, but maintaining the presence of mind to tuck her knife somewhere in his own clothes. "You speak Gaelic!"

The fire in my genitals eased a little, and I essayed an attempt to stand, using the lamppost as a prop. I felt that my good friend and bodyguard might have spared me a moment of thought rather than exclaiming over the fact that this deadly woman spoke some obscure language.

She frowned at him, and looked up and down the street as if hoping for escape or rescue. She didn't bother looking at me. "Who are you?" she asked Evan.

He replied in something that sounded like the language she had used, and I saw her eyes go wide. Really, Evan could have chosen a better place and time to seduce a woman.

Running footsteps alerted us to the arrival of others. By now, the pain had subsided enough that I could fight, if necessary. Two men raced towards us from nearby.

"Those will be my friends," said the strange woman. Then she finally glanced at me. "Are you all right?"

"Why do you ask?"

She grinned. "I was trying not to hurt you. I wanted to talk to you."

"You have a very strange way of not hurting people. I was trying not to hurt you!"

"Then we had the same goal." She really had quite a charming smile. I could see its effect on Evan. He straightened up and ran a hand through his hair.

Her two friends drew even with us, staring at the strange tableau we presented. Now that the hostilities had ceased, I took a look at our new acquaintances. The redheaded lady was accompanied by two men, one blond, one dark, all three of them about my height. With tired eyes and travel-stained clothing, they appeared to have come a long way.

"Maggie, are you all right?" asked the blond man, anxiously peering at the red-haired woman.

"Aye." She smiled and put a hand on his arm. "I was knocked into a wall twice, but I think it was a misunderstanding. These gentlemen are English."

"Welsh," Evan muttered.

"What has our nationality to do with anything?" I said, increasingly bewildered. What had begun as a quest for dinner had turned into a comedy of confusion.

The blond man looked at me. The intensity of those green eyes made me shiver a little. I could sense something here that I had never before encountered. There was power, a power I knew nothing about, but one that could easily counter any of my vampire tricks. Were these strangers witches? "We've come from England in search of an English vampire." He turned and looked at Evan. If that intense gaze affected my bodyguard, he didn't show it. "One who travels with a warrior."

The black-haired man spoke for the first time, and his voice had the lyrical inflection of the Welsh. "We shouldn't discuss this on the street, Tadg, especially in front of a place like this. I'm surprised that none of the patrons have come out to see what the fuss on their doorstep is all about."

Evan, experienced with the place, said, "They'll be cowering in there, wondering if we're all vampire hunters."

"In a sense, we are, for we have indeed been hunting for vampires," said the black-haired man.

"Then we must talk," I said. But where? Anywhere I could think of, there would be other vampires and night dwellers. I didn't think that Jean would be happy if I brought a trio of self-professed vampire hunters into his house. However, there seemed to be no other choice.

"I do apologise. Maggie Bruce." The redhead stuck out her hand.

I managed a bow and kissed the fingers that had held a knife to my throat a mere ten minutes earlier. "Gideon Redoak." It was absurd, but I trusted these three travellers from my native islands. There was something serene about the small blond man, a sense of something otherworldly.

"Evan Jones," murmured my protector, his lips lingering a little too long on the woman's extended fingers.

"Michael Fairlawn," said the blond man. "You heard the others call me Tagd, but that is my Gaelic name and shouldn't be used openly."

"Nicholas Edwards," said his dark-haired companion.

Now that we were all introduced, some of the strangeness dissipated. We arrived at Jean's door and let ourselves in. Jean and Genevieve were sitting together on the chaise. Alexander was reading a book, perched uncomfortably on one of the fragile little chairs.

"Gideon!" Genevieve said, half-rising. "You were a very long time finding your dinner." She saw the three who followed us in and her voice trailed off in wonder.

"Explain," said Jean, eyeing the uninvited guests.

I introduced everyone, but couldn't explain further than to say that these three had apparently been looking for me. Despite Maggie's spirited reaction to my initial approach, I didn't think they meant us any harm. I didn't tell anyone what Maggie had done to me. The pain was long gone. Evan was not seriously injured.

Michael Fairlawn, to whom the other two deferred, spoke up. "We mean no harm. We've come to you for help."

"Help?" Jean raised his eyebrows.

"You have an odd way of asking for it," I said.

"I'm sorry." Maggie tossed her head. She had removed the silly bonnet, and shining red hair swung down her back. Evan and Jean were watching appreciatively.

Genevieve regarded them. "What is this assistance you require? And why do you seek it from vampires? You know what we are. What are you?"

Such a direct question startled me, but none of the three seemed to take it amiss.

"We are Druids," Michael said, and I saw Evan turn to give him a very considering look. "You would call us magic users, even, perhaps, witches."

Maggie and Nicholas both made sounds of disagreement, but didn't contradict him. Michael nodded to them, acknowledging their dissent. "It isn't the correct term, but it does explain what we are."

"You are the Tuatha du Danaan. But they're all dead," said Evan.

Nicholas shook his head. "Not all of us. You are Welsh?"

"In a way. I am a Nameless One."

The three Druids made a collective sound, like in-drawn breath. "Then you truly are the ones we seek," said Michael. "For we had heard of a vampire who travelled with one of the ancient warrior race."

"Warrior!" Alexander spoke for the first time, a bark of laughter.

"Be quiet!" Jean said sharply. He turned to the Druids. "From whom did you hear this?"

Three shrugs.

"You know how it is," Michael said. "There aren't that many of us left, so we mingle among the other non-mortals in the world, and we hear things. To find the source of a rumour is like trying to hammer fog to the wall. But the stories we heard seemed to indicate that this English vampire and his warrior companion were good and honest men."

"Why would you seek our help, though?" I asked. "I've been told that it's unusual for vampires and witches or magic wielders to mingle."

"It is no longer that unusual." I shuddered involuntarily at the harsh note in Michael's tone. But we at last had some solid clues about the mysterious people who were recruiting vampires.

"What do you mean?" Genevieve said.

"We were attacked, less than two months ago, by a group of black magicians and vampires working together. There were perhaps eight or nine vampires all told, and half again that many of the magicians—or witches, if you prefer."

In the silence that fell, I looked around at the faces in the room. Genevieve's beautiful features were frozen. Jean looked thunderstruck, the storm gathering in his eyebrows. Alexander appeared confused, looking from one to another of us for some hint of how he was supposed to take this news. Evan examined the knife he'd taken from Maggie and acknowledged my glance with a sharp nod. The three Druids, knowing they had just shattered most of us, waited. Michael looked as if he was on the verge of collapse.

"Such a thing has never been," Jean said finally. "Never, in all the centuries."

Nicholas sighed. "Nevertheless, the thing has been done now."

"What is so terrible?" Alexander asked plaintively.

Genevieve turned to him. "Do the Magyars ally with the Szejekly in your country? Do you make covenants with the Turks?"

Comprehension dawned in those sea grey eyes. "Ah! So vampires and magicians are enemies?"

Michael said, "Not enemies, perhaps, but it is true that we've avoided the night dwellers, thinking them little more than monsters. Our mistake, and our shame."

Genevieve said, "And we have avoided the magic wielders, thinking them little more than shamans shaking painted sticks at the moon. Our mistake, and our shame."

Michael rose and bowed to her. "Madame, your servant."

She curtseyed. "Yours, sir." Then she grew serious. "It seems that neither of us can believe this is true, Mr. Fairlawn, but your very presence in this house seems impossible. I can also see that you have travelled far, in a great hurry, and that you are all very tired. Have you accommodation, baggage, money?"

"Yes, to all three. We're staying at the Fontainbleu."

"Then I will have the carriage brought round to take you there, and we will all discuss this tomorrow evening."

No one protested, though the four of us wished to hear the story. The Druids had endured much. Tomorrow night would be soon enough. The carriage came and took them away.

When they had gone, I found Genevieve at Evan's side.

"Your arm!" Genevieve exclaimed as she examined it.

Evan smiled bravely. "Just a scratch. It will mend."

Jean coughed loudly and Genevieve frowned at him. "And you? Are you hurt?" he hastily asked me.

I didn't want to tell either Jean or Genevieve how Maggie had dealt with me. "No. However, I didn't manage to get my supper tonight, so if you wouldn't mind..."

Jean tossed me a bottle of the much-belittled pig's blood. "Redheads are too much for you."

I pulled out the cork with my teeth and threw it at him. It seemed the only possible response.

The next evening, despite Alexander announcing that he doubted the *boszorkány*—he indicated that it meant a sort of witch—would return, we heard the carriage arrive shortly after dark. The three Druids were admitted, looking greatly rested although there were still shadows in their eyes. I suspected that something like those same shadows haunted my own expression. I knew grief when I saw it.

Once the niceties were over with, Michael spoke. "Maggie and Nicholas have agreed that I should be the spokesman for our cause. So now I must explain why we sought you out here in Paris." He paused and looked around the room. Assured that he held even Alexander's attention, he plunged into his story.

Their circle had once consisted of ten Druids, granted the gift and burden of immortality by the Goddess they worshipped in return for their services in her name. They had endured through many toils and adventures together, but immortality did not convey invulnerability. Five of them had died over the centuries from misadventure, injury or foul play.

The remaining five had been riding through the English countryside, seeking shelter for the night. Michael, as their

Archdruid—I understood that he was a sort of high priest or senior official—was responsible for finding this shelter. But it was Maggie who spotted the White Lion Inn.

When they neared the building, they realised that it was abandoned and empty. Disappointed, the five Druids dismounted anyway, to stretch and rest a bit before trying to find other accommodation. The inn did not seem to have been vacant for long, for it was still structurally sound. The occasional weed had poked its way through the boards, but nothing like the rampant overgrowth that reclaimed dwellings left untenanted for a period of years. All the windows were tightly boarded over. Nicholas walked up to investigate.

He found that the boards had been freshly nailed, and that there were footprints beneath the windows. He reported his findings to the other Druids, and they concluded that someone was living in the White Lion. Why the windows had been boarded over was a mystery. The five were weary, and it was now late and completely dark, but the inn had an unwholesome feel to it. They had just decided to travel on when the door nearest them opened.

Of the five Druids, one woman, Eleanor, was the closest to the inn. She died almost instantly, as a male vampire leapt upon her, smothering her screams with his hand and sinking his fangs into her neck. Even as the other four raced to her rescue, the vampire who held her twisted her neck and she fell. Maggie pulled out her knife, Nicholas and Gordon unsheathed swords, while Michael gathered his powers.

Magic blasted the vampire that had slain Eleanor, leaving him a smoking pile of cinders. More were pouring out of the inn, however, vampires and magic wielders. One of these lobbed power at Michael, knocking him backwards to the ground where he lay helpless.

Gordon rushed at two more vampires with his sword, but steel was ineffective against the undead. One of them snatched the sword from the Druid's grip and used it to slice him nearly in half. He was dead when he struck the ground. Nicholas used his sword to hack off a tree branch and sharpen it into a rough stake. Unfortunately, he didn't see the female vampire that had crept up onto the roof of the inn. She leapt into the tree and then down onto Nicholas' back, her fangs slicing across his neck. He rolled, screaming and thrashing, trying to dislodge her.

Three of the witches had attacked Maggie, and for a time she held her own, matching knife slash for knife slash. But she was tiring and losing blood. Michael recovered in time to see her go down, and his quick magical reflexes saved her and Nicholas. While the vampires and witches were still dazed from the green fire loosed on their ranks, Michael helped his two remaining friends onto their horses and got them safely away.

"We couldn't even bury our dead," Michael concluded, eyes downcast. I suspected that the woman Eleanor had been more than a comrade, and my heart went out to him. "We found refuge with sympathetic friends who helped us recover our health, and through them we heard the rumours of the vampire with honour."

"How can I possibly be of assistance?" I asked.

"We must destroy this coven of vampires and witches, but the three of us are not sufficient to the task. We need your help—yours, Evan's, as many as are willing to join us."

The request hung in the air. Nobody said a word, fearing that to do so would break the spell. No matter what our answer, the course of our lives would be changed from the moment someone spoke. I knew I had to be the one who did. "I will help you."

"As will I," Evan said.

Jean stroked his beard, and leaned forward. "One of these vampires, was she a woman? With long black hair and a voluptuous figure?"

"And dark eyes?" Alexander added.

"There was one such, yes," Nicholas said.

"Did you kill her?" Jean asked.

"No, she retreated back into the inn while we were recovering and escaping ourselves," Maggie said, eyeing Jean and Alexander speculatively.

"Then I am with you," Jean said. "I wish to kill the bitch myself." He glanced guiltily at Genevieve. "Your pardon, Madame. Will you come with us?"

"She is your fledgling, Jean. You must tend to her yourself."

Alexander had been sitting quietly, watching us all. Now he spoke. "If my grandfather and my great-uncle go, then what else can I do but follow?"

Michael rose and smiled at us all. "Thank you. Is there any chance that we might get others?"

The definitive "snick" of a crossbow being drawn made us all snap our attention towards Evan. "You have two powerful vampires, plus one young untested one, though I am certain he will prove a good fighter. You have the three of you, magic wielders and keepers of the secret of the Tuatha du Danaan. You have me, a Nameless One of not inconsiderable skill. And this time, we will not be taken by surprise. An army couldn't take the White Lion Inn, but the seven us can." He released the bolt and it quivered in the wall a scant inch above Michael's head. "Shall we go?"

That was how the seven of us came to be crouching in the bushes a hundred yards or so from the White Lion Inn, a surprisingly short time after the conversation in Jean's home. Our arsenal included pistols, daggers, crossbows, and wooden stakes. It had been agreed in advance that we would have to kill those in the inn. They wouldn't hesitate to do the same to any of us whom they captured. The only debate was whether it would be more strategic to lure the coven out into the open, or to storm the inn and fight within the confines of its walls.

Fighting within walls could trap us as well as our opponents. The inn was old timber, and dry. Evan soaked a rag with strong-smelling oily liquid from a bottle he carried in his pack, and wound it around the end of an ordinary arrow. He drew a long-bow from his bundle of equipment, bent it and set the string. Michael lit the rag with a green flash and Evan fired. The arrow flew in a great arc, trailing sparks and smoke, and wedged itself neatly in a joint of the roof of the White Lion. It wasn't very long before flames licked eagerly at the old wood.

There were yells and screams from within the tavern, and several people ran out, one or two still pulling on random items of clothing. We fired on them, bullets being more effective at this distance. Two bodies fell. Guns barked from their side. A bullet hit the ground beside me and sprayed dirt into my face. I crawled to keep out of range. Bullets hurt.

Noise and confusion surrounded me. Unable to see the action, I risked standing up. People still fled the burning inn. One dark-haired woman, who seemed quite inadequately clad for a chilly night in early spring, ran straight towards Alexander with a sword in her hand.

"Lucinda!" Alexander seized a wooden stake from among our weapons and ran at his turnsire. She brought her sword up. The young idiot would die with the first swing of that blade. All she need do to immobilize him was order him to stand still.

Cursing, Jean rammed a bolt into the groove on his crossbow, stood up, and fired. Lucinda crumpled to the ground as screams of outrage came from the others assembling outside the inn. Alexander had reached such momentum in his charge, he stumbled across Lucinda's body and sprawled on his face. Jean rolled his eyes at me, and went to rescue his grandson.

We could no longer hide in these bushes. The time for concealment was past, so the rest of us rose and rushed the enemy. After that, I had no opportunity to keep an eye on my friends, old or new. I concentrated on staying intact myself.

A young female, human by the smell of her and thus one of the witches, came screeching at me with a knife. Obviously they didn't yet know that we had vampires in our number—that gave us an advantage. A knife could hurt me, but not disable me, so I let her slash my upper arm, a glancing wound that scarcely hurt, and enfolded her into my embrace. My fangs were bared and I bent to drink. She screamed and struggled, but was no match for vampire strength. I swallowed gulps of her tantalising blood, sparkling with the power of her magic. I could feel the life flutter out of her, but I was torn violently away from her before I could finish.

Hands seized my shoulders and lifted me bodily. I saw the star-bedecked sky swim past my eyes and then I hit the ground, hard, causing a few more stars to dance briefly in the heavens. I managed to roll away. I gathered my wits and rose to my feet, fumbling for the wooden stake I carried. Only another vampire could have thrown me.

I barely saw the dark blur in the night an instant before he knocked me to the ground. We grappled, earth churning rapidly to mud under our struggles. I sank my fangs into his arm as he tried to throttle me. He howled and released his stranglehold on my throat. I thrust my fingers towards his eyes, long sharp vampire talons flashing in the starlight. He drew back out of my reach.

I had to get him off me. I groped in the slurry around me for the stake, which I had dropped, but nothing rewarded my search except mud. I gathered a great handful of this and lobbed it at his eyes.

Blinded, if only for a moment, he was helpless. I squirmed out from under him and kicked him in the side of the head. Enraged, in pain, unable to see me, he fumbled around in the mud. I located the stake and pounced on it just as his hand found it. We had a grim, silent struggle for that, he trying to wipe his eyes clean with his sleeve even as both hands claimed the stake.

I had not survived my father and Etienne Corbeau to die here in the cold mud in some god-forsaken corner of England. I kicked him in the groin. From his reaction, it was as effective as I remembered. I would have to thank Maggie. He screamed and let go of me. I rammed the stake through his heart. I checked to make sure it had killed him.

Someone clapped me on the back, and reached a hand down to me. I let Jean pull me back up. "Well done," he said.

Only then did I think to look around. The White Lion Inn still burned. Evan wiped a sword blade clean on a corpse that lacked a head. Nicholas and Alexander hauled limp bodies towards the burning inn. Maggie fought knife to knife with a male witch. Jean and I paused to watch true artistry at work. For this battle, Maggie had dressed in men's clothing and hidden her fiery tresses under a hood. The red-haired Druid made the encounter a dance, firelight from the burning inn reflecting along the blade. The desperate young man from the coven found his every move countered, his every stroke parried, his guard useless. Finally, she slashed his throat open, and he fell. I could feel his life sigh out of him before his corpse hit the ground.

Even as I congratulated Maggie, I felt a touch of concern that I couldn't immediately see Michael. I knew that as a high priest, he was technically a non-fighter. I also knew that he had used his magic at least twice during the fight. I had felt the use of power.

He limped into view only a few moments later, leading a pair of sweating, trembling horses. He had saved them from the inn stables, which were now on fire.

The reason for his limp soon became apparent. A sword thrust had caught him on the back of the right thigh, which was bleeding. My neck ached and chafed where the vampire had tried to strangle me, and the slash on my arm stung. Jean had a black eye and a head wound that still oozed. Nicholas suffered some missing skin, Maggie had several knife wounds, and Alexander had a burn on his leg and several cuts. Only Evan was completely unhurt.

From his mysterious pack of the miraculous properties, Evan brought out a small pewter flask. He undid the stopper and passed it first to Michael. The smell of the flask's contents made my eyes water—it seemed to have been fermented from the apples of Eden. Evan insisted that all of us take a long swig of the drink, whatever it was. I could hear Maggie gasp as she downed hers.

Evan then examined everyone's wounds. We vampires, of course, needed nothing more than blood to restore us. I could already feel my injuries healing under the influence of the blood I had drunk. So Jean, Alexander and I disposed of the bodies by tossing them into the inferno that was now the White Lion, while Evan tended the others. He stitched whatever needed stitching, and soon the Druids joined us in watching the inn burn to the ground.

"This should not be the end of it," Michael said. We all looked at him. "We worked well together. Perhaps everyone was so afraid of vampires joining with magic users simply because it had never been tried. Our powers and abilities complement each other. There is much evil in this world. We've proven that by working together, we can defeat it."

"I agree, this shouldn't end here," I said. "What do you suggest?"

"A covenant," the Archdruid said. He leaned on the stick that Evan had cut for him. "That we set darkness against darkness—vampire and Nameless and Druid against whatever is out there that abuses power and makes the night a thing to fear."

"A brotherhood, of darkness," I said.

"That's it, exactly. The Brotherhood of Darkness. We should remain together, or at least in communication, so that whenever the need arises, we can join once more to fight."

I could see nods of agreement, although Alexander looked dubious. Even Jean was rubbing his chin, which I knew meant he was at least considering the idea.

A Brotherhood of Darkness, banded together to save the world from those like my own bloodmaster. I silently savoured the irony. This could be a new purpose for me, something that would take me out of my grief and let me go forward, as my friends urged me to do. Between this covenant and my responsibility to see that Alexander became a decent vampire who obeyed the simple rules that made our lives bearable, I could move on. "I think it's a splendid idea." I clasped Michael's hand.

Five other hands joined ours. Seven voices chorused their agreement that from now on, we were the Brotherhood of Darkness.

Chapter Eight

"But you must come along, Gideon."

Genevieve pulled on her fashionable gloves and looked severely at me. Jean leaned by the door, fiddling with the buttons on his jacket. Alexander appeared suspiciously interested in the debate. I glanced to Evan for support. He shrugged.

"I don't gamble," I said. I hadn't played a hand of cards since Jonny died.

"Nonsense." Genevieve held out her hand, and I had to let her take my arm. Jean snorted.

"Ten francs, wasn't it?" Alexander said smugly to Jean.

"*D'accord.*" Jean dug out some coins and thrust them into his waiting palm.

"They wagered on whether or not I would go," I said to Genevieve.

"Do not let the children worry you, *mon cher. Viens.*"

I assisted her into the carriage, not that she required it. We three men positioned ourselves around her, trying not to step on her expensive trailing skirts. With a clatter of wheels on flagstones and the clip clop of hooves, we were off.

The casino just outside Paris resembled a palace. Awed by such splendour in a gambling hall, I gaped, my stomach tensed with phantom guilt. But the others walked in unconcerned. Inside, the casino proved a palace, indeed. Liveried servants jumped to every summons from a player. Gilt covered everything—lights, mirrors, carpets, luxury far beyond anything at either Chateau de Monet or Jean's house in Paris. I worried about the mirrors, but Genevieve assured me that they posed no threat.

Jean and Alexander drifted towards the baccarat tables. Genevieve shook her head and led me to quieter areas.

"*Chemin de fer* does not interest me. It is too dependent on luck. Can you play Brelan, Gideon?"

"I don't know."

"We shall see."

It turned out, not surprisingly, that I could not. Brelan, a game similar to poker, depended on achieving three of a kind. I wagered conservatively, and lost liberally. Genevieve showed a ruthless streak at the gaming table I never saw elsewhere. She wagered recklessly, often betting her entire pot, smiling all the while whether she won or lost. I could see the other players growing unnerved by this beautiful woman with the cutthroat smile.

Beggared at last of the money I had brought, I excused myself from the Brelan table. Genevieve gave me a nod, and turned back to her cards. At loose ends, I wandered over to see how the baccarat players fared. Alexander was in a showdown with a stranger, the only other player left in this game. A large ante lay between them, the prize glinting under the lamps. An interested crowd had gathered around to watch. I politely edged my way through.

"I gave up long ago," said Jean, making his way to my side. "The fool, look, he wagered everything. We shall have to support him for years."

The stranger, an American by his clothes and brash voice, looked at the cards he held. I saw his eyes narrow at the shoe, his brain calculating the odds on what the next card would be. Alexander hadn't glanced at his hand. His expression conveyed boredom.

"I have a deed," the stranger offered, withdrawing a legal document from inside his jacket. "Nice parcel of land in the State of Maine."

"If M. Daniels accepts," said the croupier.

Alexander, the M. Daniels in question, nodded. "I accept."

The deed joined the pot. Each man then drew a card from the shoe. Alexander had a natural nine, which was unbeatable. The stranger groaned, but stood and shook his opponent's hand. He walked away, head high. Alexander bowed to the applause.

"Congratulations, Monsieur," said the croupier, taking the house percentage and accepting the generous tip Alexander extended.

"We had best get Genevieve before she wagers the chateau," Jean said, clapping Alexander on the back by way of congratulations.

We returned to the chateau. It looked worn in the lamplight, after the gilt extravagances of the casino. It felt like home, though. Here one would not easily lose a fortune. Evan met us and asked how the evening went. In reply, Alexander emptied his pockets of coins, bills, a necklace and the deed he had won from the American.

"What's that?" Evan asked, pointing at the document.

Alexander picked up the deed and sank onto a nearby chair to read it. He glanced up. "A fresh start."

Genevieve walked to his chair and leaned over his shoulder. "What do you mean, Alex?"

"I think I am ready to test my own wings now. You, Gideon, and Jean have taught me well these past forty or so years, Genevieve. You mustn't think me ungrateful. I love you all. But I have been thinking that perhaps it is time I left. And think of it–America! A raw new country, waiting. One without the burdens of old superstitions and fear. A good place for a vampire to live."

Genevieve smiled. "Then you are ready. I give my children wings for a reason."

Our wings turned out to be a carriage to Cherbourg, then a steamship to Bar Harbor, then another carriage, and on until at last we reached a tiny fishing village called Fletcherville. My memories of my first steamship voyage consist of traveling as Evan's luggage and hiding from the other passengers. Dry land came as a welcome relief, even though the transportation arrangements on the last leg of the journey were hardly luxurious.

"I thought you wanted to try your wings, stand on your own feet, go off bravely alone in a new country," Evan said to Alexander as we approached the end of our long trip. "I don't know why Gideon and I are here."

"You're only complaining because you had to ride a mule," Alexander said.

All three of us were mounted on mules. Not only were mules more suitable to the wilds of Maine, but they were more inclined to accept vampire riders than horses were. Alexander's jackpot deed amounted to several hundred acres of forest on a low windswept cliff just beyond the bounds of Fletcherville. The inhabitants thought we were insane, taking mules to explore the property by night, but odd behaviour was expected of outsiders. "Rusticators," they labeled us, especially when they learned that Alexander planned to build a mansion on the cliff.

The mules plodded among the trees and rocks on the cliff. For reasons best known to itself, my mule drew up by a spot that offered a spectacular view. I slid from the saddle. The edge drew me nearer. I watched the play of moonlight on the surf dozens of feet below. The waves washed jagged rocks, their endless murmur soothing. An infinity of ocean stretched before my eyes. I leaned against a rock, almost in tears from the beauty.

"Gideon." Alexander's voice spoke in my ear.

"Look at that view."

"I know. Listen, I have more than enough land here. I own the entire cliff. If you would like this piece for yourself, to build your own house..."

The spell broke. I blinked. "You would do that?"

"Certainly."

"Thank you, Alexander. I shall think about it."

We remounted and rode on. I left part of my heart back on that promontory of cliff. I knew then that I would accept Alexander's offer. Here in Maine, I would be well out of Corbeau's reach. I would also have a home that did not remind me poignantly of Jonny in every corner.

"Now, this is where I will build my house." Alexander dismounted again, waving his arms to indicate his choice.

"Another pretty spot," I said. "We shall be neighbours, but not pesky ones."

I heard Evan mutter, "So much for independence."

If Alexander overhead this, he ignored it. "There is still a great deal of property left. Do you think Michael or the others would be interested in living here?"

It had been some time since I had last seen the Druids. Visits between France and England consumed time and resources and thus were infrequent. We kept in touch mostly by letter. The Brotherhood of Darkness remained solid, however. The friendships built in shared adversity had not crumbled in times of peace.

"All we can do is ask. I must return to England anyway, to settle some affairs. I shall go visit Michael and sound him out."

"Excellent, Gideon. I don't suppose Genevieve...?"

"Only if you could move Chateau de Monet here."

"Ah, well. She belongs to the lights of Paris. Go talk to Michael."

Evan and I traveled back to England. We eventually made our way to Michael's home in the Lake District, a small Georgian house he called Nuttingwood. I greatly admired the architecture of the period. My own house in New England would be built in the Georgian style. I pictured it easily nestled amongst the trees on the cliff, with a library, a conservatory for roses, a lovely guest bedroom should Genevieve visit...and I knew then that I had made the right decision.

We gave our horses over to the stableboy, and a servant ushered us inside the house. I marveled that such an informal invitation as Michael's general welcome allowed me to cross the threshold. I heard more laughter, bright music, the sounds of friends gathered for a convivial evening.

Michael greeted us both with a hug and a broad smile. "Gideon, Evan. I'm glad to see you. Come in, relax, you must be tired." He led the way into the salon. "I have a surprise for you."

There were two surprises, in fact, and more hugs. Genevieve and Jean were both waiting for us, along with Nicholas and Maggie.

"I wanted to see my friends again," Genevieve said in response to our astonishment.

Jean shrugged. "Where she goes..."

"Tell us all about America!" Maggie said.

Michael ushered us to chairs. "Let the poor men sit down and have some refreshments."

Evan and I took turns telling them everything—the steamship, and having to travel in a sea trunk, the disbelieving villagers, the mules. Laughter rang out frequently during our narrative.

When we had finished, there was silence, but only for a moment. Then Michael spoke. "You like America enough that you want to live there?"

"England is no longer home to me, Michael. France is more my home, but I feel it is time to leave Europe. And America is beyond the reach of my turnsire, I hope."

Genevieve's head came up. I felt her blue eyes bore into mine. "Perhaps."

"We'll remain the Brotherhood of Darkness, of course!" Jean said.

Michael smiled. "Of course. I should like to see this cliff top. Gideon, I have never heard you speak so movingly of a place."

"Then why not come back to America with us?" Evan said.

"What?"

"It would be the perfect place to take the Brotherhood."

The Archdruid rubbed his chin. Maggie leaned back, but said nothing. She studied each face in turn. Nicholas strummed a guitar, fingers seeking out a tune. I saw Jean and Genevieve exchange glances, but couldn't tell what they meant.

"I'll go back with you and see the place." Michael's announcement raised no eyebrows. Maggie gave him a nod. Nicholas' nimble fingers played a quick riff on the guitar by way of agreement.

"I fear we shall lose all our dear friends to America," Genevieve said, sighing.

Nicholas put his guitar down and looked at Genevieve. "You could always move there."

Her expression of horror made us all laugh, including, after a moment, Genevieve herself.

Evan and I stayed at Nuttingwood while preparations were made for the voyage back to Maine. My bodyguard went off on a mysterious mission during our stay. He returned within a few days, but told nobody why he had gone. I had long since learned not to inquire too much into the doings of Nameless Ones, especially during high cycle.

At the Dover docks, however, I discovered what Evan had done. A woman met us there, one of those thin, wiry women who look old at twenty and keep on looking old until they die at ninety, but who can do the work of three men. Evan introduced her as Mrs. Jenkins. She was a Nameless One, a Guardian who had outlived the cycles.

"I'm tired of raising the children of others. Young Evan here said there is a vampire in need of a housekeeper and bodyguard. Is it you?" Mrs. Jenkins looked me up and down, and I wished I had brushed the travel dust off my jacket.

Evan laughed. "No, he's mine. It's Alex Goldanias you'll be working for."

"Does Alexander know this?" I said.

"He'll be grateful. You'll see. Let's get on board and get you settled."

"Yes, in luggage class again."

We arrived back in Fletcherville in less than three weeks. Steamships were really a wonder. A mere century earlier, the same journey would have taken months.

Alexander met us in the tavern, where he had taken rooms . He pretended to have an illness made worse by the sun, a typical ruse for dealing with curious humans. "And who is this?" He bowed to Mrs. Jenkins.

"Your new housekeeper," Evan said.

I had to laugh—Alexander's look of dismay was comical. Michael snorted, quickly turning it into a cough.

"Don't you think I should have been the one to hire her?"

"I am right here," Mrs. Jenkins said with stiff dignity. "Kindly don't talk about me as if I was not. Mr. Goldanias, I am the one who decides my employment. I shall let you know."

Fortunately, at that point the ostler came to tell us the mules were ready.

My spirits rising, I mounted my mule in good humour. Mrs. Jenkins proved as tough as she appeared. She had refused all assistance the entire journey, and she rode the mule expertly.

Construction had begun on both houses. It was still in the early stages, of course, but the outlines of new buildings could be seen.

Michael, who had been silent on the trek from the village, spoke. "This place is truly beautiful. I feel blessed to have seen it."

"Would you consider moving here?" Alexander asked.

Michael sat in contemplative silence. "I don't know. England is my home. But I've lived there a very long time—you can't imagine how long. This is something to think about."

"We'll ride further up the trail this time. I want to show you the last tract of land on the cliff."

We all agreed to this. I hadn't seen this land. Once past the boundaries Alexander had claimed, the cliff turned wilder. We dismounted and left the mules tied to graze. Mrs. Jenkins kept pace with us on the rough trail without complaint.

In a clearing amidst the trees, we stopped to let Michael rest. He sat on a stump. Evan and I walked towards the cliff edge to view the water from this vantage point. No bad view of the ocean existed from this land.

"Look, there's England." Evan pointed. "Maggie is waving at you."

I just shook my head.

My protector leaned against a tree. "You won't be completely safe from Corbeau here, you know. If you can cross the ocean, so can he."

"I know. It is a barrier, though. Too much effort for the game."

"To quote Genevieve, *perhaps.*"

"He will find me again. I know it, Evan. I won't escape him until one of us is truly dead. But let me have the illusion."

He put a hand on my shoulder. "Of course."

We returned to the others. Michael stood up from his stump. A light shone from his face. "Look what grows at the base of the stump."

A sapling, tiny, one minuscule green leaf hanging from it. I puzzled over it. "This is a pine forest," Michael said.

Alexander examined the tiny plant. "But that is an oak."

"Look...there is a ring of these saplings, see them? The oak is sacred to us. It's a sign—a sign from our Goddess. I will move and build my house here. Her blessing is on it."

My youth had been formed by religion—sermons and lectures from spitting preachers of hellfire. Never had I encountered pure spirituality. I knelt within the ring of oak saplings. One by one, the others followed.

"So mote it be," whispered Michael.

I was the first to break the hush. "The Brotherhood of Darkness has a home."

Later that night, in the Fletcherville tavern, we raised a glass to it.

Chapter Nine

Even we undead are the playthings of time. It passes for us just as it does for mortals. It lingers, excruciating hours of boredom piling up like dust. Or it flies on invisible wings while we reach out in vain to catch it and slow it down. Time is never saved, only spent.

And so a century and more passed, in an eye blink, or an eternity.

It didn't pass idly. I sought out new vampires when and where I could, and taught them what Genevieve had taught me. The Druids established an oak grove in the forest. Sometimes seekers after enlightenment would come there. Evan and Mrs. Jenkins toiled tirelessly for Alexander and me. At first they looked after horses, then motorcars. The Cliff Road was paved. Three fine houses stood on the cliff: my own manor house, Oakwoods, Alexander's gloomy Gothic folly, Valley Mansion, and Michael's smart Cape Cod, Fairlawn. Nicholas and Maggie both lived in the town itself, Nicholas for closer proximity to several women, Maggie to assert her independence. We established a truce with Fletcherville. We didn't hunt there, and they pretended not to know what we were. It worked. We meant to see that it continued to work.

After the encounter at the White Lion Inn, the Brotherhood knew only peace. No rogue vampires, no power-hungry witches troubled our new lives. But Corbeau was not forgotten, especially not by me. The barrier of the Atlantic Ocean existed no longer. A commercial jet could now cross it in mere hours. I recalled being impressed by a fortnight's crossing on a steamship. How long ago that seemed now.

On a wet autumn night in 1979, I leaned back in the bathtub, my legs stretched out. I still appreciated the luxury of hot water flowing instantly from a tap. The Puritan preacher's voice I always carried with me began to lecture me about sloth. I drowned the bastard out by singing along with *Rigoletto,* which issued from the radio on the sink counter.

Without even a perfunctory knock, Evan came in. I rose out of the bath, taking the towel he handed me. It had to be an emergency. Nothing else would make Evan interrupt my bath.

I toweled myself dry as I spoke. "What is it?"

"Nicholas just called. Michael is in the hospital."

"Why?"

"Car accident. He's not badly hurt, but he's going to be there for a while. I'll drive you down."

I couldn't drive a motorcar. Frankly, they scared me. Evan tried to teach me once, after which we both agreed that my role in a vehicle would remain that of passenger. "Thank you. I'll be ready in a few minutes."

We drove through rain, thunder and lightning, a severe storm for October.

A wave of human misery washed over me as soon as I entered the hospital. The smells of blood and antiseptic tinged my awareness of suffering and death. Machines beeped away, measuring fragile human lives. Medicine was far more advanced now than in my youth, but pain had not changed. Tears had soaked into the very walls and floors.

Evan and I found Michael in a private room. Flowers covered every horizontal surface. The village florist's shop must have been empty. Michael sat up in bed, one arm in a cast, bandages adorning much of the rest of him.

"Gentlemen." He nodded to us serenely.

I crossed to his bedside. A whiff of antiseptic made me wrinkle my nose. "What on earth happened to you?"

"There was a report in the news about a murder in Danvers a few days ago. I read between the lines of that report. Black magic. A ritual murder, Gideon. That's the sort of thing the Brotherhood was formed to fight against."

"You went to Danvers to see if you were right. Without telling anyone what you were doing." Danvers, a small city on the North Shore of Massachusetts, had an eerie reputation.

"I could have been wrong."

Evan snorted. "Obviously you weren't. It was black magic."

A sigh from the patient confirmed this. "I saw the sorcerer. His name is Matthew. He has a whole coven he's been building up. He wants control of New England."

"And here the Brotherhood is, standing in the way," I said resignedly. "Does he know about us?"

Michael nodded. "He caused the car crash. I could feel the magic gathering, but I was in the car and it was moving. He called down this storm we're having. It brought down an old tree right on the car."

"You're lucky to be alive," Evan said.

Michael's green eyes narrowed. "Luck had nothing to do with it. Ah, here comes the nurse."

I turned my head and saw a young woman, with brown hair and eyes, entering the room. There was a twinkle in those eyes, and her smile bordered on the mischievous. I found myself smiling in response.

"I do hope you haven't brought Mr. Fairlawn more flowers," she said.

I had, actually, a bouquet from my own conservatory in Oakwoods. She took them with an exaggerated sigh and put them in a vase. I risked a glance at Evan, and he grinned.

Michael sat up a bit straighter and smiled. "Thank you, Gideon. You grow better roses than the florists do." He wasn't looking at me.

"They are lovely," said the nurse.

I noticed she was hovering slightly, as if hesitant to interrupt us. "I'm sorry, did you need us to leave the room for a moment?"

She laughed. "Oh, no. I just have to give Mr. Fairlawn his pill." She did so, then left.

Evan sat down in a chair by Michael's bedside. I looked over the collection of flowers. My roses did indeed look better than anything else. I turned when I heard Evan start to speak.

"Michael, that girl is sweet on you."

To my astonishment, Michael blushed. "I'm sweet on her, truth to tell."

"You mean you took a turn for the nurse?"

Both Michael and I groaned. Michael shifted, making a face. I suspected he was in pain, despite the pill. "To get back to Matthew, we'd better do something about him. I'm going to be laid up here for a few days. I wish the Brotherhood had someone more powerful magically on its side."

"You're powerful," I said.

"In limited ways. I'm a healer. A scholar. I work with plants, not steel. We could use a fighting mage. Once I'm up and about, I'll talk to Nicholas and Maggie. See if we can't recruit one."

"The Nameless are fighters," said Evan.

"Yes, but you have no magic. Strength alone isn't enough to fight someone like Matthew."

"He can't just throw trees at my friends and get away with it."

Michael tried to laugh. It turned into a yawn. I walked around the end of the bed and tapped Evan's shoulder. "That's our signal to leave."

Michael stayed in the hospital for several days. No more trees came hurtling at any of our motorcars. But we knew that Matthew had not forgotten us—and we would not forget him.

It came as no surprise to me that Michael began seriously dating Mary Summers, the young nurse. Nicholas, Maggie, Evan and even Alexander all took great delight in teasing Michael about this. I did not, and my reticence was noticed.

Winter arrived early on the coast of Maine. On a crisp night I trudged through several inches of snow, stars bright overhead, to visit Michael. The beauty of the Cliff Road, even lined with poles carrying electric and telephone wires as it now was, could still bring me to tears. I stood for a few minutes gazing at the pristine snow blanketing the sacred oak grove. The wind ruffled my hair. For an instant, I recalled standing on the wind-whipped tower of Corbeau's Keep, and I shivered. I knew he was still looking for me, somewhere.

By the time I reached Fairlawn, it was forgotten. I removed my boots and coat in the foyer, so as not to track snow into the house. Soon Michael and I were seated before a roaring fire, glasses of admirable brandy in our hands.

"I get the feeling that you don't entirely approve of my courtship." The pleasantries had been dispensed with. Michael spoke directly from his heart, I could tell. His green eyes bored into mine.

I leaned back in my chair and pondered my answer. "Is my approval necessary?"

"No, of course not. But I would like to know if there is a reason for the lack of it. Is there something you know against Mary?"

"What? Oh, no, nothing like that. She's a very pleasant young lady. You are obviously in love with her, and she with you. No, you should marry."

"Not without knowing why one of my closest friends feels I shouldn't."

I set my brandy snifter down on a nearby table. Getting up, I walked to the fireplace, staring at the flames. I couldn't meet Michael's eyes. "She's mortal."

I couldn't see Michael's reaction, but I heard him hiss, sucking in a breath. "Ah."

"She will age and die, Michael. You will not."

I heard a faint clink of glass on wood. Michael, too, had set his drink down. I heard his footsteps approach, and I could feel his warmth behind me.

"You still miss Jonathan."

My head rose, but I couldn't look at him. "Every night."

"And one loss means you never dare love again?"

"I..."

"I've been in love with mortals before this, and each one of them has died. That doesn't mean I can never trust myself to fall in love again. When two mortals wed, they know that sooner or later, one of them will die before the other. Even the marriage vows recognize that. Whether one partner will die after five years, or fifteen, or fifty, no one knows. I could die tomorrow. I nearly did in that car accident. If someone you love passes on before you do, that doesn't mean you never take the chance again."

I looked at him then. Concern and friendship shone from his eyes. "Are you telling me to take another lover?"

"It's been a long time, Gideon. You're lonely. And times are different, there's more acceptance now."

That made me smile, though with no humour. "Acceptance."

"For one aspect of your nature, at least."

"I'm thinking of going to Danvers. I'm going to ask Evan and Alexander to come with me. Chances are that Matthew has never seen a Nameless One before."

Michael permitted the change of subject without comment. "Just be cautious. He's strong. There may be other vampires in the area. You might want to contact them if you can."

"Perhaps. We'll be careful."

I walked home through the snow, Michael's words ringing in my ears. "It's been a long time. You're lonely."

He was right, on both counts.

I gathered my two co-conspirators together the next night. I knew the history of Danvers, the original Salem Village. It had been settled by Puritans at about the same time I was born. The American witch hysteria of the 1690s had started in Danvers, not nearby Salem. Many historical buildings of that era still stood, and had become tourist attractions. For me, a trip to the North Shore of Massachusetts was a journey back to my childhood.

Evan held the car door open for me. "Gideon? You sure you're okay with this?"

I realized that I'd been wool-gathering with these thoughts. "Yes, I'm fine. Let's go."

The limousine tires crunched over snow, then pavement once we reached the highway. I didn't glance out at the scenery. Alexander read a book to pass the time. I spent it thinking and planning. What would we do when we met Matthew? Much depended

on whether we found him alone, or surrounded by a powerful coven.

Our arrival in Salem went unnoticed. Evan checked the directions to our lodging. The Nameless Ones ran an international organization. They had safe hotels, a catering business that depended heavily on local abattoirs, and an entire network of other services for the travelling vampire. After checking in, we met in Alexander's room to discuss strategy. It would help if we had one.

I didn't want to admit that this whole adventure was more or less an impulse on my part. I unfolded a map of the area on the table and indicated a spot. "Michael met Matthew here. That should be our starting point."

"And what do we do from there?"

I glared at Alexander. Evan spared me from having to find an answer. "We ask questions. Read the newspapers for anything odd. Track down any whiff of black magic."

Alexander eyed my protector, then me. "I don't know what black magic smells like. Shouldn't we have brought Nicholas or Maggie?"

"I thought it wiser to leave them to protect Michael, in case Matthew tries to retaliate." I said firmly. Alexander finally shrugged, although he still looked dissatisfied.

We headed toward Danvers via the main highway from Salem, a short distance, but with a surprise on the way. My jaw dropped as soon as it came in sight.

On a hill overlooking the highway stood an enormous building. With gabled roofs, towers, and long wings that extended forever, it resembled a Gothic castle.

I glanced at Alexander. He, too, stared in country bumpkin astonishment. "What the hell is that?" I was glad he'd asked, because I also wanted the answer.

"The Danvers State Insane Asylum. They call it the Castle on the Hill." Evan didn't sound impressed.

"Is it still in operation?" I said.

"Oh, yes. It has a bad reputation, though. Pity. It used to be quite innovative for a lunatic asylum, now it's just another hell hole."

A trick of the moonlight cast long-fingered shadows of the "Castle" across the dark lawns. They stretched towards the limo, reaching for me. I shuddered against the window. "Drive faster, Evan, let's get that thing behind us."

Alexander stared at me, nonplused. "What's with you? It's just a building. It's not even a real castle. I'd think you'd have good memories of a castle on a hill, what with Gen's chateau..."

Evan's terse voice cut through the babble I barely heard. "Alex. Shut up."

Michael had encountered Matthew in Danvers proper, near the Congregationalist church. The Archdruid had imparted all the details of that meeting to me. Evan parked in a lot near the white steepled building. "I'll go see if the minister is available for a talk," he said.

Alexander perked up. "We can pretend we're reporters."

"That's better than saying we're nosy bastards."

With that parting shot, Evan went to investigate the church. Alexander and I, feeling safe in a New England town, separated. I watched him wander off down the street, and took the opposite way.

He was going to hate me. I found the offices of the Danvers Herald, and someone still sat hunched over a typewriter in the front room. I entered without knocking. The middle-aged woman typing away barely glanced up.

"Can I help you." She made no rising inflection at the end of the sentence.

I took a chair, dusting off the seat. "Good evening. I'm trying to find someone in town. I thought the newspaper might be able to help me."

"That so. Maybe. Who are you looking for."

A bit disoriented to be interviewed without actual questions, I got right to the point. "A witch."

She stopped typing. "Another one. There are no witches in Danvers."

"Another one what?"

"Witch hunter. Scandal monger. Go to Salem if you want witches. Leave Danvers alone."

"My information is that this witch is in Danvers. Possibly an entire coven."

A rude noise issued from her lips. "Right."

"Have there been no unusual events? Nothing unexplainable?"

I'd struck a nerve, to judge from her reaction. Her eyes narrowed. "Who are you."

"Someone concerned with coven activity."

"Talk to them at the church. Now get out."

It was pointless to antagonize her further. I left. A quick survey of the street revealed neither Alexander nor Evan. I walked back to the church and found Evan there, talking to a man in a conservative black suit—the twentieth century equivalent of Puritan weeds. My protector said goodbye to him, and we returned to the limousine together.

Neither of us questioned the other—we were waiting for Alexander to show up. Several moments passed, then he arrived, a spring in his step. He caught me staring at him, and winked.

"Beautiful girls they have in Danvers."

Evan turned to look at me. "Can I hit him? Just a little?"

"What good would it do?"

In the hotel room, we pooled our results. Evan nodded when I repeated what the reporter had said about asking at the church. He had interviewed the minister, who believed evil walked in Danvers. The town, eager to reclaim its reputation from the witch hysteria and the asylum, ignored the signs.

"What are those signs?" Alexander said.

"Ritual circles in the woods. An altar stone with blood on it. Bones, knots, herbs left on doorsteps and in mailboxes. People claim to have heard chanting from the woods on certain nights. That sort of thing."

"It sounds like black magic," I said.

Evan shrugged. "The minister didn't want to say that in so many words. But he's not happy about it."

"Did either of you hear a motorcycle tonight?" Alexander asked.

We both turned, Evan raising a puzzled eyebrow. I shook my head. "Why?"

"I thought one was following me, but I never actually saw it."

I mulled that over. It might have been Matthew, or a member of his coven, spying on us. "We'll have to keep a lookout for it. Did you find out anything relevant to our search?"

"Or were you too busy chatting up the local girls?" Evan said.

Alexander sniffed. "I talked to a couple of people who found things, like bones or herbs. The police told them to keep quiet."

Evan sighed. "We'd better try not to draw attention from the police."

"No," I said, "The questions they'd ask would be very awkward to handle."

We made plans for the following night—to talk to more people if possible, and to examine one of the ritual circles in the woods, if we could find it. Avoiding the police would be easy for Alexander and me. A simple mind trick of "you don't see me" would serve. Quietly confident that Matthew could not incapacitate three of us, we retired to our rooms.

I heard a motorcycle. It roared past the hotel, making me pause in unpacking my pajamas and toiletries. I crossed to the window and looked out, but saw no sign of the machine. With a shrug, I returned to my suitcase.

Word of us leaked through the town of Danvers. People we questioned refused to answer, or were polite and noncommittal. One man threatened to call the police if we didn't leave him alone, and we decided to end this stage of our search.

I didn't fancy the hike through the woods to the site of the one ritual circle we had managed to triangulate on our map. The old lunatic asylum on the hill overlooked this spot. It still caused me to shiver, though it bore no resemblance to my master's Keep.

Alexander paused on the snow-covered trail, head turned towards the town. "I swear I hear that damn motorcycle."

"I hear it, too." Once he'd spoken, I realized the sound had been continuous background noise to our trek, like a throbbing toothache.

Evan grunted. "It's probably a coven member, trailing us. Nothing we can do about it until he shows himself."

I pulled slightly ahead of Evan, so I could search the trail for prints or other clues with my keener night vision. The beaten path widened and ended at a ring of dirty rocks marking the perimeter of a circle, within which the snow had been trampled into mud. A large, flat stone occupied the centre. The night wind carried a scent to me, and I didn't need to ask what the dark stains on the altar were.

Someone was sitting on the altar. He rose when we entered the circle. Matthew cut an impressive figure—tall, broad and heavily muscled. The sleeves of his black shirt fluttered in the breeze. "Well. The Brotherhood of Darkness comes calling. But, gentlemen, this is not the White Lion Inn. Yes, we know that story. It made you a legend. You slaughtered some poor idiots who were half-asleep. Well done."

I saw Evan's hand twitch, and moved out of his line of fire. The Nameless pulled a gun from a shoulder holster. He clicked the safety off. Matthew raised a finger. Wind teased the sleeves of his shirt and wafted towards Evan. The gun lifted from Evan's hand, flew backwards into the woods, and crashed down on a rock. The sound of its discharge rang shockingly through the night.

Another finger lifted, intensifying the wind. A third, and I slipped on the mud as I fought to keep my balance against the gale. The intense wind was not aimed at me, however, but at Evan. I gasped as sturdy Evan, caught in the storm, flew. His head smashed into a tree and he slid bonelessly down the trunk to the ground.

"One down," said Matthew.

I wanted desperately to go to Evan and see how badly he was hurt, but I didn't dare turn my back on our adversary. Matthew turned to look at me, then Alexander.

"Vampires. Strange alliances your friend the Druid makes."

He raised his fingers again. The wind obeyed, battering against me, upsetting my balance, making it impossible to move towards Matthew. I tried to look at Alexander. He, too, fought the unnatural force Matthew had called down on us.

Above the howling, whipping sounds of the forest being torn apart, I could hear something else: the loud gunning engine of that motorcycle. It drew closer. Did it bring reinforcements for Matthew?

My fangs prickled at my gum line, my nails grew and sharpened into talons. I snarled, hunched against the wind, fighting it with vampire strength. For the first time, I saw Matthew look uncertain. He took a step away from me and lowered his hand. The wind died down, now sending leaves flying rather than twigs and branches. I leapt at Matthew, trying to knock him off balance. We grappled. His shirt slipped away from me, the material as hard to catch as water. My fangs grazed his cheek. He flung up a hand and pushed my chin back. The force of his blow tumbled me off him onto the altar stone. That hurt, momentarily stunning me. I looked around for Alexander. He had grabbed a downed tree branch, and was trying to knock Matthew off his feet. My friend's eyes were blazing red, his fangs extended. Matthew at least showed true bravery by standing and fighting two maddened vampires.

He called up his wind again, and I had trouble regaining my feet. Lightning forked overhead, illuminating the hilltop. The motorcycle engine drew closer. A flash from the sky reflected off chrome racing up the hill.

Matthew whirled, distracted. Alexander's tree branch caught him in the stomach, and he went down. The wind stopped, though the lightning continued. The engine of the hurtling machine whined. The rider, crouched low over the handlebars, aimed directly for Matthew. The witch scrambled to his feet at this new threat, turned, and ran.

"Let's go after him!" Alexander shouted.

I shook my head. Despite supernatural powers, I felt exhausted and sore. There was nothing left in my energy reserves. Released from Matthew's relentless attack, I ran to Evan's side. He had dragged himself up into a sitting position, but his hair was matted with blood.

"Are you all right?" I asked.

"I hit a tree. My scalp is all over the trunk. What do you think?"

"You're conscious and you're talking. I think you'll be fine." I helped him up. He wobbled, but stayed upright.

"Who's the kid?" he asked.

I thought at first he was hallucinating before I recalled our rescuer. Turning, I saw a young man, one hand laid possessively on his motorcycle, talking to Alexander. The moon reflected off his long, fair hair. Tall, though not so tall as Alexander, and slim, he looked to be no more than a teenager. He dressed like one, as well, in denim and leather. He was a vampire.

He realized Evan and I were looking at him and nodded at me. "Hey. I'm Francis. Francis Calvert. Alex here tells me you're a baron."

"I was a baron, in my breathing days. Gideon Redoak, at your service. Why were you following us?"

"Because I want to join the Brotherhood of Darkness. I figured sooner or later the witch activity around here would bring you to check it out. I kept my eyes open, and sure enough, you guys came. So I trailed you."

"Why do you want to join the Brotherhood?"

Alexander hissed, "Gideon, don't dissuade him."

Francis Calvert leaned against his motorcycle. "Hey, word's out about you guys, you know. You're famous. Kicked some serious ass. And I'm one of those who thinks vampires don't have to be monsters. I'm on your side."

Evan, holding the back of his head, looked the boy over. "We owe you one for helping us. Come on back to Maine with us, then, if you're that determined."

Our new friend scrutinized my protector, nose wrinkling. "Your blood smells funny. You're one of those weird things, aren't you?"

"Kid, I got thrown into a tree tonight and knocked out of a battle I should have fought in. Don't push me right now. I'm a Nameless One, if that's what you mean."

Francis nodded. "Yeah, one of them."

Alex's head turned. "Sirens. Matthew must have called them to try to make trouble for us."

I heard them, too. "Time to go."

We made our way back to the limousine. Evan insisted he felt well enough to drive, but Alexander made him sit next to me and took the wheel himself. Francis followed us back to the hotel in Salem.

Evan patched himself up with the first-aid kit and accepted the whiskey I poured. Alexander telephoned the Druids back in Fletcherville to tell them we that had a new recruit.

"What do we do about Matthew?" Alexander asked dejectedly.

We all just looked at each other and shrugged. Nobody knew. We needed a witch ourselves. The Druids were magic-users, but their magic was not the same.

Evan felt the bandages on his head. His hand came away dry, and he nodded in satisfaction. "Next time, I wear a helmet."

I glanced at him. "There will be a next time?"

"Count on it. Or baron on it, in your case." A grimace crossed his face.

Alexander was studying our new recruit. "So, Francis, what's your story?"

His eyes shifted evasively. "I was bumming around the country, got pulled into some stuff, made some bad moves—at least I guess that's what happened. I woke up this way one night, that's all I know." He grinned. "Hey, you know what they say, if you remember the 60s, you weren't really there."

Neither Alexander nor I could fault Francis if he had been tricked by a vampire and was too embarrassed to admit it. We didn't need to know the details—at least not at the moment. His actions tonight provided him with all the bona fides we required.

We returned to Fletcherville the next evening, not quite the triumphant homecoming we hoped for. Matthew was still alive, and he would be seeking revenge.

Francis, with his modern slang and modern ways, was an odd fit for the Brotherhood. We all liked him, however, and made him welcome. Until he could build a place of his own, he moved into Valley Mansion with Alexander. The Gothic splendour of my friend's mansion tickled the boy, or so he claimed to me. He said he thought Oakwoods was too pretty for him, and Fairlawn too domestic.

That winter turned into the spring of 1980 without a sign from Matthew. There was none of Corbeau, either, but I had word that he still travelled Europe, spreading evil and pain. He had not forgotten me. I doubted Matthew forgot us, either. Yet summer breezes caressed the cliff peacefully. They brought no breath of dark magic with them.

Michael Fairlawn married Mary Summers in August, twice. The first wedding was in a church with all her relatives present, plus important civic guests and those members of the Brotherhood who could attend. The other ceremony proved far more interesting: a moonlight handfasting, held in the sacred oak grove, presided over by Nicholas. Never before had I witnessed a Pagan wedding. The ceremony, with its solemn invocations to the four directions, and binding of wrists, moved me more deeply than the Puritan wedding between Prudence and Jamie. The words spoken in that grove were of love and honour, not obedience and serving God.

Still no magical reprisals came down upon us. Evan and I went back to Danvers, where I ignored the looming asylum, but found no sign of Matthew or of any coven. There was no hint of where they had gone.

"Maybe we scared him off?" Evan said hopefully.

I looked meaningfully at the back of his head, and he shrugged. "No, he's gone underground. He must be preparing something."

"Be nice to know what."

We returned to Fletcherville, and reported our lack of results.

"We'll keep our eyes open," said Michael.

He and Mary adopted a baby girl, not long after their marriage, and named her Elizabeth. Never lived a child so spoilt by indulgent "uncles" and one "aunt."

Fidgeting for independence, Francis built a rough but sturdy shack just the other side of my property, on a narrow spit of land Alexander gave him, and moved out of Valley Mansion.

But for all our vigilance, there was no sign of Matthew, and no hint of Corbeau.

Ten years passed, and, we dropped our guard. We accepted the status quo. Matthew had moved on, giving up his plans to control New England. We wanted to believe that. Why would he wait so long, otherwise? One year blended into another with no hostilities on any front. We marked the time watching Elizabeth grow, and speculating about Matthew and his coven.

Late one spring night in 1990, Alexander and I walked together along the cliff side trail. I never tired of the ocean view. The Atlantic changed every time I saw it. Tonight it lapped peacefully at the rocks below. A waning moon showed its prongs in the sky.

My friend broke the silence. "Gideon, you know I've been searching for my family."

I nodded. It had become a hobby of his, not one I fully approved of, but it kept him busy. His own children had married, but their family lines vanished into the chaos of Eastern European history since 1815. I worried that he might learn something that would hurt him.

"I've found someone. A descendant in a straight line from one of my uncles. She's Canadian. Her name's Janine. She's an orphan."

"She has no other family?"

"Not that I can discover. Her aunt raised her, but the aunt's gone now, and the poor child's on her own at eighteen. I thought I might ask her to come and live in Valley Mansion."

"With Mrs. Jenkins as chaperone?" I asked before I could stop myself.

He put a hand over his heart, to show I wounded him. "I'm shocked that you think I would need a chaperone with my own cousin."

"A distant cousin, removed by many generations. Eighteen years old and alone in the world. Probably impressionable, and here you are, the rich, handsome cousin swooping her off to his Gothic mansion in New England."

"You make her sound like Jane Eyre."

I watched him silently for a few moments, trying to penetrate the mock indignation to his true motives. "If you wish to do this, Alexander, then nothing I can say will change your mind. Do try to consider the effect on the poor girl, though, will you?"

"You worry too much."

Michael and I talked this over a few nights later, after dinner at Fairlawn. Mary and Elizabeth drifted upstairs for that mysterious maternal ritual known as bath and bedtime, leaving us two men to ourselves. I brought up the subject of Alexander's cousin.

Michael sighed. "It sounds to me as if the girl has nobody else. We'll all act as Alex's chaperones, and hope he behaves himself. I think we really don't need to worry about Janine getting seduced. Unless she wants to be—she is legal age."

"Alexander would be hard for an impressionable girl to resist."

"Then he better make sure he doesn't impress her."

I nodded, and leaned back in my chair. "Elizabeth is growing up so quickly. You must be proud of her."

The Archdruid's face smiled so broadly I thought it might crack. "Very much. Never a dull moment with children around. She's bright and funny, just a treasure. I couldn't love her more if she were my own."

He told me long ago that he couldn't father children. I, of course, couldn't either, but I couldn't fathom the desire for children and had never wanted any. "She's very sweet."

"Speaking of my own children, how do you think Mary looks?"

I blinked. The question made no sense, but I ventured an answer. "She looks well. Rosy."

"She's pregnant."

My jaw dropped. "I-I...what?"

He nodded. "Yes, I know. I told you there could be no children of my own. But we have been blessed. Mary carries twins."

"Congratulations?"

Michael laughed. "That's more or less how I feel. As if someone slapped me. The Goddess chose to give us children, Gideon, and I am humbled before her."

Once again, I found myself speechless in the presence of his spiritual connection to his Goddess.

Michael recognized this, and changed the subject. "Janine will be fine. I can always offer her a job babysitting."

That made me laugh. "All right, you've persuaded me. I won't worry about Janine."

Alexander started the necessary immigration process, and before long, Janine arrived with her pitifully few belongings. Her cousin hosted a welcome party for her at Valley Mansion. My first glimpse of her reassured me somewhat. A pretty blonde girl, she made the rounds of the room with assurance and grace. She tossed her head back and laughed at Francis's attempt to flirt with her, and she gave Nicholas a playful push when he tried the same. The mostly male Brotherhood obviously didn't intimidate her in the least. She danced with us all in turn.

I bowed to her, and she accepted my hand for a waltz. I guided her steps, since she confessed unfamiliarity with such an "old-fashioned" dance.

"You dance very well, Gideon. I may call you Gideon?" Her eyes laughed at me.

"Of course, and thank you. I had a good teacher."

"And you're gay? Alex told me that."

I was taken aback that she knew this, and even more by the casual way she asked. "Alexander had no right to give you such personal information about me."

She looked into my eyes. "It's okay, I don't care. I think you're very nice. And a great dancer."

"Thank you."

The waltz ended. I bowed to her, and handed her off to Francis for a far faster number. I walked over to Alexander and kicked his ankle.

"Ow! What did you do that for?"

"No reason at all." I stalked off.

Maggie stopped me by the windows. "Now what was that about?"

I sighed. "Everyone has to know my personal business, it seems."

"What, that you're gay?"

"Thank you so much, Maggie."

"Oh, come and dance with me, Gideon. Nobody cares, you know. Everyone likes you. We all think you need a lover."

I thought I needed one, too, but didn't feel it was a matter for general discussion. Yet, my friends cared about me and my happiness. As I considered this, warmth flooded my heart. Friends: what would I do without them? "Will you have this dance?"

"I've been waiting all night."

Chapter Ten

I walked the quiet streets of Fletcherville at one in the morning, the only person stirring at that hour. On fine summer nights, the weather tempted me outdoors. Though I never tired of the path along the cliff, I enjoyed variety. The sleeping town did not heed my soundless footsteps.

I wandered without any purpose in mind, and found myself on the far edge of town. A derelict cannery, relic of more profitable fishing days, stood alone in a field littered with industrial debris. Many residents had petitioned the Board of Selectmen to have the cannery demolished as an eyesore and hazard. The property's ownership, however, was in legal limbo. At night, the place was both spooky and dangerous.

I was startled to see that a figure knelt in the dead grass in front of the cannery. A woman, stark naked in the moonlight, raised her hands to the sky. I froze in place. If she glanced this way, she would see me. Vampire mind tricks were useless on those with real magical power. I doubted she would believe this was a chance encounter with the local undead population.

Fortunately, she rose without turning her head and went into the cannery. I wasted no time at all heading back to Cliff Road to report to the Brotherhood.

"There has to be some connection to Matthew," Michael said. "I was wondering if he was training some younger witches to set against us."

"Great," said Francis. "An army."

"And we never have found that warrior witch we need," Maggie said wryly.

"No doubt there's a young coven holed up in that cannery," Michael said. "There's no sort of cover anywhere around it to spy from. It's a miracle you weren't seen, Gideon."

"She had her mind on other matters."

"I know that cannery pretty well," Francis said, and we all turned to look at him.

Alexander almost smiled. "I bet you do."

"Why would that be?" I asked.

A dramatic sigh issued from our Count. "Gideon, even I know that the old cannery is a good place to score drugs."

We looked back at Francis, who just shrugged. "Nothing wrong with it. And like I said, it means I'm probably the only one here with any knowledge of the layout of the place—unless Mags here smokes dope or Alex shoots up."

Maggie innocently said nothing, but Alexander looked offended. Michael quickly regained control of the meeting. "Then you're our expert on the cannery, Francis. Can you draw at all?"

"Um, no."

"If Francis can describe the building details to me, I can draw them adequately for our purpose," I said.

Michael nodded. "Thank you, Gideon. If we have a good idea of the building layout, perhaps we can come up with a plan. Now the rest of us should try and find out what we can about this woman and anyone else seen around that cannery. Ears to the ground—you know how rumour spreads in this town. It would be unbelievable if nobody was talking about a beautiful new redhead in Fletcherville."

I found paper, pencils, rulers and other drafting supplies in my office. Francis and I set to work at the dining table in Oakwoods, with Evan looking on in case he was needed. Francis watched with interest as I picked up a soft-leaded pencil and drew a quick sketch of the outside of the cannery as I had seen it just a few hours earlier. It was rough, but fairly accurate. I did eliminate the detail of a naked young woman out front.

My young companion took the paper and studied it. "Not bad. So, how come you can draw?"

"Drawing or painting was considered an essential element of a gentleman's education. My father couldn't ignore this expectation, but he regarded art as frivolous. If I had to learn to draw, it should be something worthwhile. He hired tutors to teach me architectural design."

"Bit of a control freak, was he?" Francis nodded knowingly. "Mine, too."

By the end of that week, the Brotherhood knew more not only about the redhead, but about the others who had moved into the old cannery. They had rented the cannery under the guise of a film crew, claiming to be scouting it for a shooting location. Nobody had seen so much as a camera, but the townspeople expected film crews to be mysterious and secretive. They were not surprised to see no obvious external sign of any movie-making activity.

The redhead, who was the apparent leader, went by the name Gemma Bannerman. All of us doubted it was her real name, just as we all had no doubts she had been trained and sent by Matthew. When the coven started following and threatening our non-combatants the Brotherhood realized we had to act, and quickly.

Mary, now extremely pregnant with twins, was the most vulnerable. Michael loaded her down with protective spells and amulets. When he couldn't be with her, either Nicholas or Maggie would accompany her. The coven, or Gemma alone, tried to get past these defenses. Bones and gris-gris bags were found in Mary's car, and in her locker at the hospital.

Elizabeth and Janine also received shares of hostile treatment. Elizabeth was dropped off and picked up at the school door each day. This put a severe cramp in her social life—devastating for an eleven-year-old.

When her kitten Vance was found dead we knew we couldn't wait any longer. If we didn't take action against the coven, the next victim would be human. Vance's throat was slit, to show us there was no possible way this was an accident.

"Francis and I have the plans all drawn up," I said as we sat down in the meeting room at Fairlawn.

"All we need is some cover," Francis said. "I don't suppose Druids can create a forest overnight."

Maggie and Nicholas grinned at each other, but didn't explain. Michael just shook his head.

"I can create cover, though," he said. "Fog, rain, clouds…make it a dark night, keep them in the cannery and make it harder to spot us closing in."

We debated and argued for hours, proposing, discussing and rejecting one plan after another. Sketches and diagrams covered half the table, and my cannery map was festooned with squiggly lines and Xs in several colours. As the levels went down in the bottles of Scotch and brandy, our hand gestures and voices both rose proportionately.

At one point Evan whispered in my ear, "If I didn't know you better, Gideon, I'd say you were actually having fun."

I glared at him. It had no effect. I was, in fact, having fun despite the seriousness of the situation. After so many years of watching and waiting—for Matthew, for Corbeau—it was a relief to be doing something at last. I eagerly anticipated a good fight.

Michael and the other two Druids needed time to brew up their magical weather, so once we had a firm plan, the date for the attack on the coven was set for two nights from our meeting. Nobody was to make a single move against the coven until then, not even to acknowledge their existence. Agreed on that, we broke up the meeting. Nicholas and Maggie both agreed to spend what was left of the night at Fairlawn, neither one being in any condition to drive back home.

As promised, fog and rain covered our approach to the cannery on the night we had chosen for our attack. The Brotherhood members drew collars close or huddled in their jackets, but made no complaints as we drifted into our positions according to plans. The weather would keep the prey inside, and that was what we wanted.

I leapt up to a broken window, crouching on the ledge and for once grateful that I was short. From this vantage point, I could see and hear what was going on inside the cannery.

Alexander and Francis copied my move, finding their own window ledges, while Evan stayed below my window, checking his arsenal.

The entire coven appeared to have assembled. Gemma Bannerman was definitely their leader. At least tonight she was wearing clothing, barely. The nine coven members were all very young and bore the unmistakable look of fanatics.

"The filthy undead are on to us," Gemma said. "Matthew warned us about that."

Another scantily clad young woman said, "Let's slay them all."

Perhaps one or two of the participants had some actual intelligence, for there were murmurs of protest and fright at this proposal.

Gemma looked at them all. She didn't sneer or scowl. Her glance was proud. "We have been training ten years for this. I'm growing tired of simply harassing the humans who associate with the undead. It's time we moved against them all. First, we kill the women—the Druid's wife and daughter, and that orphan the count so kindly took in."

It was then I made a costly mistake. I looked at Michael, to see what his reaction was to this cold-blooded plan. I should have looked at Alexander. Michael was far too experienced a hand at intrigue to be taken in by someone like Gemma. Alexander, on the other hand...

With a scream of pure outrage, Alexander launched himself off the window ledge where he had been crouching and down onto the cannery floor. All our carefully laid plans dissolved into total chaos. Gemma threw back her head and laughed.

"Did you think I didn't know you were here all along? Get them!"

The rest of us emerged from our hiding spaces, already in fighting mode. Evan cleared two burly males from my path as I tried to make my way to Alexander, who was now attempting to strangle the red-haired coven leader. She was putting up a good fight, considering that she faced a tall, strong vampire as an opponent. Someone tackled me from behind, and I had to turn away from my goal in order to fight. Alexander could look after himself.

I gripped my assailant by the arm and shook her off, sending her sprawling to the floor. I had long since learned to ignore niceties of gender in a fight. She swung out and up with her legs, trying to trip me and bring me down with her, but a kick to the ribs dissuaded her. She jumped to her feet with the resilience of the young, only to meet my fist driving into her stomach. Down she went, and this time, she stayed.

I availed myself of the opportunity to look around. Michael was checking on anyone, friend or foe, who had fallen. As a healer, he couldn't help it. Nicholas was still fighting off one of the strong-arm bullies of the coven. Evan made his way to the struggling pair and dispatched the coven member with a nasty neck-twist. Francis and Maggie had nobody left to fight. All the witches were down—all but one.

A stern, cold voice rang out. "Everyone stop where they are, or he dies now."

Gemma Bannerman had somehow managed to capture Alexander. She had him effectively bound with some magical force that was beyond our calculations.

"What is it you want, then?" Michael said.

"Your heads, all in a row."

Alexander tried hard to escape, I will grant him that. "Don't you dare surrender on my behalf, Michael!"

Evan glanced at me. "Didn't occur to me for a second," he whispered.

"Evan!" But I had to suppress a grin at this black humour.

Michael shook his head at Gemma. "I don't think so. Go back and tell Matthew to send someone a little more experienced next time. You're all far too young for this."

She laughed. "You would say so, being an immortal freak. The old can never accept defeat."

"No, it is the young who cannot. The old are used to it."

"Then let us see, old man."

Gemma made a hand gesture as we watched. Alexander writhed and screamed, though nothing appeared to touch him. Then he suddenly slumped in his invisible bonds. Several gasps escaped from the Brotherhood, including me. There was a wooden stake driven into Alexander's chest.

"You can take it out if you want, but he'll be mine to control," said Gemma.

Michael's eyes narrowed. He too made a gesture and suddenly the cannery was filled with dense fog and blowing leaves. "Francis, Gideon, Evan...get Alex and get him home," Michael said. "We'll keep the coven busy."

Reluctant though the three of us were to leave the fight, we knew he was right. We were the only ones who could take care of Alexander.

Whatever spell Michael had cast, it had removed Alexander's bonds, and Gemma was too busy fighting the fog spell to pay attention to her prisoner. She had already done her damage.

As much as we wanted to remove that stake, all three of us knew better. We were careful not to let it dislodge as we picked up Alexander's fallen body and carried it out of the cannery.

Pausing to look back, I could only be grateful that the place was so isolated from the town. Strange fogs and lights flickered through the ruined building, and a wind from nowhere blew leaves in great bunches where there were no trees to have shed them. Yells and screams filled the air and the sounds of fighting continued.

"It's going to be one hell of a movie," Francis said.

Evan shifted the oblivious Alexander, whom he was carrying as easily as a child. "It'll be the news at noon if we don't get him inside."

We made our way to where the various vehicles had been parked and stowed Alexander carefully in the back seat of my Cadillac. Francis and I squeezed into the front with Evan.

"So how come we can't pull out the stake?" Francis asked as we headed for Cliff Road.

"We can't be sure old Gemma was bluffing," Evan said. "We can't pull out the stake until she's dead, or she might be able to control Alex."

"Isn't he dead, though? True dead?"

I shook my head. "Take a closer look. Matthew should have been teaching his replacement basic anatomy rather than world domination."

The stake had missed all the important chambers of the heart. Alexander was not true dead, merely in a state of suspended animation due to the shock. Of course, Gemma would have done this intentionally to gain zombie control once she pulled out the stake.

We arrived with our sad cargo at Valley Mansion, wondering how to get it inside without disturbing Janine. We had no qualms about disturbing Mrs. Jenkins. Evan went and fetched her to help us.

The housekeeper sniffed at us. "You'll just have to bring him in. It's not like the girl doesn't know there are strange things going on."

If Janine knew there were strange things going on in the mansion that night, she gave no sign. We were undisturbed as we took Alexander down to his Spartan furnished bedroom on the dungeon level of Valley Mansion. We laid him out as comfortably as possible and cleaned him up a bit.

"Idiot," Evan sighed at him.

I shrugged. "We all act impulsively from time to time."

"What do you think is happening in the cannery?" Francis asked.

"Hopefully our Druids are winning," I said.

It was an unanswerable question, at least at the moment. Dawn was drawing near, and a decision had to be made. The four of us in Alexander's somber bedroom consulted with each other. It seemed safe enough to leave Mrs. Jenkins to guard both Janine and Alexander. Should Gemma escape from our Druids, she wouldn't make any moves against Alexander during the day. There's little point in making a vampire your fetch and then waking him in daylight. With the promise that Evan would return to Valley Mansion in the event of an emergency, he and I went home to Oakwoods and Francis to his shack.

"Quel jour," I said, heading upstairs to my bedroom.

Evan shrugged. *"Oui. Bon nuit."*

The next evening, Evan and I returned to Valley Mansion. We found the Druids, looking a bit battered, and Francis already in place. Janine sat next to Maggie, looking pale but defiant.

"Michael's told me everything," she said to me.

"Good," I said.

Evan looked at her, then at Michael. "Everything?"

"As much as she needs to know."

"I'd like to know what happened to you lot last night."

The Druids explained that there had been a magical and physical battle, and that they had finally prevailed over the coven and chased them out of town. "Experience triumphs again." Nicholas grinned.

Maggie sniffed, and shook her head. "Children. Gemma does have genuine power, mind you."

"Genuine enough to have let her escape, and circle back," Michael said.

"Fuck." Everyone looked at Francis. He expressed what we were all thinking quite well.

"So she's going to come to get Alex?" Janine asked.

"He's a powerful vampire and will be under her control once the stake is removed. With him, she could wipe out the Brotherhood." Michael got up and helped himself to some of Alexander's Scotch.

Francis said helpfully to Janine, "That would be a 'yes'."

I spoke up. "So how do we best protect Alexander?"

Michael swallowed his drink. "Maggie, Nicholas and I can run some magical interference. But bear in mind that we worked hard last night and have only had a few hours' sleep. Most of the hard work will be up to you."

"I can do anything you want me to," Janine said.

"Good. Because what I want is you out of the way and safe. Maggie, please take this civilian and lock her in her bedroom. Mrs. Jenkins, I believe you have a key?"

I had to admire Janine just then. The expected responses of screaming or protesting didn't happen. She stood with dignity, and joined Maggie. She smiled at us all. "Best of luck. Goodnight, gentlemen."

Maggie saluted her. "I would never go that quietly."

"You're not aware of your value as a hostage."

"Oh. Ah."

Once Janine was safely tucked away on the second floor, we stationed ourselves around the mansion. Francis and I, with our night vision, kept a watch on the outdoors. Evan guarded Alexander's body. Nicholas prowled the back rooms of the house, Michael and Maggie split the rest.

It was a windy, damp night. I was near the garage when I heard a rustle of movement on the left. A fleeting shadow slipped past me, easily dismissed as imaginary. But there was a sense of presence and a slight tinge of bloodsmell.

"What was that?" came Francis' voice.

"I believe we have a caller." I slipped as quietly as the shadow into the trees on the lawn, following the wind.

She ran swiftly around the mansion to the back, where the windows overlooked the cliff and the ocean.

It was indeed Gemma. She stood exposed in the moonlight, seeming totally unconcerned that both Francis and I were only a few feet from her, staring up at the windows on the second floor. Francis almost got close enough to lay a hand on her, but then she jumped. She leaped at an angle calculated to smash through one of the windows, though I swear the glass shattered and fell away before Gemma went through it. The sound of breaking glass brought Mrs. Jenkins and the Druids running. There was a scream from the room Gemma had entered.

"Janine," said Francis.

Moments later, the back door opened and Gemma emerged with Janine held hostage by a very sharp knife at her throat. Janine's eyes were wide. Gemma dragged her hostage to the edge of the cliff. Nobody moved.

The wind whipped past us, smelling of leaf mould and dead fish, what the tourists referred to as "fresh air." Far below, the tide had receded, leaving bare, jagged rocks.

Michael was the first person to speak. "Very well, then. What is it you want?"

Gemma rolled her eyes. "I should have thought that was obvious. The vampire for the girl."

"His life is not ours to give you. Let the girl go. She has nothing to do with you."

Gemma laughed. "You think I would just give up a hostage? I want Goldanias. He will help me control this valley."

"We can't let you do that," said Michael.

"Then we have a stand-off."

"I will be your hostage."

"That's just a trick. Do you take me for an idiot? Incidentally, if you don't stop that spell you're casting to raise a fog, I may lose my grip."

Michael raised an eyebrow at her, apparently impressed. "You seem to have the advantage of us. It appears the only thing we can do is give you Alex. But we want Janine back."

"This useless little thing?" Gemma let Janine dangle over the edge for a moment, then pulled her back and shoved her towards us, sending her stumbling into Evan. He grabbed her and wrapped her in a protective hug.

We all went back inside Valley Mansion. Mrs. Jenkins and Maggie were now soothing Janine. Nobody went near Gemma, who seemed oblivious to the reality of her position.

The seven of us made quite a crowd in Alexander's dark bedroom. Gemma's attention was all on her potential fetch. Alexander lay motionless with the stake in his heart, like some bizarre clockwork toy.

"How amusing it will be to see him turn on his friends," Gemma said. "And Matthew will be avenged for the indignities he has suffered. Say goodbye to the Brotherhood."

"Goodbye," said Evan, and hit her quite neatly on the back of the head. "Stupid bitch," he added as she crumpled to the floor.

Nicholas tsked and shook his head. "Never forget that you are standing in a room full of enemies."

"Sound advice," Evan said.

"So, what do we do with her?" Janine asked.

I glanced at Alexander. "Someone is going to wake up hungry." I reached down and pulled out the stake. Blood gushed, and Evan grabbed a shirt to staunch the wound.

"Welcome back, Alex," he said as the Count's eyes flickered open.

"Need blood," Alexander moaned.

Evan and Francis helped him sit up. I lifted Gemma and carried her to the bed. He drained her dry. We threw her body off the cliff.

Chapter Eleven

It had been far too long since I had visited my "Maman" in France, and I also had business in England, so Evan and I closed up Oakwoods and headed for Europe. When Genevieve saw us emerge grinning from our rental car, she gave us such fierce hugs that even Evan winced.

"Tell me everything," she said as Jean took his chance to greet me.

We talked for hours, sipping the excellent wine and watching the night breezes caress the grape vines and orchards of Chateau de Monet. Genevieve passed on what news she had of Etienne Corbeau and his whereabouts and doings. She carefully refrained, however, from dropping any clues about the source of this information, or the activities of Le Societé des Gardiens. I knew that as Corbeau's get, I posed a risk to Genevieve and the Gardiens if I knew too much and Corbeau should trap me.

It was hard to leave Genevieve, but my business affairs in England were pressing. Evan and I opened up the house in London, and I noticed that it was showing signs of age and neglect. But since every piece of furniture, faded cushion or worn panel reminded me of Jonathan, I was reluctant to make any changes or renovations.

I performed a small ritual whenever I was in London. I went to Jonny's grave and laid fresh flowers on it. This time I noticed that the gravesite seemed better tended than my house. Very well, then, I would have the house redecorated. It was time to let go. Long past time, really, but letting go caused such an ache. The caretakers of this little plot must have wondered why someone had been paying for its upkeep since 1815.

I said my goodbyes and went to the business meeting I had to attend. It ran late, long past the hour scheduled, and we were all tired and disgruntled by the time it concluded. I stopped in a pub on the way home to have a whiskey, and stopped again later to take more suitably vampiric refreshment. I left the young man alive and healthy, not much the worse for wear, and went home before Evan could start to panic.

Having reassured my protector that I was in one piece, I went upstairs to draw a bath and get ready for bed. It was early, and

I wouldn't fall asleep before dawn, but I could lie in bed and read a bit.

The tub was filling nicely and I was partially undressed when I thought I heard a scuffle downstairs. I turned off the steaming water and pulled my shirt back on, reaching for my bathrobe. As I shrugged into the plush velour, I heard the commotion again and knew I hadn't been imagining it.

Evan would have the situation, whatever it was, well in hand, but I should find out what was going on. There was time before dawn, so I went downstairs. In the living room, I found Evan standing near a window with a vise-like grip on what could only be a cat burglar. However, there was a taint of the occult about him, some nebulous factor that let me know he was not human.

"So," I said, "What have we here?"

Evan pushed his captive around to face me. I saw a very young man with unruly dark brown hair and the most extraordinary amber eyes. I wondered if they were a trait of his kind, whatever his kind might be.

"Get your bloody hands off me!" he spat. His accent was lower-class English, with a veneer of higher education laid on top. I could also perceive from several feet away that he hadn't properly washed for some time, or done his laundry recently.

Evan's face wrinkled with distaste and he shook his prisoner, who was already showing marks here and there that would turn to bruises by morning. "Watch your mouth."

"You are hardly in a position to make demands, young man." I took a seat in the nearest chair that was upwind. "It would be useless for me to threaten you with the police. I fear neither of us desire the meddling of...humans."

His face went pale beneath the dirt he'd smeared on as a disguise. "Well, if you're not going to call the police, what are you going to do with me?"

"I haven't quite decided. Why did you come here? What were you looking for? Who sent you?"

"Nobody sent me! As for what I'm looking for, I'll know it when I find it."

"What makes you think I've got this..." I held my palms up, "...whatever it is?"

He smiled tightly. "Because no human could have what I'm looking for."

I was becoming angry. "Enough of these evasive games! Explain yourself."

Evan tightened his grip and gave the young man another shake. "Tell the nice Baron who and what you are."

"I'm a werewolf," said the would-be burglar defiantly. "All I want to do is find a cure. I'd hoped you might have something that would give me a clue."

"Are you sure there is a cure?" I asked.

"What can be made can be unmade."

I could only shake my head and feel very sad for this young man. What was I going to do with him? Tomorrow night was the full moon, and I could not, in all conscience, simply turn him loose on an unsuspecting London. He might destroy half the city, or he might not, but I couldn't take the chance. There was also the danger that he might attempt to burglarize some other home and be captured by police. Should he turn into a wolf while in prison...it was unthinkable.

"You'll stay here," I said. "At least during the phase of the full moon. After that's over, we'll speak again."

"What if I bloody well don't want to stay?"

"My dear young man, I'm not giving you a choice. Evan, kindly show him to his room."

Evan took a firm grip on our reluctant guest. "This way," he said, hustling the young man down to the cellar.

There was a specially-designed room down there, twin to one Evan had installed in Oakwoods, with the doorframe inlaid with silver. It locked with a silver key. When I asked Evan why he had built an escape-proof, silver-warded cell in each of my houses, he had only looked wisely at me and said, "You never know what you're going to need to lock up."

The werewolf slunk past the silver wards. Evan shut and locked the door, ignoring the gutter language that came from within the cell.

There was no time now to take a bath, so I let the water out of the tub and simply undressed and retired. Evan followed the young thief's trail, which would have been invisible to even the best human tracker. He found a battered van and evidence that the young man had been living in this vehicle. He hadn't been occupying it alone, however—when Evan opened the door, a large and hungry timber wolf stood up, growling in a menacing manner. Evan withdrew before he lost his throat.

Evan, however, has a way with animals. He offered it food and shelter and assured it that its master was safe. The wolf agreed to come with him, although it wouldn't let him touch it.

When I came downstairs the following evening, I found my protector playing on the floor with a wolf. My first thought was that the prisoner had somehow gotten loose, but the friendly way this lupine was romping with Evan precluded that notion.

"This is Warg." Evan grinned up at me as the wolf came loping to sniff at my shoes. "He belongs to our friend in the cellar."

A chilling howl from the nether regions of the house made Warg whine and my hair prickle. "Our friend in the cellar is not himself, I gather."

"I took a peep. He's silver, and glows, and he's twice the size of Warg, here. A truly frightening creature."

It howled again. "Poor thing." I shuddered. "No wonder he wanted a cure."

Throughout the very long night, the werewolf howled. Warg joined him once or twice in a quavering lupine chorus, and I was surprised that none of the neighbours called to complain, or reported us to the police. Perhaps they saw the full moon and thought I had taken up raising Alaskan huskies. I always liked the sound of howling wolves, a chorus that has sadly diminished in today's world, but not in my house.

At last the sky began to turn paler, and I felt the tug of weariness. The chorus from the cellar had stopped, and Warg was asleep on the rug in front of the library hearth. I went up to bed, wondering what on earth I was going to do with a werewolf.

Evan left the young man in the cell for most of the day. The thief was exhausted and sick, and Evan felt it was better to let him sleep as much as possible. Finally, as dusk was nearing, Evan went and unlocked the cell.

Naked and filthy, the young man emerged, blinking in the light. He snatched the blanket Evan held out to him, and wrapped it around himself.

"You had no bloody right..." he began furiously.

"Shut up!" Evan said. "What makes you think you had a bloody right to roam around London as a werewolf?"

"I can take care of myself."

"Obviously not. You were living in a van, for crying out loud, and stealing to survive. Look, you're a mess. Go upstairs and wash up. There's a bath waiting for you, and clothes in the middle bedroom. When you're clean and dressed, come down and eat something."

Evan turned before the boy could answer him and walked back upstairs. The thief stood undecidedly, until he felt a tug on his hand. It was Warg, trying to lead him after Evan.

"Oh, all right," he muttered, just loud enough for the wolf to hear. Warg led, tail high as a banner swinging gently, all the way to the bathroom door.

When I came down and joined Evan at the dinner table, he filled me in on what had happened.

"The middle bedroom window opens with easy access to a tree," I said.

"I know. But I didn't want him to think we were going to hold him against his will."

"Which way do you think our young thief will choose to descend?"

He nodded towards the stairs. "The right way."

Evan had deliberately left out clothing as unlike a cat burglar's black guise as possible. I barely recognized the young man descending with the wolf at his heels. His hair and face were clean, he was wearing a white sweater and blue slacks that were a bit undersized—Evan was shorter than he by a couple of inches—and as he drew nearer, I could see that his eyes were now blue. He stopped at the bottom of the staircase, obviously wondering if it was too late to bolt.

I waved my hand over the table. "Come and eat something."

He entered the room and opened his mouth as if to speak.

"Not now. Eat first," I said.

He stared for a minute, and slid into the chair behind the place set for him. He fingered the fine linen of his napkin wonderingly, and looked at the place setting with trepidation.

"They aren't silver," Evan said, taking the lid off a serving dish of roast beef. He served a plateful of food to the open-mouthed boy. "Go ahead," my protector said, eyes dancing, when the thief stared with hesitation at the bounty before him. "It's not poisoned. But take it slowly if it's been awhile since you last ate a good meal."

Evan began eating as if it was of no consequence whether the other joined him or not. The lad threw me a puzzled glance, obviously wondering why I didn't have so much as an empty plate in front of me, then began eating.

From the way he methodically tucked away his food, I could tell that it had indeed been a while since his last good meal, or since anyone had looked after him at all. He appeared to be scarcely twenty years old, if that. Where were his parents? How had he been struck with the curse of lycanthropy, and why had he fallen upon thieving for a living? But I had told him to eat first, so these and other questions would have to wait. I realized that I didn't even know his name.

Finally he finished eating, and fed his wolf from the table scraps with Evan's permission.

We withdrew from the table and went into the library for our discussion. The living room was too formal and might remind him of his capture the other night, and the parlour had been shut off years ago.

"Well, young man, I think the time has come to talk," I said, as Evan indicated the chair our guest should take. He stood directly behind the chair, making the boy rather uncomfortable. I had not asked how Evan had treated the thief upon capturing him, but I didn't imagine that my bodyguard had been gentle. There were fading bruises visible here and there on the werewolf, but none on Evan.

"Yes, sir, I suppose it has." The thief's tone and demeanour were quieter than they had been the night of his capture.

"I am Baron Gideon Redoak. This is Evan Jones, my bodyguard. And you are...?"

"Mitch Pritchard."

"Is that short for Mitchell?"

He turned a dull red colour. "Mitchell's me... my middle name. My real first name is Gaylord." He winced, expecting mockery.

I knew perfectly well what the word "gay" had come to mean. It no longer meant "cheerful, happy and carefree." His accent betrayed a lower-class background, so perhaps his parents had thought that "Gaylord" sounded grand and hadn't realized that "gay" was a euphemism for "homosexual." His distaste for his first name gave me pause for thought. Was he a homophobe? I saved that question for later.

"Will you tell us how you became a werewolf, Mitchell?" I asked, deciding that no one deserved to be called "Gaylord." He looked grateful.

"I won a scholarship to Cambridge to study animal science." He sounded a little boastful. "I just finished my first year, and they asked me if I wanted to do a wildlife survey on the Continent. Of course I was keen to go. I was one of a team, three blokes, and we were sent to the Carpathians in Hungary. The country's opening up now that the Reds are backing down, and we were to catalogue the wildlife population in that area, hadn't been done since the First War. We left some gear at a youth hostel, and we'd drive or hike up into the forest to camp while we collected our data.

"A couple of weeks in, my mates and I were settling for the night when we heard a wolf howling in the distance. We hadn't seen any sign of wolves up to then, and we were excited that some might have survived. I went out to the Rover to get the tape recorder, and all of a sudden this huge white wolf the size of a horse came ripping into the tent and killed my two mates."

Tears welled up in his eyes but didn't fall. He swallowed hard and continued. "I threw the tape recorder at it. It was all I had for a weapon. It jumped me, and I thought I was gone for a burton. But all it did was chew my leg up, and then it went howling off into the night. I don't know why it didn't kill me."

Evan stirred. "Sometimes the werewolf has the desire to create more of its kind."

The young man sighed. "I woke up the next day. My leg was a bloody mess. I couldn't even look at what was left of the other two chaps. I dragged myself into the Rover and drove to the nearest town. I got to the clinic and passed out again. I spent the next three weeks in hospital. I got an anonymous note while I was there, an invitation to go out to a cabin in the woods when I was released. It said I mustn't go home, and that I would get some answers when I got to the cabin. Well, when I got out, that's where I went, because I wanted to find the blighter who told me I couldn't go home and punch him.

"There was no one there, but I found another note. It told me to wait. There was food and a water supply, so I waited. And I noticed that I started feeling very strange—restless, sick to my stomach, and I kept thinking that something terrible was going to happen. When I looked in the mirror, I saw that my eyes had changed colour. They were amber. The next morning, I woke up outside, miles from the cabin and stark naked. I was very tired, and I couldn't stop throwing up. I made it back to the cabin, and slept for the rest of the day. By the next morning, I was fine again. And my eyes were normal. They hadn't taught Lycanthropy at Cambridge, but I knew what I'd become. It didn't take me long to realize that the wolf that attacked me was a were. There'd been food in the cabin, but it was running low. I went back into town and restocked on everything. I tried to trace the owner of the cabin. It had been rented, but nobody knew by whom."

"I know," said Evan softly.

"What?"

"It was the werewolf, trying to make amends. He couldn't make himself known to you, but he knew what he'd done, so he gave you a safe place to go for the change."

"I hadn't thought of that. I went back to the hostel that we'd been using as our HQ to get my things, and found the place had burnt to the ground while I was in hospital.

"Twenty people died in that fire, and I was one of them. None of the survivors knew we'd been camping out, you see, and I was reported dead along with everyone else who'd been killed in the hostel. I found out my mum and dad had already had a memorial service for me back in Liverpool." Now the tears did start to slide down his cheeks. "I thought it was better that they go on thinking I was dead, than know that I'd become a werewolf. So I went back to the cabin."

"And the wolf?" I looked at Warg.

Mitchell smiled, and wiped his eyes. "I found him alone in the woods. I think he thinks I'm his alpha leader or something. He won't leave me, at any rate, and he's fairly tame." His expression darkened. "There was one morning I woke up, covered in blood, and even sicker than usual. I found out later that some people camping in the woods had been savaged to death by a wild beast. I knew it had to be me. There was nothing else in the woods big enough to have attacked anyone, and Warg wouldn't hurt a cat. So I packed up Warg and headed back to England, hoping to find a cure. I've been spying on those I know have occult powers, breaking into their homes and going through their books and things, trying to find something that will break this curse."

"You're both incredibly stupid and tremendously lucky." Evan said. "Breaking into the homes of those with occult power could have left you a toad, or the evening's sacrifice, or very dead. There are far worse things to be than a werewolf."

"I think I'm beginning to realize that." Mitch pointed at me. "What, for example, are you?"

"I'm a vampire."

"You're right, then." Mitch turned to Evan, "There are worse things to be than a werewolf."

"You're about one word away from finding out what one of those things is," Evan said conversationally.

"What's that, then?"

"Put across my knee and taught some manners," Evan said grimly.

"No, Evan," I said. "I would like to know why you feel that way about vampires, Mitchell."

"I can't control the wolf, or remember what I do when it takes over. Maybe I killed those people in the woods, but that was once.

I don't kill people, every night, just to feed my appetite." He glared at me defiantly.

I sighed. "You watch far too much television. I don't kill when I feed. Most vampires don't, in point of fact. The best way to have mortals start vampire-hunting is to leave a trail of blood-drained bodies lying around, and I'm too old to be on the run all the time. Nor do I feed every night, there's no need to. There's much you have to learn about other occult beings, Mitchell."

I was pleased to see that he looked ashamed of himself. "What sort is Muscles, here? And why does a vampire need a bodyguard who's into hitting things?"

Evan's fists clenched, but he restrained himself.

"Evan is of a race that acts as protectors to vampires. And I need him just in case any young werewolves take a fancy to break into my home near dawn."

A slow smile spread across the lad's face. "I reckon you're the right sort, after all. So now what? Am I still your prisoner?"

"I'm prepared to offer you employment."

"Employment?" He looked astounded, as did Evan.

"Yes. You need a decent post with an employer who understands your...special needs. I need an employee who understands mine."

"I don't know if I want to work for a vampire."

"Why not give it some time? We could both be on trial."

I could see Mitchell compare the comfortable house to his van, the excellent meal he'd just eaten to starvation, and the offer of employment to a life of thieving. "A trial period sounds all right. What's this employment, then?"

"I have need of an assistant in my business concerns. I have multiple investments, and you would help me run them. It's now mostly done by computer and fax, and I have little understanding of such machines." I saw Evan "tsk" at me for the white lie, but he was beginning to grin at my plan. "I would also require you to act as my chauffeur or butler upon occasion. I will train you in whatever aspects of the business you require. You will receive a generous salary, room and board and a clothing allowance. I will expect you to dress appropriately. In return, you will allow yourself to be confined during the full moon for your own safety and that of others, as well as conducting yourself like an executive-in-training—at least in public and at business meetings. I don't use my title in public, therefore you will address me as "Mr. Redoak" or "sir" on such occasions. In private, you may address me as Gideon. Is this agreeable to you?"

His grin broadened, and was mirrored on Evan's face. I could tell that my protector was already anticipating the fun of trying to smooth this rather rough diamond. I could only hope that Evan's methods didn't include a good beating.

"Yes, sir," Mitchell said. "But, please, couldn't you call me Mitch?"

"Not at the moment, at least."

"Oh, well. Anything else I should know?"

"One or two things. I live in New England, and keep this house only for occasional visits. You have no objection to living in the United States?"

"No, sir. What else?"

This was the tricky part. "I take it that you object to the use of your rightful first name because you do not follow that particular persuasion?"

He took a moment to work this out. "If you mean am I gay," he said hotly, "I bloody well am not."

I took a deep breath, even though I didn't need to, and faced him squarely. "I am."

His eyes went wide and he looked at me incredulously. "You? But..."

"You were expecting pink shirts with frills and lace?" Evan said harshly. "Or a 'swish' accent?"

Mitchell's eyes swerved to Evan. "Are you...?"

"No, I'm not," Evan said bluntly. "But it's never been a problem for me, working for Gideon."

The young werewolf swallowed and looked at me again.

"If you feel this will cause a difficulty in our working relationship, tell me, and some alternative arrangement will be made for your welfare. While I don't currently have a lover, there is always the possibility that I may find one, and I can't have an employee living in my house who objects to my sexual preference." I crossed my arms and looked at him steadily, awaiting his reply. Drat the boy, I was already growing fond of him, and if he turned my offer down, it would hurt my feelings. It wasn't sexual attraction, either. It felt more like I was adopting a son.

"If Muscles here doesn't have a problem," Mitchell said, gesturing at Evan, "then I don't, either."

"Good," I said. "Now, there are some other things you need to know." I told him about the Brotherhood.

When we had finished talking, and my new employee had gone to bed, I found my old friend and protector staring at me incredulously.

"What is it, Evan?"

"Why did you tell him that? About being gay? I've never heard you be so open about it before."

"I told him because I anticipated trouble if I did not. His aversion to his own name suggested that he might be homophobic. I had to be open with him to find out if he was."

"All right, I can accept that, but why that bit about finding a new lover? That's the first I've heard of it."

I crossed to the window and looked out. "I'm lonely, Evan. It's been more than a century and a half since Jonathan died. Perhaps it's time I came out of the closet."

Evan's mouth twitched.

"What's so funny?"

"I just never expected to hear you use that phrase," he said, grinning. "Gideon, you don't have to announce yourself in public. It's no one's business but your own."

I sighed. "Let's discuss our new employee. Tomorrow, I need you to go to the American Embassy..." There was a great deal of legal red tape to be untangled before I could take officially dead Mitchell Pritchard and his wild wolf home to Fletcherville. Both the Gardiens and the Nameless were adept at forging passports and paperwork, but these took time to handle properly. The wolf, of course, presented a considerable problem, but like most problems this one was solved with money.

At last, I was able to bring the two new members of my household to Oakwoods. Warg took one look around the house and settled down on the hearth rug in the drawing room as if he'd always lived there. Mitchell looked around his bedroom, next to Evan's, with a stunned expression, as if he was staying in an expensive hotel on someone else's bill.

"Too rich for my blood," he whispered, testing the mattress. "Pinch me," he asked Evan, who complied. "Ow!" He rubbed the spot Evan had pinched. "All right, it's real. I never thought I'd be living in Buckingham Palace." He grinned at me. "It's almost like having a family again."

I resisted the urge to pat him on the head. "Welcome home," I said instead.

Chapter Twelve

Bodies of Confederate and Union soldiers alike littered the edges of the battlefield, where they had been dragged out of the way. The remaining troops were demoralized, their taste for battle long since sated. Few officers were left, and only one army chaplain remained, moving diagonally among the wounded offering words of encouragement.

"Checkmate, I believe."

I looked down at the chessboard again. Damn. That "chaplain," Michael's remaining bishop, had indeed moved so that no matter where I tried to place General Lee, he would be captured. "The South has fallen again."

"You'd never make a good Confederate soldier anyway." Michael chuckled.

"It's a beautiful chess set. They come in all sorts of armies now. I've even seen them with movie characters."

We were in the library at Fairlawn, Michael's masculine retreat in his household. Mary had recently given birth to fraternal twins Galen and Vivain. I had paid the expected respects and tried my best to enthuse about the babies, but if truth be told, I found it difficult. Two little lumps with vestiges of red hair and large red squalling mouths, the babies looked alike to me. I declined the honour of holding one. It was a relief to go and play chess with Michael.

There was a knock on the front door. We heard it opening, and voices. One sounded like Francis, and moments later, he appeared at the library door.

"Can I bring in someone to meet you both?"

"Yes, of course," Michael said.

"Uh, keep an open mind, ok?"

"Francis, just bring him in. Or her, as the case may be."

The young man withdrew for a few minutes, then returned with a slightly older male. He was average height, with a wiry build, and had scars on nearly every bit of exposed flesh I could see. A pair of cold blue eyes returned my stare with amusement. He was dressed entirely in black.

Francis made the introductions. "This is Ray, Ray Griffin. And these are Michael Fairlawn and Gideon Redoak."

"Good evening," Griffin said.

"Have a seat," Michael said. "And tell me what I can do for you. What does Matthew want now?"

If Griffin was at all startled, he hid it well. "Mind if I smoke?" Without waiting for an answer, he took a cigarette package out of his shirt pocket. "I'm here to propose a truce," he said as he lit his cigarette.

Michael eyed him silently for a moment. I looked at Francis, who shrugged.

"And is this what Matthew wants?" Michael asked.

"I doubt if Matthew wants much of anything," Griffin said. "Seeing as how he's dead." He blew smoke towards me.

Michael showed no reaction. "How did that happen?"

"I killed him in a magical duel. Damn near killed myself, too."

Michael said nothing for a moment, trying to read Griffin's tone and posture for a clue as to the veracity of his statement. He got up and crossed over to a table where he kept liquor decanters. "Would you like a drink?"

Griffin shifted, looking impatient. "This isn't a social visit."

"This isn't a social drink."

The sorcerer grinned. "In that case, whiskey would be fine. Straight up."

"It's your liver." Michael poured straight Scotch for Griffin and a brandy and soda for himself. Francis accepted some whiskey, as did I.

"If that's true," I said, raising my glass to Griffin, "we owe you thanks."

"It's true, and you owe me nothing," Griffin said. "For all you know, I'm worse than he was and this is all a ploy."

Michael looked at me. "Is it?"

Vampires can't truly read minds. We can detect strong emotions, and generally are able to determine if someone is telling the truth or not. It's a gift that takes centuries to develop, and I had only been able to employ it consistently for a few years. I'd detected no contradiction between Griffin's feelings and his words. "No."

"Why did you kill Matthew?" Michael asked our guest.

"Besides the fact that he was fucking insane? He raised me, more or less, from the time I was fourteen and tried to make me what he was. I decided I'd had enough. See all these scars?" He pulled up the sleeves of his black sweater to show enough scars to make a map. "I've got a lot more of these, all over. Some are from my father, but most are from Matthew. His teaching methods were a bit medieval. But he shouldn't have taught me how to kill someone in a magical duel."

"Oops," said Francis, with a grin.

"So now you would like a truce." Michael ignored Francis. "Between the coven and the Brotherhood?"

"The coven is disbanded," Griffin said. "It's in a shambles. They wanted me to reorganize it and take over. That's when I packed up and left. I'm no coven leader. And frankly, without me, there's nobody powerful enough to run it. So you don't have to worry about the coven. I just want a truce so you don't come after me."

"Gideon and I need to speak privately for a moment," Michael said. "Would you mind?"

"C'mon, Grif, I'll get Mary to make you some coffee," Francis said, pulling on his new friend's arm.

Once they'd vacated the room, Michael and I looked at each other. "That young man ought to come in a package marked 'handle with care,'" the Archdruid said.

I nodded. "He must be a very powerful witch."

"In fact, a warrior witch, wouldn't you say?"

I looked at him. "Do you really think he'd consent to join the Brotherhood?"

"He certainly can't go home again. He seems a bit lost. He might agree if we make the deal sweet enough. We'll build him a house here on the Cliff Road, and make sure he's looked after."

"Let's give him a try, then."

Griffin listened intently to our proposition. He kept his face carefully controlled, but was not quite so successful with his emotions. I could sense that he very much wanted to accept our offer, because otherwise he was homeless and on the run.

"And you may stay in Oakwoods until we get a house built for you," I said.

"I don't want to live in a mansion," he said quickly.

"That's just as well," Michael said with a laugh. "Since what you'll get is a bungalow."

"I didn't mean that, I just—" Griffin's lip curled. "Matthew had a mansion. I can rig up a shelter in the woods, you don't have to worry about me."

"Oh, give me a break, Grif!" Francis rolled his eyes. "You're crashing with me, you idiot."

"Then it's all settled," Michael said cheerfully. Griffin looked at Francis, who grinned at him, and shrugged his agreement.

It only took a few weeks to build a small but cozy bungalow for Griffin, and he moved in with gratitude. He had very few possessions and almost no money, and was a bit embarrassed to have to rely on the generosity of the Brotherhood. We reassured him that he need not pay us back monetarily. We intended to use his power mercilessly.

October 31st that year was a perfect Hallowe'en night. The sky was an eerie, painted black backdrop, decorated with thin streaks of grey cloud and bright stars. The moon, three-quarters full and orange, rode high in the dark heavens. The temperature was chilly, carrying more than a hint of snow on the wind, but not so cold that it forced the small goblins and ghosts to leave off their trick-or-treating.

While these miniature monsters terrorized the village, their elders held parties. Adults enjoy dressing up just as much as their children. There was a dance at the community centre, with refreshments and prizes for the best costumes.

Some of the Brotherhood attended, unable to resist. Evan had participated on the decorating committee, and ensured that no mirrors were left in embarrassing places. Francis, Alexander, Mitch, Evan, Janine and Elizabeth attended the party, the last with strict instructions to come home at a decent hour.

The Druids, of course, did not attend, nor did Ray Griffin. Samhain is one of the major Pagan religious holidays, and the followers of such faiths have better things to do than pretend to be exactly what they are. I felt that I had more important things to do than condone such frivolity, but my staff cheerfully deserted me in order to have fun.

Around midnight, Warg let me know that he needed to go outside. Normally, I would merely have opened the door for him, but I found the silence of the house unusually oppressive, and so I decided to take the wolf for a walk. He thought this departure from routine was great fun, and frisked at my heels like a puppy.

I set off down the path along the cliff's edge, confident that Warg knew enough to stay well back from the drop-off. Just behind Oakwoods, the cliff juts out quite a ways into the ocean, and there is a nice view from this point. I walked out to look at the lights from the harbour in the village.

It was much colder, and the wind was cruel off the sea. I leaned against the iron railing that had been erected here and stared towards the distant town center. The wind didn't trouble me, but Warg, for all his thick fur, whined and shoved his head between my knees for protection. I reached down and scratched his ears, wishing idly for some companionship other than a wolf's.

How long I stood there, lost in thought and loneliness, I don't know. A low growl from Warg roused me. Someone was coming up the path. I saw that it was Ray Griffin.

"Evening, Baron. Hello, pooch." He did a slight double-take. "Uh, that's a wolf."

"This is Warg," I said as the wolf ventured out to sniff this newcomer.

"Oh, right, Francis told me about him." He looked uncomfortable, huddling down into his jacket. Obviously he had not expected to run into anyone on this path. "Why aren't you at the party? Not your scene?"

"You could put it that way," I said dryly, wondering whatever had happened to the English language. "I was raised to believe that dancing was a sin."

"Really?" He looked briefly intrigued, then his expression closed up again. "Want a smoke?" He produced a package of cigarettes. "Guess not." He put them away again. "I can't believe I'm standing at the edge of a cliff, talking to a vampire. Didn't Gemma get tossed off of here?"

"Only after she was already dead. And you are definitely not she."

"No," he said softly. "She was Matthew's little darling."

I wondered whether or not to invite him in for a cup of coffee or something stronger, but didn't know how he'd take the invitation. I had no idea what Francis had told his friend about me, but I imagined that my sexual preference had been mentioned. I felt no attraction that way towards Griffin, but I did feel a certain amount of sympathy for someone who had apparently been through many of the same experiences that I had. However, I knew of no way to explain this to him. I had never spoken of what Corbeau had done to me to anyone other than very close intimates.

We stood watching the sea in silence for a while, both of us on the verge of saying something but holding back.

"Well," he said, sensing the awkwardness, "It's cold out, so I'd better be getting home."

He patted Warg tentatively, and the wolf didn't growl.

"Good night, then," I said.

He turned and started back towards his new house. He paused and looked back at me. "There's trouble in the wind," he said cryptically, and walked away without another word.

"What a strange young man," I said to Warg, and took the wolf home.

The night after Hallowe'en, Oakwoods hosted the Brotherhood for its traditional post-Samhain meeting. It was customary to attend in formal dress for this occasion, as a countermeasure to the silliness of the night before. Even Francis wore a tuxedo jacket and bow tie, although he did look rather like a boy on his way to his high school prom, right down to the purple and black Nike running shoes.

"Oh, I do like those," Alexander said as he glanced down at Francis' feet.

"First class all the way. I can get you a pair at a discount."

Alexander rolled his eyes and turned to give his compliments to Maggie, who looked stunning. She responded by kissing him passionately on the lips and running her fingers through his thick black hair.

"I've been wanting to do that for a century," she said, and smirked at me. "You're next."

"Not likely." I slid behind Evan, who was grinning.

"How about me, Mags?" said Mitch. "I'm a better kisser than the boss." To my dismay, Mitch had done his best to lose his Liverpudlian accent and pick up the worst Americanisms possible. I had repeatedly told him not to call me "boss," to no avail.

"I don't do wolves," she said. "Not your kind of wolf, anyway."

"I'm not asking you to kiss Warg."

"Children," Michael intervened, "Let's take our seats now, shall we?"

As always, the Archdruid looked rather odd in formal evening dress. Michael is the only person I know who wears a tuxedo as if it were tweed.

Nicholas sauntered in, grinning as he looked at everyone else. "Looks like a full-page ad in *GQ*."

"Fine," said Michael, "Next year, you can all come in jeans, for all I care. I hate this stupid tux, anyway. Who started this tradition?" For some strange reason, everyone looked at me.

"I think it's nice to dress up once in a while," Maggie said. "Besides, I happen to think I look terrific in an evening dress— like a beautiful bird of paradise amongst so many penguins."

"That's what I like about you, Mags," Nicholas said, laughing, "Your modesty."

"How was the Hallowe'en party?" Michael asked.

"I didn't win best costume," Francis said grumpily.

"Serves you right," Alexander said with a snort. "You went as a vampire."

Francis shrugged. He turned to grin as Ray Griffin came into the meeting room for his first meeting of the Brotherhood. Obviously, Francis had not told his new friend about the tradition of wearing formal dress, for Griffin was in his ubiquitous black jeans and a black turtleneck sweater. He stopped, dismayed, in the doorway.

"Francis," he said, and shook his head. "Thanks heaps."

"Come in and be welcomed," Michael said. "It doesn't matter what you're wearing."

Griffin sat awkwardly in one of the empty chairs kept for guests. Maggie turned and spoke very nicely to him, trying to put him at ease. The young man seemed somewhat lacking in social graces and small talk. Not even Maggie could penetrate his nervousness.

Around him, the conversation about the village dance swelled up again. It seemed to have been a success, judging from the reports of those who had attended. But all at once, the talking and laughter stopped. I half-rose from my chair, a name on my lips.

The door had opened and Genevieve walked into the room. She was closely followed by Jean, but all eyes were on her. She wore a deceptively simple blue gown and her hair was swept up. She looked gorgeous. The men in the room were staring openly, even though most of them had seen her before.

I rose to greet her, being the first to recover my wits. "Genevieve," I said as I kissed her.

"Gideon, *mon fils.*" She hugged me so hard, I knew something was wrong. "It is so good to see you. Introduce me, please?"

I introduced her to the members that she didn't know, and she greeted the ones she did politely but gravely. Jean was not meeting my eyes at all, and I knew that was not a good sign.

"My dear." She squeezed my hands. "I had to come to you the moment that I knew."

"Knew what?" But I already guessed. In more than a century, Genevieve had never visited the Brotherhood's sanctuary in Maine. Only one thing could have brought her here so precipitously, without even a telephone call beforehand.

She confirmed my worst fears. "Corbeau is coming for you."

The room was absolutely silent. Of all the faces at the table, my eyes sought Griffin's, and he raised his eyebrows resignedly.

Now we both understood what he had sensed the night before. "How soon?" My voice didn't sound like my own.

"I do not know for sure," Genevieve said, "but within two days, without doubt. He has squandered his fortune over the years, and cannot travel as rapidly as I have done. Les Gardiens have been trailing him closely for some time. They are certain of his intentions—he is coming now."

Before I could speak, Evan's hand slapped the table, not loudly, but as decisively as a judge's gavel. "Then he walks into a trap. This will be the last mistake he ever makes."

"That is my hope," Genevieve said. "I am determined that he shall meet the true death. He has chosen the time and place." Her blue eyes glittered like the fire in a diamond.

I sank slowly into my chair. "This is Etienne Corbeau, not a coven of witches."

"One vampire," Michael said quietly, "against the Brotherhood of Darkness. You're not facing him alone, Gideon. No matter what he may have heard, he won't be prepared for what he'll find." He looked around the table. Francis and Mitch wore serious but puzzled expressions, but the others nodded grimly at the Archdruid. If Corbeau had seen the looks in their eyes at that moment, even he would have quailed.

"We'll need to make plans," I said, and suddenly everyone was talking at once.

For the next several hours, we discussed and rejected strategies. Unlike the evening when we had plotted our attack on the cannery, I felt no excitement. For our ploy to work, everyone would have to cooperate smoothly. But most of all, I would have to face and defy my old master. It was the confrontation I had dreaded for more than two centuries.

Our formal dinner became an impromptu supper as we talked and argued, then scattered around the house to make arrangements and put weapons and other elements of the plan into position. At last, the house and the Brotherhood were as ready as possible. Most of the guests went back to their own homes. It would make Corbeau suspicious to see several cars or sense too many presences around Oakwoods. Tomorrow, the Brotherhood would return on foot, as stealthily as possible.

Dawn was approaching, and I accompanied Genevieve and Jean to the guest room I had offered them. Evan and Mitch, yawning, followed with their few pieces of luggage. They had obviously left France in great haste. But before I bid them good day, there was something I needed to ask Genevieve.

"I don't understand. Why now? He's left me alone for all these years. I hoped he had forgotten me, or found some new play-mates to amuse him. What made him decide to come for me after all this time?"

"I do not know." Genevieve's voice was sober. "The last time, it was because you had found a new lover, but I sense this is not the case now?"

"No, there's no one. Although I have been thinking about it quite a bit."

"And it is about time," she said with a sniff, and I thought I saw Jean grin for a second.

"I wouldn't dare to take a new lover as long as Corbeau is still my master."

"This time, we will kill him," Jean said.

"And there will be nothing left of him but ashes, if I have to burn myself to achieve it," Genevieve said harshly. "We want no accidental resurrections."

I shuddered. "I should think not."

My dearest friend hugged me. "Be brave, *cheri,*" she whispered. "I would rather meet the true death myself than let any harm come to you, *mon fils.*"

I hugged her back, breathing in the scent of freesia. "You've changed your perfume, *Maman.*"

She chuckled and released me. "I think you will stand up well to this test, Gideon. You have already dared much."

"I couldn't dare this test without the help of my friends."

"You have loyal friends. And strange employees." She laughed at Evan, who grinned back and winked. She turned to Mitch. "I have not met many werewolves, and it is always a pleasure."

Mitch, who had been uncharacteristically subdued since Genevieve's arrival, brightened up instantly. "Gideon talks about you a lot. I'm really glad to meet you finally." They gravely shook hands.

When I went to bed at sunrise that morning, I prayed for the first time in over three hundred years. Whether I petitioned the Puritans' God or Michael's Goddess I could not say, but in either case, I heard no answer.

When I arose at dusk, I had no doubt that Corbeau would come that night. The wind outside stank of blood and warnings.

Genevieve, Jean, my two housemates and I were in the living room, with its willow-patterned wallpaper, mosaic fireplace and the portrait of Jonathan that dominated the room. I didn't give the portrait so much as a glance, fearing to lose my resolve.

We had agreed that the three Druids, Alexander, Francis and Ray Griffin would return separately and hide at a discreet distance while we waited for Corbeau to arrive. He would know Genevieve and Jean were with me, but that would only serve as a further spur to him. He was arrogant enough to dismiss Evan and Mitch as mere servants. Genevieve didn't think that my master had ever met Evan's kind. The Nameless Ones despised him.

I was wearing down the nap of the Aubusson carpet in front of the fireplace. I passed Genevieve without even seeing her, and she reached out to halt my pacing.

"Gideon, sit," she said, much as one would speak to a dog. I sat stiffly in my favourite wing chair, my fingers pulling at the stitching where the arm was sewn shut.

The atmosphere of the house, which hitherto had been one of waiting, seemed to draw itself together and stand, hushed and fearful, on tiptoe. The fire flickered in the hearth, and I heard Warg begin growling. Mitch got up without a sound and grabbed the wolf by the thick ruff of fur around his neck.

"Time to put you in the basement." Mitch's own voice resembled the wolf's growl more than a human sound. His eyes had turned amber and glowed in the firelight.

Evan rose, so focused that he flowed out of his seat, his hazel eyes narrowed. He began methodically checking his store of weapons and the various other things we had laid out.

I got up again, barely noticing that I did so. No one stopped me, but all watched me carefully. The sharp click of a crossbow being drawn back diverted my attention to Evan. He nodded when I caught his eye, and looked down at the deadly quarrel. "Ash wood." Involuntarily, Genevieve and I both shuddered, as if he'd mentioned poison.

A caressing and irresistably magnetic voice entered my head, compelling me to come to the door of the house. I obeyed, even though I knew who summoned me.

"Be strong," Genevieve called after me.

They were easy words to say. Thoughts of my friends, the Brotherhood, steeled me. I did what I had to do. I opened the front door.

"Hello, Gideon," said Corbeau casually.

I stood still, not reacting. I don't know why I'd expected him to have changed in some way. He leaned confidently against the door jamb, his white teeth flashing at me and his blue eyes points of ice. His black hair, like raven's feathers, ruffled slightly in the breeze. He was still beautiful. His voice scalded with derision.

"Well? Aren't you going to invite me in?"

There was no need, as he could enter my home, or any vampire's home, without an invitation. Only the houses of living mortals were barred to us. He'd proven that in England, when he had raped me.

"Come in," I said.

He brushed past me with a smile, bringing the tang of the sea with him. Sea salt was encrusted on his leather clothes, and I wondered when he had started dressing in such garments. Knowing him, he'd likely been hunting in an establishment that catered to those with such tastes. He liked to go for easy prey before taking on a challenge, to whet his appetite.

"You've changed." He sneered as he reached out to touch my temple. I stiffened in anticipation of his icy fingers on my face. "Grey hair? At nineteen?" He taunted the illusion I'd willed to age my appearance. Without waiting for an answer, he grabbed me by the neck and shook me. "Who else is in this house?"

Calm and dignified, Genevieve said, "I am."

Corbeau flung me away from him, and I made a rapid acquaintance with the hall carpet.

"Genevieve," Corbeau said. "How very nice to see you again. What a pleasant surprise, my dear." The sarcasm made me wince. He began walking towards her. "Come for a visit?"

"I have some house cleaning to finish," she said, stepping back from him.

It may have looked to him as if she was afraid, but she was luring him into the living room, where the trap was set and waiting. I rose quietly to my feet, so as not to distract him. Despite my fall to the floor, I was calm. I had already won a large part of the battle. I had faced my master, my nightmare, and I was not afraid.

"House cleaning?" His voice growled, but he was lured by her ruse like a toy on a string. He was following her right to where she wanted him. Noiseless and unnoticed, I shadowed his steps towards Genevieve.

"Yes. This house is infested with vermin."

He bowed mockingly. "You belittle yourself, my dove."

Her eyes blazed. "You killed my husband!"

My own emotions were racing, as I found myself less and less under the hypnotic influence of my master. Was I truly breaking free? It seemed incredible.

"Both husbands, I believe." Corbeau smiled cruelly.

Genevieve stiffened. "Gaspard was no threat to you. At least Claude faced you as an equal, but Gaspard's murder was needless." She continued to slowly move backwards as she spoke.

"He was in my way."

"It was the act of a coward, Corbeau. You torment the helpless and flee from any true fight. You have always been a coward."

Corbeau lunged at her, but she side-stepped him neatly. His momentum took him to the center of the living room before he saw Jean and Mitch in battle-ready attitude. I looked around for Evan, and spotted him behind a chair, with his crossbow pointed at Corbeau's heart. Corbeau's face twisted. "What is this?"

"This," I said, "is the last place you'll ever see."

"Silence, slave!" He turned on me, his eyes glowing and his fangs sliding out of his gums. His taloned hands once more grabbed for my throat, but I reached up and blocked his arm. "How *dare* you..."

"I dare," I said, and laughed. I had never laughed at him before, and it was liberating. Corbeau, reacting to my laughter, failed to notice that the rest of the Brotherhood had entered the room like ghosts and were putting the pieces of the trap into place.

"You think you can defy me?" Corbeau was looking at me as if he'd never seen me before. "You're laughing at me. It's time to teach you another lesson." He jerked his head at Genevieve without looking at her. "Kill her."

I actually took a step towards her, for one second intending to carry out this command. Then I stopped in horror, realizing what he had told me to do.

Kill Genevieve? Harm my mentor—my mother?

I spat in his face. Both of us recoiled in surprise, and he backhanded me before I could move out of the way. I fell to the floor, and he whipped around to face Genevieve. But the sight of several people who had not been in the room a moment earlier stopped him in his tracks.

Genevieve stood, smiling slightly, not bothering to show her fangs. She was composed, as beautiful and cool as a sculpture, while her opponent was a slavering beast. "Get back. You may not touch me, or Gideon, or any of those here."

Corbeau looked around him in a fury, and tried to move towards me. He found his path blocked by fresh roses, their heady scent perfuming the air. Interspersed with the roses were twigs of ash and thorn. He stopped, eyes blazing impotent hatred at everyone in the room, but especially at the Druids. They had scattered the barrier on the floor.

He was old, and had many of the old beliefs. He still slept in a dirt-filled coffin. He cringed away from holy symbols. Roses and thorns were ancient ways of obstructing a vampire's progress, and the wood of the ash tree is poison to us. He believed. He could not cross the barrier.

"Bound by your own foolishness," Genevieve said. "A rose is only a flower. But this…" she raised her hand. She was carrying a sharpened wooden stake. "…this is death."

"Gideon," I heard Evan whisper. I turned and saw him crouching below Corbeau's eye level. I accepted the stake he handed me. "Use it well," he said.

"If I fail, use the crossbow bolt on me." I didn't think I would survive if I failed, and the crossbow would be a cleaner death than anything Corbeau would do to me. Evan didn't argue.

Corbeau's hesitation broke and he lunged at Genevieve, but drew up short at the barrier. I walked up to it, and calmly stepped over it. Corbeau's mouth opened, and he staggered back, stunned that the trap had no power over me. Neither did Corbeau—not any longer. The others in the room were smiling, or looking surprised, according to their natures, as it became evident that I had finally been liberated from my master's influence. Genevieve's face was full of love and pride, almost hurtful to see. Ray Griffin gave me a brief nod and a smile that was almost compassionate, and I remembered that he had slain his master. Then I forgot everything except Corbeau. "Face me," I said.

Corbeau turned, his talons ripping across my cheek. "Put that down."

I looked at him. Nothing of what I had once loved remained. His voice no longer mesmerized. Even a direct command provoked no response in me. I was free. I wanted to laugh. I wanted very badly to do what I did.

I raised the ash wood stake and drove it through his heart. As I did so, memories came flooding into my mind, even as the blood came flooding out of the wound on my master's chest. As he screamed and pawed frantically at the stake, I was remembering the past: a young man, barely more than a boy, who only wanted to be loved, and a handsome, mesmerizing stranger who had at first supplied that love, and then betrayed it. I had loved him.

It had taken a long time for him to kill that. Even when he had put me in chains and beaten me, I had loved him. When he had given me to his twisted lieutenant, Graydon, who liked things that whimpered in pain, I had still loved him. What had made me quake in fear was not the thought of another session with the whip or worse implements, but the agonizing notion that he might leave me. That was what had finally burned away my love for him, cauterized the ancient wound—that he had abandoned me.

Genevieve, Jonathan, the Brotherhood: these were all loves more precious by far than whatever I had felt for Corbeau. But he had been the first, and his betrayal hurt.

The echo of that pain still resounded in my heart. When I had awakened in that buried coffin and realised what he'd done, it had broken me. Evan had pulled me out of my prison, but he had not rescued me whole. My love for Corbeau had been left in that lonely grave in France. Without it, I was crippled and it had taken more than a century before I found healing with Jonathan. Whatever agony Corbeau felt now, he had earned.

He screamed again, and I blinked, recalled to my present surroundings. The danger was far from over. He was reaching for me, one taloned hand scrabbling for my face while the other continued to worry at the stake like a dog with a burr. His eyes were pleading, begging me to help him. It was an expression I had never seen in them before, and it disturbed me. He seemed to be trying to remind me of the love I had borne for him.

Genevieve had watched me drive the stake into my master. She looked down at the stake in her own hand. With an air of at last putting paid to an old debt, she advanced across the barrier and drove her stake into her enemy's back, severing his spine.

More blood spurted across the floor. Corbeau must have fed well before arriving at Oakwoods, and I could only hope that he had not preyed on the citizens of Fletcherville.

He dropped to his knees, his crimson-tinged eyes rolling back to look at Genevieve. "You bitch," he spat, blood spraying out as he spoke. His eyes reflected horror and disbelief that this could be happening to him. His own egotism had betrayed him. He was not invincible. The shock must have been a worse blow than the two stakes.

Genevieve stepped back, as did I, both of us disturbed that he could still control his own body so well with two ash stakes in vital areas. He was an incredibly old and powerful vampire.

Those horrible eyes, the dark light in them dimming far too slowly, came back to rest on me. "Gideon," he whispered, the power still vibrating in his voice. "Come to me, young lord. Come and pull these stakes out."

I was able to resist the plea in those eyes, recalling all the times I'd begged him to stop the pain. I turned my back on him. Looking down at my hands, I realized I was shaking with delayed reaction. I was free! That voice, those eyes, no longer commanded my obedience. Relief overwhelmed me, shuddering through my system.

"Gideon!" Corbeau was imploring now. No doubt there were tears in those eyes. I refused to look.

Evan's crossbow bolt took him through the throat, rendering him mercifully silent. I dared to look back, and saw him begin dragging his paralyzed body across the floor towards me, like a grotesque snake. Three stakes now transfixed this evil mirror of Saint Sebastian.

Mitch, carefree sarcastic Mitch, made the move none of the rest of us seemed to consider. I hadn't seen him leave the room, but he must have done so when he realized that one stake was not going to be effective. He came running in from the direction of the dining room, brandishing the firewood axe. It took three blows, and even after the head was severed, the body continued to crawl for a few wrenching moments. Maggie had turned distinctly green by the time it stopped moving. Mitch looked appalled at what he had done, and started to cry. He collapsed slowly to the floor. Michael, startled out of immobility, moved to his side. Evan also went to Mitch's aid and the two of them picked the young man up and carried him out of the room to treat him for shock. Maggie excused herself and followed.

The others stirred, then, shaking off the transfixed state of shock and horror that had held them in place. Griffin looked at the mess on the floor and shook his head, as if it offended his professional sensibilities. Alexander came to my side, slowly, as if approaching a dangerous animal, and looked at me questioningly. I was too stunned to do more than give him a small smile, which didn't seem to reassure him. Nicholas was humming softly, likely not even knowing that he was doing it. Jean was holding Genevieve, comforting her or seeking comfort—it was hard to tell which.

Francis gingerly touched the severed head with his boot toe. "Yuck. Was it this bad when you killed Matthew, Ray?"

The sorcerer shook his head. "Matthew was messy, but not like this. Our fight was mostly magical."

"For all our sakes," said Genevieve sharply, "don't reunite the body with the head, or let it get too much blood in its mouth."

Evan returned, bringing cleaning supplies that he left in one corner until it was decided how best to handle the remains.

"Surely the danger is past?" Nicholas asked.

"I do not trust him, even now," Genevieve said. "We must burn the body and scatter the ashes, widely."

Part of the preparations had included building a bier out on the promontory of the cliff. Alexander and Francis carried out the body, and I very cautiously carried the head. I held it at arm's length, by the hair, so that I couldn't see the wide-staring eyes, after one stomach-wrenching glance into them by accident. The blood had drained from them, leaving them a dull blue that was by far warmer than their colour had ever been while Corbeau lived. Taking the head from my hands before it was put on its final resting place, Michael stuffed garlic and ash twigs into the mouth and quickly sewed it shut. We laid the pieces well apart on the pyre, and covered them both with roses and thorns. The wood pile had been soaked with gasoline.

We all stood in silence around the pyre for a moment, unable to believe that our enemy had been defeated. Blood soaked my suit, Genevieve's dress, and Mitch's sweatshirt and blue jeans. Blood had lightly sprayed all those who had been close to the slaughter scene. Mitch was rubbing at his shirt with his elbow, as if trying to rid himself of the stain. His eyes were still amber, glowing ferally in the darkness. Genevieve didn't seem to care about her ruined designer gown, although Jean was dabbing at her cheek with his handkerchief, playing the gallant even now. Michael, Maggie and Mitch had rejoined us, so that everyone could watch the burning. Evan passed out torches made from wood sticks topped with thickly-wrapped gasoline-drenched paper. His harsh features solemn, Ray Griffin lit his torch with his cigarette lighter. We passed the flame from torch to torch until a small semi-circle of smoky light enclosed the cliff side of the pyre. With one accord, we tossed the burning brands into the pile of wood.

By the time the flames died and nothing was left but ashes, I was feeling the emotional backlash of the night's events. I tore my gaze away as Evan began, gingerly, to rake the ashes and check that no small fires had started in the scrubby brush that eked a living out of the cliff. The hot smell of burnt vampire flesh hung over the still-smoking coals.

I'd been watching Corbeau burn, and hadn't once glanced at anyone else. Now that I was finally able to look away from the mesmerizing flames, I saw that Mitch was sitting on a rock near the edge, his head in his hands. Michael was scattering fresh roses onto the ashes as Evan raked them into a pile. Nicholas and Maggie were talking softly with Genevieve, and all three of them kept shooting surreptitious glances in my direction. Alexander, Francis and Ray Griffin also appeared to be deep in a discussion, but at least they weren't staring at me. Jean was walking the perimeters of the fire, looking for stray embers. Occasionally he would stop and point out a spot to Evan.

I swallowed, suddenly in need of a drink. Blood, brandy, beer—it wouldn't have mattered what at that moment

He was gone. The ashes would be scattered, with roses, garlic and thorns, at sea. There would be no accidental resurrections. The True Death had finally claimed Etienne Corbeau—or whoever he had been, long ago, when he was young and innocent and a vampire had come to him, promising power and eternal life.

Evan had succeeded in gathering all the ashes, and the Druids had made certain that these remains were well-seeded with roses, thorns and garlic buds. I felt all the eyes of the assembled company turn on me, but no one spoke.

As one, the Brotherhood walked to the head of the treacherous set of stairs that had been carved out of the side of the cliff. We began a shaky descent, made all the more perilous by frost and sea foam. Cold, wet wind assailed us. I heard Ray Griffin mutter under his breath behind me, and a moment later the wind stopped.

"That's dangerous, you know," Michael said calmly. "Tampering with nature."

I could almost hear the sorcerer grin. "Lots of things are dangerous, Michael."

Down we went. Alexander was helping Maggie to climb down, and she was accepting his assistance without a word of sarcasm for his chauvinism. They were very steep, slippery stairs. Nicholas was humming again, and I wondered how he could spare the lung power. It was a tune that seemed to encourage weary, tentative feet to find surer grips and to go down just one more step towards the bottom.

Then we were there, soaked with the foam, salt crusting on our skin, inhaling the smell of fish. It was a relief after the smell of burning vampire.

Evan handed the oilcloth sack that held the still-warm ashes to me. "You first. It is your right."

I took the bag, and bowed my head over it. "For your betrayal," I said, and took a handful of the contents and tossed them out, over the rocks, into the water. They hissed slightly, then sank out of sight.

Genevieve took the bag from my shaking hands and hugged me briefly. "For Claude," she spat at the oilcoth. "And for Gaspard." She, too, hurled some of the ashes at the Atlantic, which swallowed them.

Everyone took turns, all being very careful not to prick fingers on the thorns and shed blood onto the ashes. Finally, it was over. Mitch was shivering in his wet and still-bloody clothes, and nearly everyone else looked rather ill.

"Dawn comes," Genevieve said, sensing the rising glow in the east. "It comes quickly here. Let us return to the house at once."

"At once," meant something slightly different to the vampires than the rest of the Brotherhood, but even Maggie was not that far behind us.

Chapter Thirteen

As Mitch parked the Cadillac, the driver of the Volvo emerged from his own vehicle. From a distance I could only observe that he was taller than I but shorter than Mitch and warmly dressed against the chill November night. I got out of the car and walked up to greet him. Close proximity revealed him to be lean and handsome, perhaps in his late thirties, with neatly trimmed sandy hair and warm brown eyes. His long blue coat and the grey suit under it were of good quality and business-like cut, but he also had a jaunty red scarf wrapped around his neck.

"Mr. Redoak?" His voice was clear and pleasant. "I'm Joshua Trevallion."

We shook hands. "It's very good of you to make an evening appointment for me. This is Mitch Pritchard, my assistant."

"I'm pleased to meet you." Trevallion shook Mitch's hand, and turned back to me. "I don't work typical business hours, Mr. Redoak. I'm honoured to be called for an opinion. Shall we go in?"

We went into the shop. I noticed Trevallion pause just inside the door and inhale. He smiled slightly when he caught me looking at him, but offered no explanation for his behaviour. All I could smell was old wood, aging varnish, and dust.

The reason I'd requested our meeting stood before us. A lovely little Chippendale table...or was it? I had spotted it in this shop earlier, and asked my acquaintances in Boston to recommend an antiques expert who could appraise it. I was given Trevallion's number and he agreed to examine the table.

The shop owner bustled forward to meet us, and I saw the anticipation of a sale light his eyes. The light was abruptly extinguished when Joshua Trevallion introduced himself.

"I assure you..."

"Assure me all you want," Trevallion said evenly. "I would like to see the table in question."

The other man seemed to deflate. Mitch snickered, and I shot him a reproving look. This outing represented a promotion of sorts for Mitch—Evan, with some misgivings, had stayed at home while Mitch took on the role of my chauffeur and bodyguard. Abashed, he went in search of the store's friendly cat, and Joshua and I went to look at the table.

Trevallion examined it thoroughly. He got down on his knees and looked up at the base from underneath, using a flashlight. He took out a measuring tape and held it against various parts of the table, shaking his head and muttering to himself. It was quite an interesting process to watch, and I had to admit that he looked rather appealing when he was down on his knees. I quickly suppressed that stray thought.

At one point, he actually produced a magnifying glass and studied some detail or other with it. The owner of Everything Old Antiques stood to one side, hands in his pockets, staring glumly at these proceedings. I also stood to one side, so as not to block the expert's light.

The careful way in which he worked impressed me very much. I've always appreciated true professionals and the way they approach their tasks.

Finally, Trevallion stood up. He brushed off his knees and put the tools of his trade back into their respective pockets. His face was set in a grave expression. "Mr. Redoak, you were right to be dubious of this table's authenticity."

Mitch appeared from behind a pine wardrobe, the cat at his heels. "You mean it's a fake?"

"It's a very faithful reproduction," Trevallion said. Then he smiled, and winked at Mitch. "In other words, if it's being sold as genuine and not a reproduction, it's a fake. If a Chippendale had anything to do with this table, he strips clothes, not furniture."

Mitch snorted. The shop owner was trying very hard to hide behind a large, hideous blue and green ceramic vase. Joshua Trevallion fixed him with a look that showed there was steel under the gentle warmth I had already noticed.

"Mr. Robins," he addressed the sorry creature, "I suggest that you either re-label this piece or remove it from your shop. I'll be reporting you to the Better Business Bureau and the Art and Antique Dealers League of America. Good night, sir." He turned and left the store. Mitch and I followed closely behind.

"Thank you, Mr. Trevallion," I said when we were at his car. "You saved me from making an expensive mistake."

"Believe me, it's my pleasure to expose frauds and forgers."

"May I compensate you for your time and trouble?"

He hesitated, and then glanced at his watch. "There was very little of my time involved. I'll settle for your promise to pass along a recommendation to your friends." He dug into his wallet and handed me several business cards.

"Of course." I gave him my own card.

"If you need an appraisal done again, I hope you'll call me. I also buy antiques for clients who trust my taste."

"It is a pity about that table, I would have liked a mate to the one I have."

Instant enthusiasm lit up his face. "You already own a Chippendale?" He seemed to realize that this was an obvious question, and went on, "I mean that good Chippendales are scarce. I know very few people who own one."

Mitch laughed. "There's not a stick of new furniture in the house."

I gave Mitch a sidelong look. "I own several fine pieces, including the table."

"Boss," Mitch said, "If you're going to talk furniture, can we go somewhere warm?"

I had forgotten that Mitch, despite his were blood, and Trevallion would both be feeling the cold. There was a small café just down the street, and we retired to its shabby warmth to continue our conversation. Mitch, who was driving, almost dove into his generous mug of hot chocolate, and apparently tuned out what Trevallion and I were saying.

"If you're interested in seeing my collection, perhaps you would like to come for dinner?" I liked this quiet, self-assured man already, and didn't want him to simply fade into the tapestry of those I met and never saw again. His eyes were so warm.

"That's very kind of you..." I could almost hear the "But..." forming behind his words.

I forestalled him. "It's worth the trip, and I should like to repay you for this evening in some way, if you won't take more ordinary payment."

"Thank you, then." He smiled. "I accept."

His eyes met mine, and for a moment I saw a half-interested, half-puzzled look in them. He broke eye contact, but not before I could have sworn I saw a faint blush tinge his cheeks.

I gave him directions on how to find Fletcherville and Oakwoods, and we agreed that he would come the evening after next. That settled, I rescued Mitch from drowning in a third cup of cocoa, and we walked Trevallion back to his car, then returned to our hotel.

Mitch and I drove back to Oakwoods the following night. Evan met us at the door, subjecting us both to careful scrutiny. Warg barged out the door, jumping up on Mitch. Evan shooed him off, then reached out and ruffled Mitch's hair.

"Well done, little thief."

"Don't do that!" Mitch said. "And don't call me that, either."

"It's what you are," Evan said, throwing his arm around the young were's neck. He looked over at me. "Did he behave well, or should I thrash him for you?"

"Let him loose, Evan," I sighed. "He behaved very well. I'm quite pleased with him."

Mitch broke free of Evan's grasp and tried not to show how flattered he was to hear those words. But the way he straightened up, squared his shoulders, and blushed gave him away.

"Boss," he said, then ducked as Evan swung a hand at him. "I mean, sir, shouldn't you tell Evan about our guest?"

"'Guest'?" Evan said. He'd started down the steps to retrieve the luggage from the car, but stopped on the third step.

"Yes, of course," I said to Mitch, then turned to Evan. "A Mr. Joshua Trevallion will be joining us for dinner tomorrow evening. If you would make the necessary arrangements, I would appreciate it very much."

"No problem," Evan said. "Lobster okay?"

"I believe so." I turned to go into the house, but not before I caught the look that passed between my housemates. I knew that the moment I was safely out of earshot, Evan would quiz Mitch severely about the dinner guest. There was nothing for Mitch to say, beyond the obvious. I was repaying a favour, nothing more.

Had I really seen a look of interest in Joshua's warm brown eyes? They were such unusual eyes, the colour of dark butterscotch...no, such speculations were foolish. I barely knew the man. I felt that we could easily become friends, and friendship was rare enough in itself.

Still, he had blushed after holding eye contact...no, that was merely a typical human's discomfort with being caught looking someone else in the eyes. Ah, this line of thought was foolish!

I walked through my big, empty house looking for comfort. Whatever had possessed me to build a mansion up here on the cliff? Oakwoods was far too large for a lonely bachelor and his two housemates, even with a timber wolf. It was full of beautiful things, but at the moment none of them appealed to me. I paused before the graceful Chippendale table, whose pale imitation had allowed me to meet Joshua Trevallion.

Jonathan had liked that table, too.

Almost guiltily, I cast a glance at the portrait of my long-dead lover that hung above the living room fireplace.

The living room was also where Corbeau had died. The carpet had been replaced and all traces of that night obliterated, except in the memories of those who had been there.

I went out to the cliff. Warg followed me, happy to see all his people back, but it was so cold and windy that he soon left me to return to the warm fireside. It was snowing again, but the wind was so wild that very little accumulated on the cliff top. There was none at all covering the greasy black spot where we had burned the body of Etienne Corbeau.

Unsatisfied and lonely, I went back inside. What else was there for me to do? My brief trip to Boston had not cured the despair that had settled on me, after all. The small hope that had kindled when Joshua had smiled and blushed was too faint and nebulous a thing to even be acknowledged, let alone nurtured. I didn't even know if his tastes were the same as mine. There could have been several explanations for that blush. Tomorrow night, I would greet him as merely a potential friend.

I arose the next evening in a good mood, looking forward to entertaining my guest. Scrubbed and groomed, I went back into the bedroom and dressed in my best suit and a striped tie. For the first time in years, I had trouble with the knot. I couldn't seem to make my fingers cooperate.

After winning the battle with the tie, I went downstairs, my feet lighter on the treads than they usually were. I saw Mitch come around the corner with Warg, both shaggy heads cocked to see who had come down the stairs with such an unfamiliar gait.

"You look good," he said, grinning at me. "We spent the whole day cleaning the house, what do you think?"

I took a walk around the first floor of Oakwoods. The furniture, paneling and doorknobs all gleamed. Not a speck of dust had been allowed to linger on any surface that I could see. "It looks wonderful. Thank you both."

"Come see the dining room."

The table had been set with our finest linen, china and cutlery. Glowing candelabra held white tapers that only awaited the touch of a match. A bottle of wine cooled in the bucket of ice beside my place.

With some difficulty, I said, "Thank you, you and Evan have gone to a lot of trouble. We're not entertaining royalty, after all."

Mitch hid a smile as I turned and walked unseeing right into the table, jarring the careful arrangements.

"A baron is royalty," he said.

"Please." I held up my hand. "Don't use my title tonight." I backed away from the table, only to bump into the sideboard.

Mitch was grinning openly by this point. "Better come and sit in the living room, before you wreck the table."

At last I heard the sound of a car, its tires crunching on the driveway gravel. I stood up as Mitch went to the door, hissing at him to straighten his jacket and tie. He ignored me and hurried to let Joshua in. I heard them bantering in the hall about the condition of the road and the length of the drive as Mitch took Joshua's coat. I still didn't feel quite ready when Mitch ushered our guest into the living room.

The tall, handsome furniture expert greeted me with a warm, friendly smile and a quick handshake. He seemed fully at ease and genuinely happy to be welcomed into our household. Suddenly, I was no longer nervous.

The evening flew by like a dream. Joshua complimented the house, and was quiet and attentive when I conducted him through the rooms. He asked intelligent questions about the history of Oakwoods and some of the pieces I showed him. He praised the cooking and the choice of wine, and didn't seem to notice my lack of appetite.

I did catch him giving me an occasional puzzled glance, however, and he was embarrassed to be caught. I wondered what he was thinking, but his facial expression gave me very few clues as to what, exactly, was puzzling him. Did he sense something different about me?

Did he find me as attractive as I found him?

The conversation at dinner flowed easily. Joshua had traveled around the world many times, and could weave exciting and amusing stories from his adventures. He was as much at ease discussing sports as he was speaking of furniture or the antique trade. He revealed very little of his own background, however, and I noticed that he didn't inquire too closely about the personal histories of me and my housemates. He and Evan fell into a discussion about cooking, and I could see that my protector was impressed by Joshua's knowledge of this subject. Evan was in high cycle at the time, and intensely interested in anything related to food, but it was a hopeful sign that he took to Joshua. I knew Mitch already liked him.

When the meal was over, Joshua and I retired to the living room for brandy while Evan and Mitch cleared away. I invited him to smoke if he wished. He smiled and said that he had never picked up the habit.

"This is excellent brandy." He set down his empty snifter. "But by now, I wouldn't expect anything else."

"Thank you."

He rose and came over to my chair. "Gideon Redoak..."

"Yes?"

"Tell me you didn't invite me all the way out to some god-forsaken cliff in Maine to look at furniture and drink good brandy."

"I..."

He leaned down and kissed me. It tasted of brandy and hope. I returned the kiss, with interest.

"I..." That was as far as I seemed able to get. Our eyes met, but I had to look away from him after a second. Joshua burst out laughing.

"You're shy," he said, "and wary. I should warn you, I'm a persistent hunter when there's something I want. But right now, I'd better get on the road. I've got to catch a plane out of Logan tomorrow. I'll call you when I get back from my buying trip to Europe. Goodnight, Gideon."

I walked him to the door, mostly feeling grateful that he hadn't pushed. I wasn't ready for a new relationship, or so I told myself. So why did I also feel vaguely disappointed?

A week or so passed by with its normal routine, and I once more grew restless in Oakwoods. The house seemed to echo my loneliness. It needed the presence of a soft-spoken expert in antique furniture to make it complete. These thoughts were going to drive me mad. I needed to get away from the house and its memories for longer than a few days. Where to go, however? Boston had not been nearly enough of a diversion, even though I had met Joshua there.

As I sat pondering whether to go and open the house in London, the telephone rang. Hoping to hear Joshua's voice, I answered it myself. The sound of Alexander's familiar doleful tones brought me back to reality quickly.

"How'd you like to go to Venice?"

Alexander had applied the lessons on business investing he learned from me and Genevieve to great effect, amassing a fortune that was frequently boosted by his indecent luck at gambling. His villa, La Casa di Fontani, occupied a small private island just outside of Venice. It was a beautiful spot, full of gardens and a multitude of fountains, and I accepted his invitation with a sense of relief.

"I thought you needed a vacation," Alexander said to me as we walked along the Grand Canal by the Piazza San Marco. "I need to do some business here, but more than that, I needed to get away and I thought you did, too. That's why I asked you to come."

"I'm very grateful to you. But why did you think I needed a vacation?"

"Well—after what happened—"

I turned my head away. As much as I tried not to react to any reference to Corbeau's death, I still flinched every time someone mentioned it.

"Gideon..." Alexander reached out, but allowed his hand to falter and drop before he touched me. "I can't deal with you this way. You've always been the strong unemotional one who tells me to snap out of it when I'm in one of my moods. I'm sorry I mentioned that night. Please forgive me, and try to remember that we're here to have a good time."

"Of course I forgive you. But I can't absolutely promise that I'll have a good time. I'll do my best."

We were just opposite one of the many sidewalk cafés that accumulate in the piazzas like leaves in autumn. There were quite a few people at the tables, for it was a lovely evening. Several beautiful young ladies were among the customers.

"Now there is the reason I came to Venice," said Alexander with a smile. "To admire the works of art."

There were also attractive men in the crowd, not a few of whom I recognized as sharing my sexual preference. The overtly homosexual type didn't appeal to me, but I felt no attraction even for those whose signals were far more subtle. I realized that I was looking for only one face, with sandy hair and butterscotch-coloured eyes. I shook my head violently to rid it of this vision. "I prefer the buildings."

"You would."

That night, we went to the Casino Municipal. I couldn't help comparing this excursion with my first introduction to the world of gambling, so many years ago in France.

"Why are you smiling?" Alexander asked suspiciously.

I shook my head. He would never understand.

There were far more women in the casino than would have been common or allowed in the previous century. The older ones wearing deceptively expensive gowns tended to be serious gamblers. Those who boasted younger faces and more daring necklines often had other objectives. One of the latter spotted

Alexander and me and liked what she saw—half of what she saw, anyway. Her carefully practiced welcoming smile at Alexander led to a calculating frown at me.

I had no reason to stand in her way. "I see a clear table over there," I said, pointing to a route that would take us right past the woman.

As Alexander strode past her table, the woman, with an awkward arm gesture, swept her beaded evening bag off her table. I controlled the impulse to pick it up myself, and let Alexander have the pleasure.

"You dropped this," he said with a little bow.

"How clumsy of me." She smiled invitingly at him. She took lipstick and a compact from the bag, and fixed an already perfect face. She caught me watching this procedure and gave me another one of those frowns. Now I was not only "gay best friend," I was "annoying gay best friend." Alexander, whose eyes had been following every stroke of the lipstick and powder puff as though entranced, remained oblivious to our little subtext. He finally remembered to say something.

"Hello, I'm Alex Goldanias."

She held out her hand. "And I'm Brier Snow."

"And I'm apparently extraneous," I said under my breath. "Gideon Redoak." Miss Snow couldn't have cared less had I said "Prince Charles." I added to no one who was listening, "I'm going to get a drink."

There was a bar in the mezzanine from which one could look down on the scene below. One end seemed reserved for those like me—the non-gambling, skeptical single—and the other end was monopolized by courting couples. I glanced over the railings to see if I could spot Alexander and Brier. He was already sitting at her table, holding her hands and speaking to her earnestly.

"I'd love to surprise you by saying 'I bet that tall, dark-haired lout is your friend', but the truth is I saw you come in together."

I turned my head. "Joshua? Whatever are you doing in Venice?"

"I'm on a buying trip for a client. What on earth are you doing here?"

"I came for a vacation with Alexander. And he's not a lout—at least most of the time."

"I'll bet you five bucks American he asks her to come over to the table of whatever game he prefers and has her blow on his dice or cards for luck," Joshua said.

"Cards. And no bet, it's too much of a sure thing."

Within minutes, Alexander was at the baccarat table, with Brier behind him to blow on his cards.

"Where are you and Mr. Smooth staying in Venice?" Joshua asked me.

"At his villa, La Casa di Fontani."

My companion let out a surprised whistle. "I could retire to the Caribbean on the auction of the contents of that place. Must be nice. Still, he's a pretty poor host to desert his guest at the first drop of a clutch."

"Really, I don't mind. Better he finds a pretty girl to spend the night with than spend it trying to understand me. It's quite painful to watch."

Joshua laughed, and we chatted some more while watching the baccarat table. Alexander lost three games in a row, which made him give up gambling for the night. He did remember me at that point, and sent a runner to find me. "Signore Goldanias wishes you to know that he is leaving now for the island. If you wish to stay here longer, he will send the launch back for you."

Ten to one he'd totally forget, though of course Evan would come back for me. But I'd had enough of casinos, although for a change, I had quite charming company.

"Go on," Joshua said, apparently reading my mind. "I'll be in touch once I'm back in the States. We'll have more time to talk... and other things." Then he kissed me again. I tasted whisky and soda and his promises on his lips. The runner showed no reaction, nor did anyone else at the bar. This was Venice, after all.

Unexpectedly, I felt the vampire trying to break through. My fangs grew and I knew my eyes were red. I hadn't lost control like that for years. I fought the monster back, and looked up when I could feel that my eyes were normal.

"Everything okay?" Joshua asked.

"Fine."

I followed the runner back downstairs after bidding Joshua goodbye, and found Alexander and Brier waiting for me. Since Brier pouted but said nothing when I rejoined them, I assumed Alexander had explained the situation to her. We returned to the villa, and Alexander and Brier went off to the former's lush bedroom. Evan and I exchanged looks that consisted mostly of rolled eyes.

"You would think he might remember that he was turned in the first place because he couldn't resist—"

"I know," Evan said with a resigned sigh, and he disappeared to tinker with the launch.

Hours later, as I worked on some papers that I had brought with me, Alexander appeared in the doorway of my bedroom.

"Gideon..." he said tentatively.

I examined him critically. His hair was rumpled, and he was clad only in his housecoat and a pair of pajama pants.

"Yes?" I said, in my least encouraging tone of voice.

"I'm sorry I neglected you."

"Don't be ridiculous. How can you possibly be sorry that you met a lovely young woman?"

"But I ignored you in order to get to know Brier."

"I hope that I am not so conceited as to believe that my charms can possibly compete with those of Miss Snow for your attention."

Alexander blinked. "Don't be like that. For once, don't pull a Baron Redoak on me. Can't you just be Gideon, my friend, this once? I want to apologize for paying so much attention to Brier that I made you feel uncomfortable and unwanted."

"I didn't feel that way in the slightest. I ran into Joshua Trevallion."

"Oh, really? What's he doing here?"

"On a buying trip."

"Are you going to see him again?"

"That, Alexander, is none of your business."

"Damn it all, Gideon...I...you...you don't make things easy to say, do you? I just wanted to tell you...damn."

"It's all right, Alex." I was unable to resist feeling smug. "I love you, too."

Chapter Fourteen

Only Alexander, outside of my household, knew that I had met Joshua in Venice. He was kind enough not to ask too many questions about my relationship with the antiques expert, questions I couldn't have answered. Certainly we had expressed interest, and the potential was there to move beyond friendship and into new and exciting territory. But what had happened in the casino worried me. What if the next time I couldn't control myself?

When Joshua called to tell me that he was back in the United States, I invited him to come for dinner again—and to stay for the weekend, should he so desire. I heard myself say that and stared at the phone, but I couldn't retract the words.

He accepted, although he said he could only stay one night. He said he would be happy to stay in a guest room, and left that sentence open to interpretation.

When Joshua arrived, he presented me with a bottle of fine Italian wine. Our fingers brushed when I accepted the gift, and we kissed. This time, no fangs appeared. He and I chatted about Venice until Mitch summoned us to dinner.

This dinner was less formal than our first one had been, especially as Mitch seemed to think he need no longer put on his company manners. I was relieved to see that Joshua took the young werewolf's behaviour in stride, joking right back at him. They seemed to get along quite well, in fact.

At bedtime, I gave Joshua the usual excuse of an exotic skin disease to pardon my absence during daylight hours, and he looked at me very closely. This was someone from whom I couldn't keep my secret for very long, I feared. If I continued to lie to Joshua, it wouldn't be a good foundation even for friendship, let alone anything further.

But what would he do when he learned the truth?

Alexander had lapsed once more into a deep brooding mood, no doubt missing his villa in Venice, and the readily available young ladies in the casino. He moped around Valley Mansion like a tall, lean cloud of despair. Janine confided to me that sharing a house with her brooding cousin was not unlike living in a Gothic novel. Francis started calling her Jane Eyre.

"I'm so lonely," Alexander said gloomily, draping himself over the back of the leather sofa in the study of Valley Mansion. He lit one of his infernal black cigarettes.

"I wish you wouldn't smoke." Janine waved away the fumes.

"What's it going to do, kill me?" Alexander asked with a ghastly smile.

"No, but it might kill me. Haven't you heard of the dangers of second-hand smoke?"

He ignored this and brooded.

"Alexander," I said, "if it's love you crave, you're not going to find it by sitting here smoking those wretched things. You must get out and meet young women who are interested in more than a one-night stand."

Janine came and stood behind my chair. "That's right," she said, putting her hands on my shoulders. "Maybe you need to go shopping for an antique table. It worked for Gideon."

"Now wait a minute," I said. "Nobody has mentioned love."

"So why is he coming for the weekend? Because he admired your collection of nineteenth century bottles? I don't think so."

If I could have flushed, I would have. I took refuge in pompousness, rather a failing of mine. "That's none of your business, young lady."

She laughed.

When I arrived back home after my social outing to Valley Mansion, I found Mitch grinning at me. "There's a phone message for you."

"Well?"

"Someone named Joshua wants to know if you'd like to go see opera with him. I told him you were more into country and western. He seemed to think that was funny."

"You know, Mitch," Evan popped his head around the corner. "It is one of my greatest regrets that you are too old to spank."

"Here, he left his number."

I snatched the piece of paper from Mitch's hand. "Shoo," I said to both Mitch and Evan. I called Joshua from my study.

"I know I'm coming to your place tomorrow night, but I got unexpected tickets to the opera in Bangor, and thought you might like to see it with me. You could have Evan drive you over, and I'll drive you home since I'm staying for the weekend anyway. Sound like a deal?"

"It's a deal," I said.

"I'll see you outside the opera house at seven-thirty, then. I'll be the one wearing the green carnation."

I snorted. *The Green Carnation,* a scandalous novel, had fictionalized the relationship of Oscar Wilde and Lord Alfred Douglas with disastrous results for them both. Fortunately, I doubted that anyone remembered that connotation now. We exchanged goodbyes and I hung up.

Although I knew hardly anybody still dressed for the opera, I put on my tuxedo. Alas, I no longer owned an opera cape, nor did my hairline come to a widow's peak. All in all, I looked more like a banker than a vampire.

I barely spoke to Evan during the drive to Bangor. He seemed to understand. Outside the opera house, he drew up at the passenger drop-off and ran around to open the door for me.

"Behave yourself. Have a good time."

"Aren't those two mutually exclusive?"

I spotted Joshua, whose buttonhole was earning him some amused attention. "Nice carnation."

"Thank you. I've been getting lots of friendly reminders that St. Patrick's Day isn't until March."

"I should have worn my green bowler hat."

"Do you really have one?"

"No."

We both laughed and went arm in arm into the opera house. We found our seats and settled down. I chuckled when I saw the program. The performance was *Die Fledermaus.* "Joshua, where did you get these tickets?"

He shrugged. "They came anonymously by courier. That happens occasionally, when you work with the kind of clientele I do. Why?"

"Oh, no reason." I strongly suspected that I knew who had sent the tickets—two meddlesome matchmakers named Evan and Mitch.

The opera was excellent. Joshua and I both enjoyed it very much. In the protective darkness of the theatre, our hands met. His warm fingers curled around mine, and I saw his eyes turn to me. I was content.

After the opera, we stopped at a café on the way home for coffee and an incisive analysis of the performance. After we had praised the staging and the orchestra, we discussed the cast.

"I thought the soprano was quite good," I said, sipping gingerly at my coffee. I had to drink slowly for my system to accept the beverage. "She sang very well."

"Pretty, too," Joshua said with a shrug. "If you like little blondes."

"I take it you don't?"

"Not my type." He winked. "I prefer dark hair."

I felt myself grinning, a rather unusual expression for me. But his wry humour appealed to me.

It was very late by the time Joshua's car pulled up the driveway to Oakwoods. We decided that it was worth a brief walk to the cliff, despite the cold and snow, to see the view. Our hands safely entwined, we stood side by side on the promontory and looked southwards to the few lights that still twinkled in Fletcherville.

"My God, it's beautiful here," Joshua sighed. "A perfect ending to a perfect evening."

"Did you really think it was perfect?" I looked at him anxiously.

"There's only one way it could be more perfect," he said, his eyes searching mine for something.

"What would that be?" My voice sounded husky on the salty air.

His arms went around me and drew me close to his body. I raised my head, and his lips lowered to mine. A delicious warmth spread through me, and I returned his kiss, pressing against him with all the longing of the lonely years.

Of course, we had kissed before, but not with this depth of passion. And this time, the vampire remained caged. My head fit perfectly on his shoulder.

"We should go inside," Joshua said finally, dropping his arms with regret. "We wouldn't want the kids to worry."

I laughed softly. "They're likely watching us out of one of the windows. But yes, we should go inside." Dawn would come in a very short while, for one thing, and it was too cold out for a human to tolerate for long.

"It's late," Joshua said in tones of regret. "And we're both tired. The first time should be special, and take all night."

"Let's hope that it won't also be the last time."

"Gideon, you are the slowest person to pick up a hint that I've ever met. I love you. I fell in love with you in that antique store. I've been trying to seduce you ever since. And now that I finally have the perfect opportunity, it's too late. I want to have sex with you, frequently."

"I'm in love with you, and I would like to sleep with you. But there's not enough of tonight left."

I showed him to one of the guest rooms.

We spoke on the telephone, of course, and he sent me postcards from wherever his travels took him, but it wasn't the same as his being here. I found myself wanting him to move in as a permanent resident.

I crossed the living room one night, and chanced to look up at the portrait of Jonathan that hung above the fireplace—Jonny, my lost love. But it was time and past to move on.

I kept as close an eye as possible on Alexander after that conversation in the den of Valley Mansion. I'd heard him speak that way before, and it was almost invariably followed by a suicide attempt. This time, he seemed to sink very low indeed, according to my spy Janine, spending most nights in his study, pacing and smoking endless cigarettes. He left Valley Mansion only to hunt, and either Francis or I accompanied him to ensure that he did nothing foolish.

One night, after a fortnight of this, we were in the town Common of the next village down the highway from Fletcherville. The Common was deserted on this cold January night. Alexander had hunted amongst those staggering home after too convivial an evening at one of the local bars. I had contained my own hunger, not wanting to hunt the same evening as another vampire. Francis had claimed he wasn't hungry at all. I would invite him to come and share my bottled stock later, although he usually disdained animal blood.

"You needn't follow me around like my keepers," Alexander suddenly snarled at us.

Both Francis and I stepped back. Alexander was in a dangerous and unpredictable mood. I might have more centuries than he, but I couldn't match his physical strength should he attempt violence. Francis must have had similar thoughts.

"We're here for your own safety," I said.

"My own safety!" Alexander's mouth twisted in mockery and he leaned against the trunk of a convenient tree. "Why do you bother? Why not just let me wait here for the sun? I'm not worth all this trouble."

Francis' angelic face snapped up at those words, blond hair flying. Something sparked in his blue eyes and he hauled back and slapped Alexander across the face before I could stop him. Alexander looked as stunned as I felt. Francis had been a vampire less than thirty years, while Alexander had nearly two centuries seniority. Such an assault was unheard of, and very unlike Francis.

"Sometimes," the fledgling vampire spat into the snow, "you make me sick, Alex. All you ever do is moan about your lot. Look at what you've got! You've got wealth, power, social position, a house, a beautiful girl, a great little cousin who loves you—and you want to wait for the sun because you think you're not worth anything! All you need to do to get Brier back is apologize to her and tell her the truth. If that scares her off, she was never meant for you in the first place, but at least you'll know that! Get with the program, Alex! Or I will just leave you here for the sun." He shook his head. "I wonder if you even know how good a friend you have right here." He put an arm around my shoulder. "Why do you put up with him, Gideon? You've had it a lot worse than this sorry bastard, and you never complain. Come on—I'll buy you a brandy at the Inn, or we'll go to the China Clipper and party a bit. Let's leave Sad Sack here on his own, since that's what he wants. If he decides to wait for dawn, that's his lookout. I'm tired of babysitting."

I felt myself being pulled along in Francis' wake. I looked back and saw that Alexander was still leaning against the tree, stunned. No, not stunned, gobsmacked is the term, I believe. He looked rather silly, actually.

Francis' unorthodox treatment seemed to work. Michael called a meeting of the Brotherhood the next night, and when we all had assembled, save Alexander, the Archdruid looked at the two vampires who were present.

"Where's Alex? I thought you were keeping an eye on him."

"I'm here," said a rough voice. "I don't need a babysitter any longer." Alexander came in, wearing a baggy old sweater and worn denim blue jeans that hardly came up to his usual sartorial standards. "I've come to a decision. No more suicide attempts, I swear. I have to say thank you." He finally looked at Francis. "But if you ever hit me again, little one, I'll hit back."

"Fine," said Francis with complete equanimity. "That's what I was hoping you would do."

During the short ride back to Oakwoods, the conversation was all about the Fairlawn twins, Galen and Vivain, now nearly one year old and growing like little saplings.

"Be sort of fun, having two little tykes running about," Mitch said as he hung up my coat in the front hall.

"I already have two tykes underfoot." I glanced slyly at each of them in turn.

"But you must admit that your life isn't boring when we're around," Evan deadpanned.

"A little boredom might be nice once in a while."

"Get out. You wouldn't last a minute without us."

I looked at them both seriously. "You're right."

"Let's not get all mushy here," said Mitch. "Speaking of mushy, do you think Alex will ever find a girl?"

"I believe it's likely," I said, sitting down in my chair to think it over. I noticed that the seam at the end of the arm was frayed where I absent-mindedly picked at it. In fact, the whole house was looking a little shabby. Three men were not, perhaps, the most scrupulous housekeepers. "Alexander is a persuasive man who is used to getting his own way."

"The fact that he's also obscenely wealthy and ridiculously handsome doesn't hurt," Mitch said.

"So cynical, so young," Evan said with mock regret. "Just wait 'til you're centuries old, like Gideon and me. Then you'll have every right to be cynical."

"Well, I won't live to be centuries old," Mitch said, "so I've got to express my cynicism now, while there's still time."

"Of course you'll live to be centuries old, with any luck," Evan said. "Werewolves are immortal. Didn't you know that, little thief?"

Mitch went very still, his face pale. All the usual humour and roughness seemed to drain from him at once. "No," he said, too quietly, "I didn't." With a sudden violence that neither Evan nor I expected, Mitch hurled himself away from us and ran from the room. We heard his feet pound up the stairs, and the door to his room slam shut.

"Shit," said Evan, most uncharacteristically.

I started to rise, but he stopped me. "No, I'll go talk to him. I'm the one who upset him."

My protector left the room in Mitch's wake. Warg had started up abruptly when Mitch fled, looking anxiously at Evan, and decided to follow him to see what was wrong with his master. I was left alone to mull over this turn of events and hope that Mitch did nothing drastic.

I adjourned to the parlour and turned on the television, hoping to find a program worth watching. The invention of late-night television was an unexpected boon to vampires. It gives us something to do, which explains the number of horror movies broadcast at three a.m.

However, it was early yet, and the so-called "prime time" programming was still on the air. I watched an alleged comedy about a family with three delinquent children. Their father was exceedingly lenient—mine would have beaten me raw for behaving in such a manner. This show was interrupted by endless commercials for embarrassing hygiene products. I tried the public broadcasting station, only to be told, in lurid detail, several disgusting facts about the personal habits of an obscure species of wildlife. Other channels gave me mindless comedies, overstretched dramas, violent crimes, and commercials for everything from knives that could cut through tin cans to a cream intended for use on a body part not mentionable in polite society. I turned the television off, wondering what the world was coming to. Admittedly, I was suffering a general feeling of dissatisfaction with everything.

The telephone rang, and since my staff was otherwise occupied, I answered it. To my relief, the caller was Joshua. After I'd greeted him, he asked, "Why are you answering the phone? Where are the kids?"

"Mitch isn't feeling well," I said, scarcely able to tell him why, "and Evan is with him."

"Nothing serious, I hope?" Joshua sounded genuinely concerned.

"I hope not, too. How are you?"

"Fine, thank you. I called because I'm going to an estate auction up there in Maine next week, and thought I would invite you out for dinner."

"You will stay here, won't you?"

I heard him draw in his breath. "Yes, and I think we need to talk."

"I concur. When are you arriving?"

"A week from Thursday. I can stay for a few days, if that's not an imposition..."

"Not at all. I'll see you then."

I hung up just as I heard footsteps on the stairs. Mitch and Evan were coming down again. The young werewolf looked calmer. By unspoken agreement, we drifted into the kitchen, where Evan made a pot of strong sweet tea spiked with whiskey and we all sat at the table.

"You're all right, then?" I asked Mitch. Although the joy of Joshua's upcoming visit was crowding other concerns from my mind, I was still worried about the young man.

"Why should I be any different from everyone else in the Brotherhood?" Mitch said. I could see that he'd been deeply shaken, despite the bravado of his words. I reached out and touched his hand, briefly, and was rewarded with a smile. "Thanks, boss. It's good to have support."

"And just think," Evan said, ruffling the boy's hair, "we've got all those years to mold him into a reasonably presentable person."

"Frankly," I said, taking in Mitch's tousled hair, rumpled clothes and unlaced sneakers, as well as his dreadful American slang, "I don't believe eternity is long enough for the task."

After ensuring that Mitch really was accepting the news that he was immortal, I went up to my study to concentrate on some work that needed doing. I thought about the young man's horror at learning his fate, and how generally uncomfortable he seemed with his lycanthropy.

I knew that it was very painful when the full moon caused his limbs to warp and his body to contort, grow fur and become the wolf. There was, however, nothing I could do for him, except continue to supply a safe place for him during the change. My knowledge of werewolves was very limited. Mitch was the first of his kind that I had met.

My private line was ringing when I entered my study. Assuming it was a business call, I picked up the phone. "Gideon Redoak."

It was Joshua. "Gideon? I wanted to talk to you privately."

I sat down, heart dropping. Had he reconsidered his request to visit me? Had he found someone else, someone less reserved? It had only been about half an hour since his last call, but the heart is not always rational in these circumstances. "I'm listening."

"When I come to visit this weekend, I don't want to stay in a guest room. I want you, Gideon. All of you. You're incredibly sexy, did you know that? I want to have sex with you, and not just for the weekend."

I took an unnecessary breath. "I feel the same way about you."

"Then we'll talk about this some more, in person. But let's not do too much talking."

We exchanged a few more words, then he had to go to do some work. I sighed, rolled up my sleeves, and began to tackle the mountain of paperwork on my desk. Thursday. I had to wait until then before my questions would be answered. If I stalled my work until then, however, I would no longer have a comfortable fortune to play with. Sternly upbraiding myself for allowing my mind to wander, I knuckled back down to the stock market reports, letters, faxes, and other paraphernalia of the business world. Thursday would come in its own time.

One thing I could not put off, though, was telephoning loved ones in France. Just after I arose Wednesday evening, I dialed Genevieve's private line.

"*Bon soir, Maman,*" I said when she answered.

"*Bon soir, mon cher fils.*"

"Genevieve, I'm in love."

"You have no idea how happy that makes me, Gideon. Who is the most fortunate man?"

I told her all about Joshua. She listened patiently, even though there must have been a hundred other things for her to do. At the end of my recital, she laughed.

"He sounds perfect. May I be the one to give you away at your wedding?"

I was being teased, and unlike so very long ago when I had first met her, I knew that and could retaliate on the same terms.

"Only if I'm the one to give you away at yours."

"I am having a wedding?"

"Aren't you going to marry Jean?"

She snorted "Be serious, *mon cher.*"

We both laughed. She assured me all was well in France, and I told her all was well in Maine. We said goodbye with my promise to come and visit soon.

Thursday came, finally. When the brass knocker sounded, Mitch rushed to answer it, then went through an elaborate ritual of straightening his clothes and smoothing his hair before he opened the door.

"Good evening, Mr. Trevallion," he said formally, bowing from the waist. "Welcome to Oakwoods. Please, come inside. Allow me to take your wraps. I trust you had a pleasant journey, and that you continue to enjoy good health?"

Joshua's jaw dropped, then his eyes twinkled. He slowly removed his long winter coat and jaunty red scarf, and handed them carefully to Mitch.

"Thank you, Mitchell." His tone was equally formal although his mouth was twitching. "I had a very pleasant journey, although I encountered a patch of ice that was somewhat worrisome. My health is quite good, thank you for asking. I see that you have recovered from whatever illness you had recently."

Unable to keep up the pretense of sophistication any longer, Mitch grinned. "I'm fine, thanks."

Joshua grinned back. "Glad to hear it. Now scram."

Mitch backed away. "I think I hear the phone."

"Joshua," I said when the dust had settled, "that was cruel."

"But effective." He smiled, and our eyes locked. "It's good to see you again," said Joshua, cocking his head inquisitively to one side.

"You, too."

There was an awkward pause. Then we both laughed and I held open my arms. He flowed into my embrace and our lips met as our arms encircled each other. It felt like heaven.

"You promised to take me out for dinner," I said when we finally disengaged.

"So I did. What on earth did your doorman do with my coat?"

I retrieved it for him, but it took quite a bit of time for him to get into it, for some reason. This operation finally achieved, I found my own coat and, holding it over my arm, went into the kitchen to tell Mitch and Evan that I was going out.

"Have fun," Evan said.

"Be sure he drives carefully," Mitch added. "And don't stay out too late." He guffawed, and Evan nudged him.

"Good night, children."

Joshua insisted on helping me into my coat, and the ensuing tangle left both of us slightly breathless and laughing like schoolboys. Arm in arm, we walked out to his car. He drove to a town a little way down the coast, where he had found a superb Italian restaurant. I ordered a vegetarian pasta dish and hoped that Joshua wouldn't notice I ate almost none of it.

"Oakwoods feels more like home every time I visit," he said, twirling his own pasta expertly. "It's become very difficult to leave."

"Then don't leave." I astounded myself with those words, but realized I meant them.

"Gideon, I do love you. And I love the kids." He smiled. "Sorry, I should say that I love Mitch and Evan. Well, I like Evan, I guess, he's a hard man to know very well. The house is gorgeous, and I could learn to live in such an isolated spot."

"But?"

"I've been alone for a long time, managing my own affairs, keeping my schedule as it pleases me, being able to take off on a buying trip on almost no notice. I need a home, but I need that freedom, too. Would you be willing to share me with my clients, put up with my leaving for long trips and conducting my business?"

"Of course. I often leave for business trips myself, usually to England where I have a lot of my portfolio. I want a lover, not a house pet."

His eyes lit up, glowing soft amber. Then he took a deep breath. "There are questions one has to ask these days."

I knew what he was broaching, but how could I satisfy him without revealing my true nature in a crowded restaurant? I wanted to wait until a private moment, until we had actually committed ourselves to a permanent physical relationship. "I want a long-term relationship, not a brief fling. Since that is what I'm looking for, I'll give you any answers you need."

"That was one of my questions." He smiled, abandoning his own nearly-empty dish and frowning at my nearly-full one. "Don't eat much, do you?"

"Have to watch the waistline." I patted my rather solid middle. The turning burns body fat, but when one has a naturally stocky build, there isn't much that becoming a vampire can do to help one's figure.

"You look fine. I don't do one-night stands. Too dangerous, for one thing."

Ah, that was a subtle way of introducing the next question. But how on earth could I assure him that I did not, and could not possibly, have AIDS, or any other contagious disease? "I agree. I've only had two lovers, Joshua, both a very long time ago—long enough ago that, had they been infected, there would be signs by now. You'll have to take my word for it."

"I do." He toyed with his glass of wine. "I've only had one lover, and that was in my undergraduate days, which were longer ago than I'll admit." His eyes danced, the crinkles at the corners the only sign that he was in his late thirties. "I'm clean," he went on, more gently. "And since I believe you, it's only fair that you believe me."

"I do believe you," I said softly. Our hands met on the stem of his wine glass and I felt a glow that had nothing to do with the alcohol. "I love you."

After dessert and coffee, we left the restaurant and drove to the shore of the Atlantic. Despite the sub-freezing temperatures, Joshua parked on a wharf and we sat in his car like two teenagers at Lovers' Lane, arms about each other, fingers teasing hair, lips locked together in passion and tenderness.

He finally broke away and started the car. "Not yet, love. Not in a car, at any rate."

"No." I was amazed that my voice still worked. "Not in a car."

"Shall we wait until I can move in permanently? That way it won't seem as if we're rushing things."

"Good idea. Do try and move in tomorrow, won't you?"

"Why, Gideon, I never pegged you as the impulsive type."

We returned to my home, which hopefully I would soon be sharing with this wonderful man, and sat before a lively fire in the den. We pretended to play chess, but neither of us paid very much attention to the board. We reluctantly called off our other game before it went too far. After one last, lingering kiss, Joshua took himself upstairs to his guest bedroom. I banked the fire for the night.

I didn't hear from Joshua for a few days after he left for New York, but that didn't worry me overmuch. I knew what it was like to travel. He would contact me when he had the time.

Then a postcard arrived in the mail, from Japan. "Dear Gideon," it read, "I'm sorry that I didn't call you, but I had to rush to Kyoto to meet an important client. Very last minute deal, no time to tell anyone. Japan is lovely. Will call when I get back. Josh."

I looked up from perusing this message to see both my housemates gazing at me inquiringly. I knew perfectly well that they had both read the postcard, given the public nature of these missives. Joshua had not added any personal notes for that very reason.

"What is it?" I said.

"It's not signed 'Love, Josh,'" Mitch said worriedly.

I sighed. "I think it's time to have a serious discussion with both of you. Come up to the study, please."

Evan and Mitch looked at each other, and shrugged. Mitch looked slightly scared, as if he'd been summoned to the headmaster's study. They followed me up the stairs and into my private office.

"Sit down, please." I took my own place behind the desk.

Evan perched casually in one of the chairs, but Mitch slumped into another, his shoulders sagging in anticipation of a lecture. I smiled at him, much to his surprise.

"Joshua and I are not lovers," I said.

"Gideon, I'm sorry—" Mitch began, his perturbation showing in his use of my name, which seldom passed his lips. He obviously was feeling very guilty.

I raised my hand, and he subsided. "But I am in love with him." There was absolute silence. "When he returns from Japan, he will be moving into Oakwoods permanently, as my lover. If either one of you has a problem with this, I want to know now." I crossed my arms and regarded them both steadily.

"I have no problems with that," Evan said. He looked completely serious.

"Me, either," Mitch said. "What do you think we've been— ow!" He yelped with pain as Evan kicked him on the shin. Mitch glared, rubbing the traumatized limb.

"You two..." I shook my head. "Have you really been playing matchmaker?"

Mitch pulled his legs out of Evan's reach. "Sure we have. Who do you think sent those opera tickets? Or arranged that Josh should conveniently hear of auction sales in the vicinity?"

"Or made up the guest room that's right across the hall from your bedroom door?" Evan added, his hazel eyes gleaming with glee.

I leaned back in my chair and looked at them for a moment. "Thank you. Thank you both."

Two weeks later, the telephone rang, and Mitch fetched me without any nonsense. He handed me the instrument with a flourish, and retreated out of earshot—I hoped.

"Gideon?" Joshua sounded as if he was next door, and I wished he was. "Did you get my postcard?"

"I did indeed, thank you. Are you back in New York?"

"Not yet, I'm still in Japan. But I had to call you, it's lonely here."

"It's lonely here, too. Joshua, when are you coming home?"

I heard an indrawn breath on the other end of the line. "Home. Say it again."

"Come home."

"I wish I could be on the next plane. My business here should wrap up in a week. I'll call you from New York. I love you."

"I love you, too."

Never before had seven days passed so slowly. I suppose I wasn't easy to live with for that week. Alexander threatened to take me back to Venice, by force, to pass the time. Mitch could be heard muttering that perhaps I needed to be locked in the cell in the basement. Warg whined and slunk out of my path whenever he saw me coming.

When he finally arrived at Oakwoods, Joshua greeted me fondly. His coat slid to the floor of the hallway as he wrapped his arms around me. Cold air blew unnoticed past us, because he had neglected to shut the door behind him.

"I missed you," he said, when he had to come up for air.

"And I you." I untangled my fingers from his sandy mane.

"Where is your loyal staff?"

"I sent them out for the night." I reached around him and shut the front door, then faced him again. "Do you think you can live with them, Joshua?"

"Why don't we go upstairs, and talk about it?"

"I haven't prepared the guest room," I said, as we walked up the stairs, entwined like two cats.

"It's about time I saw the master bedroom, anyway."

As we entered my room, I said, "There's something I have to tell you."

His eyes were darting around, taking in the decor. "What a nice room. A little dark, maybe...sorry? You were saying?"

"Joshua, there's something I must tell you before we go any further. You may not want to go any further when you hear what I have to say."

He stopped wandering around the bedroom and came to the side of the bed. "No matter what it is, Gideon, I'm prepared to listen," he said, sitting down. "I agree, it's high time you and I had a really serious talk."

It was my turn to wander around the room, looking at familiar objects as if I had never seen them before. Where had that brass horse come from? How long had I owned that painting? How could I calmly tell the man sitting on my bed that I was a vampire?

"You see," he was saying, watching my every move with concerned eyes, "I've noticed so many strange things about you. I have to be extremely observant in my line of work."

"Of course you do." I raised my head from contemplating the brush set on the top of my dresser, wondering if this revelation was going to be easier than I thought.

"I can't talk to the back of your suit jacket, Gideon. Come and sit down with me. Why do you wear a suit around the house, anyway?"

As I turned, he raised a hand, smiling. "Never mind. That answer can wait. But, whatever it is you're going to tell me, I'll understand. I hope it explains some things."

I walked slowly over to sit next to him. "What things?"

He smiled, and reached out to touch my hand. "Don't look so alarmed. You'd have to be a close observer to notice. I think it's your stillness that's hard to explain. You don't make any unnecessary movements, and the ones you do make are quiet and

studied, somehow. And, love, you might want to remember to breathe once in awhile when you're in private."

"Good lord, you noticed that and it didn't alarm you?"

"Not after I noticed other things, like the fact that you don't eat, and the way you move. I just added up all the facts and suppositions and decided that you were somebody very special, and when you were ready, there'd be a logical explanation." .

"I'm a vampire."

He took a deep breath. His face showed surprise, but no fear. His eyes widened, but he didn't pull away from me. "I think I need a drink," he said quietly.

There was a decanter of brandy on the dresser. I got up and poured him a snifter, and handed it to him. His fingers brushed mine as I passed him the glass. Again, there was no pulling away, only a quizzical smile. He looked as if he'd had some great puzzle partially solved and was only looking for the final piece to fit.

"You're a vampire."

"Yes."

"How old are you?"

"I was born in 1622, and brought over in 1642."

"And it's now 1991, so you're either twenty, or three hundred and sixty-nine. You don't look either."

"Actually, I'm nineteen. I was turned before my birthday. But I've found it more practical to appear older." I looked at him closely. He was trembling slightly, but he wasn't running. "You do believe me, don't you? It's the truth."

"I believe you," he said, giving himself a little shake. "But, um, would you prove it for me? Just so that I see what I'm getting myself into?"

As much as I hated it, I showed him the vampire—the glowing red eyes, the fangs extended, the fingernails turned into talons. He took it very well. He only needed one large gulp of brandy to compose himself.

"So what happens now?" he asked, when I'd reverted back to my regular appearance. "Are you going to drink my blood?"

"Not unless you want me to, and only then. And I would only take enough to fill a wine glass, less than you would donate to the Red Cross. Joshua—I will never hurt you."

Joshua sat for a few minutes, pulling at the bedspread. "Gideon," he said quietly, "we belong together. I've known it since we met. You seemed so reserved that I didn't want to push it, and I wasn't ready to give up my freedom. I don't know if I can take living with a vampire. Being gay is hard enough in today's society. Having two alternative lifestyles seems rather excessive. But there's only one way to find out if I like it." He stood up, setting down the brandy snifter carefully on the bedside table, and took my hands in his. "Convince me."

I undressed him slowly, admiring each bit of his body as it was revealed. He returned the favour, although a bit faster. When we were both naked, we explored each other with fingers and lips. I bore him down to the bed, and my teeth, without fangs, nibbled at his neck. He would have quite the hickey in the morning. He moaned, but with pleasure. My tongue moved over the great vein, then slowly moved down to play with his hardened nipples. Something further down was hardening as well, but I ignored that for the moment.

I tickled his ribs with my fingers, and he choked with laughter. He reached up to touch my own erect member, as if to say "hurry up." Ah, well, if that was what he wanted…

He gasped as I entered, but with pleasure. He wrapped one leg around me and our bodies found the perfect rhythm. I was the one who gasped now. It had been so long, I was worried that I had forgotten the mechanics. I need not have feared. Making love to Joshua was as easy as getting dressed. He knew how to move, how to encourage me onwards.

When the climax came, we both cried out. Then, deeply satisfied, I withdrew and we lay side by side, he sweaty and tired, I feeling like I had gone to heaven.

Joshua sat up, and I wondered if something was wrong. Then he took my right hand between both of his and kissed the edge of it.

"I'm convinced," he said.